A SENSE
OF JANE

by

V J Cooper

First Published in Great Britain in 2023

Published by First Spark Publishing

Copyright © 2023 VJ Cooper

A CIP catalogue record for this book is available from the British Library

Certificates used with permission from the NRS © Crown copyright, 2023

ISBN 978-1-7394501-0-6 (hardback)
ISBN 978-1-7394501-1-3 (paperback)
ISBN 978-1-7394501-2-0 (ebook)

Cover Design by Creative Covers

Typesetting by Book Polishers

For Jane, Margaret and Sarah.

May your voices be heard and your spirits be free.

CONTENTS

WHEN YOUR HEART IS HEAVY,
LET THE WIND CARRY IT.

AS HOPE WHISPERS IN YOUR EAR;
LOOK AHEAD.

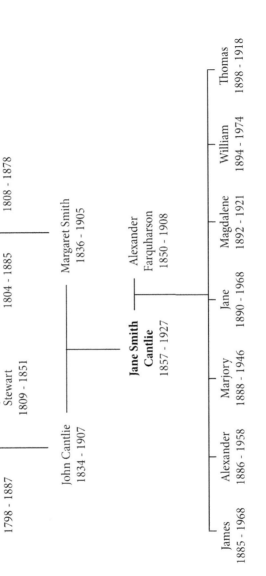

Francis Cantlie
1798 - 1887

Mary Elizabeth
Stewart
1809 - 1851

John Smith
1804 - 1885

Sarah Stuart
1808 - 1878

John Cantlie
1834 - 1907

Margaret Smith
1836 - 1905

**Jane Smith
Cantlie**
1857 - 1927

Alexander
Farquharson
1850 - 1908

James
1885 - 1968

Alexander
1886 - 1958

Marjory
1888 - 1946

Jane
1890 - 1968

Magdalene
1892 - 1921

William
1894 - 1974

Thomas
1898 - 1918

ACCOUCHEMENT, 1857

SECRETS ARE HELD. Sometimes they are passed on; sometimes they are not. The ghosts of the past live quietly amongst the living, and in Victorian Scotland, Milton Cottage was no different.

*

MARGARET'S RELENTLESS JOURNEY ended with one final push and Jane emerged into the world, earlier than expected. A surprisingly robust looking bairn with a shock of dark hair and strong sounding lungs, she was wrapped quickly in a man's shirt, as was the custom, and a thick woollen shawl to ward off the cold that lingered inside Milton Cottage. As Margaret held her child for the first time, absorbing the tiny features, an immense feeling passed over her that she had no words for, but her mind was still and her heart full.

Sarah smiled at her daughter and new grandbairn, relief apparent on her face, thankful that all was well in the end, as her dreams had withheld their secrets.

But with little time yet to wallow, the women in attendance scurried. There was work to be done in order to protect both mother and child.

The friends and neighbours in attendance set quickly to work to sain Margaret and her daughter. Belief in fairies was strong, their power feared, so the rituals had to be carried out quickly and precisely to prevent mother and child from being carried away. There was many a tale of the fairies taking a newborn or its mother, and replacing them with one of their own, a changeling, but only the unsained and unbaptised could be taken, so both would be closely watched by those around them until Margaret had attended church and her quine been baptised.

Every seven years the fairies had to pay a teind, or payment, to Hell, and a newborn was the perfect substitute for one of the fairies themselves. It was well known that mothers were taken for their milk as fairies had a great liking for it.

Ann lit the fir candle and handed it to Isabella who held it over the heads of mother and bairn and birled it round them both three times, whilst Sarah set the Bible alongside some bread and cheese under the pillow, chanting the old words passed down through the ages:

"May the Almichty debar a' ill fae this umman, an be aboot ir, an bliss ir an ir bairn." (May the Almighty prohibit all ill from this woman and be about her and bless her and her child.)

The food was then given to Ann and Isabella, as both were unmarried, to be placed under their pillows to evoke dreams. The small heart-shaped brooch, a treasured heirloom, was taken from the drawer and pinned to the petticoat worn by Margaret during her accouchement, and carefully the newborn was passed three times through the garment to ward off the fairies and the Evil Eye, and also to prevent the sin of being overpraised, something that would never be tolerated.

Sarah washed the child, being careful to avoid wetting her tiny palms as to do so would wash away her worldly luck, and the water was disposed of under the house. Once dressed she was turned three times head over heels and blessed, then held upside down and shaken three times to protect her. Only the wee one herself could tell what indeed that felt like.

Finally Margaret could hold her daughter again. She alone knew that the quine was to be called Jane but no name could be uttered aloud until she was baptised. Meanwhile Sarah called her husband to fetch the old, borrowed cradle into the room. Donald, the blacksmith, had delivered it at the break of day on hearing the news - a live cockerel within it as custom dictated, removed now of course - and the cradle was placed at the side of the bed.

And so it was, on a mild spring morning at ten minutes to three, on Thursday 21st May 1857, in Milton of Auchindoun, Mortlach, the illegitimate daughter of John Cantlie was born to one Margaret Smith, daughter of John and Sarah, poor folk with little of anything and one more mouth to feed.

Page 14.

1857. BIRTHS in the Parish of _Montrose_ of _____ in the County of _____

No.	(1.) Name, and Surname of Child. Name, when given or altered after Registration of Birth.	(2.) When and Where Born, with Hour of Birth.	(3.) Sex.	(4.) Name, Surname, and Rank or Profession of Father.	(5.) Name, and Maiden Surname of Mother.	(6.) Signature, Qualification, and Residence of Informant, if out of the House in which the Birth occurred.	(7.) When and Where Registered, and Signature of Registrar.
40	Smith Jane	1857	F	illegitimate	Margaret Smith	Margaret Smith mother	1857
41	Nicholie Alexander John	1857	M	Nicholie Robert	Nicholie Alexander Father (present)	1857
42	Reindie James	1857	M	Reindie Father	Reindie mother (present)	1857

Registrar

Census 1861

Jane awoke to the sound of voices drifting through from the kitchen, combined with the clattering of rain on the little window. Her toes crept their way to the edge of the bed, peeking out from under the blankets, testing the temperature of the air. Had they been given the choice the bairn would have stayed snuggled in bed but the mind was impatient and it was in charge. The wind whistled and walloped against the glass but did not frighten her, in fact only the day before she had enjoyed playing outside, the wind nudging her, making her walk like old Mr Macpherson up the road, after too much whisky.

Eager for the day to begin - and oblivious to the significance of it - she clambered out of bed and used the chamberpot, careful not to soak her nightclothes and toddled across the room towards the door. Pulling back the curtain that separated her and her mam's beds from George's, she smiled at the woman sitting cradling a bairn and said, "Morning," to the old man passing through the door.

Jane knew not to expect an answer but she liked to speak to the other people who lived in her home. It was a busy cottage and Jane never quite knew who to expect from day to day. There was a sense of busy calmness that filled the air, so much hustle and bustle but very little noise, which enveloped Jane in a blanket of comfort which at the age of three she had no words for. Skipping through the door, her brown curls bouncing, Jane launched herself into the kitchen with a tongue full of chatter and a belly full of anticipation.

The kitchen was quiet that morning, only an old woman standing beside Jane's mam, watching her disapprovingly as she made porridge over the fire, the spurtle being used, stirring over enthusiastically. Either side of the hearth a chair sat idly and granda's pipe and tobacco nestled in a nook. A dresser on the adjacent wall housed the basic accoutrements a kitchen needed in the way of crockery and pots and pans, and a box bed nestled itself opposite the hearth, where Jane's granny and granda slept, the top used for storage and where an old fiddle lay in wait.

"Well here's a ray o' sunshine on a dreich April morn'," proffered her mam as she ladled some porridge into a bowl for Jane, placed it in front of her and kissed the top of her head. The peat fire that was smouldering in the hearth gave out a modicum of heat but it was nothing compared to the creamy warmth meandering down to her belly. As Jane ate, the wind blustered and bellowed causing the door to rattle and whine on its hinges and the rain spattered through cracks, wetting the earth floor.

The newspaper lay on the table where granny was sitting peeling vegetables. Margaret joined her, having removed the pot from the fire, and her eyes widened as she looked again at the picture of the train engine dwarfing the man standing by it. There had been much news of it in the paper on how it would benefit the area but some were sceptical, scared even, of change and what that could bring. Miles of track had been laid between Aberdeen and Inverness transporting goods and folk up and down the land and now Dufftown was to join the metal road of progress.

"Imagine being able tae travel fae Dufftown tae Keith in a matter o' minutes," Granny was saying.

"I ken, Mother. It disna seem possible."

"Aye, but what an adventure it would be, and goodness knows I've had little of those in my fifty three years on this earth. I dinna suppose I will get the chance tae travel on one though. I imagine it will cost a fair bit o' money."

"Aye, it's nae for the likes o' us, I don't suppose."

The two quines fell into a wistful silence and Margaret looked at Jane and wondered if her life would be different - better- instead of living as she did, grappling for every penny, poor in possessions but rich in the beauty of the surrounding countryside.

Nestled in the undulating hills of the parish of Mortlach, in Banffshire, Milton of Auchindoun consisted of several cottages facing south, with the Meal Mill at one end and the bridge over the River Fiddoch at the other. Milton Cottage, in which Jane was born, was in the middle, next to the old schoolhouse, the school master, Charles Stuart, long gone and her uncle John biding there with his own family. Her home consisted of a stone built, thatched roof dwelling with an earth floor and clay plastered walls, whitewashed with lime, which absorbed the Scots language of Doric, interwoven with the remnants of Gaelic words that still lingered, the threads like the weft and warp of cloth.

Surrounded by fields full of grain, flocks and herds, it was an enchanting landscape, at times wild and windswept with deep snow underfoot and at others calm and tranquil with warmth in the sun and rich greenery. The river and burns quenched the land and the softness of the water flavoured the best whisky, illicit or otherwise. The farms of Clunymore, Coldhome, Boghead, Keithmore and Bakebare enveloped Milton, Clunymore being the childhood home of Jane's father, John Cantlie, his own father being a farmer and feuar -a land proprietor- at the time of her birth, providing the Cantlies with more food in their bellies than most.

Jane finished her porridge and hopped off the chair, her bare feet scuffing the flattened earth, making tiny indentations on its surface and blackening her wee toes. There were chores to be done before play and she liked to tell her granda how well she had done them when she saw him in the evening.

Granda and young George had long since left for a day's labouring on Boghead Farm, their bellies filled with porridge, but they would be cold and hungry for supper on their return in the evening. Sarah peered out the small window at the lashing rain.

" I hope there will be enough peat to dry oot the coats tonight."

"Aye, Mother. Once dinner is past we'll let the fire die doon a bit and save the peat for later. It's nae too long till the Feeing market so things will be a bit easier wi' George bringing in steady money."

Sarah sighed, " I hope he manages tae get a job wi' a local farm. I'm nae good wi' my bairns being far away."

Sarah's face hardened as memories of her losses surfaced.

It was a poor home, cantankerous in its workings and lacking in the physical comfort of some, but there was an abundance of love and kindness, sitting quietly among the thrawn determination to make life better, intertwined with a gentle sense of humour.

Sarah shook off her memories and turned to Jane.

"Through you go and get yersel' dressed, quine. George needs some socks so you can help me to rip back the wool fae an old jumper."

Jane thought of the last time she had to hold the wool for granny, so it could be wound into a ball again, and her heart sank.

"Oh Granny, my arms hurt holding up the wool."

"Nae girning now Jane, it needs tae be done and afterwards you can wind up the eight day clock. I ken how you like that."

Jane took great responsibility for the clock and was proud of being able to hold and turn the large key in reverent motion. She had no understanding of how to read it but she was aware that it told folk when to eat and when to go to bed and that seemed quite magical to her. With her mood lifted she skipped through to get dressed deciding that sore arms were worth the promise of being given such an important job.

And so the morning passed, each quine engrossed in some household activity or other and as the clock hands approached the midday hour and the Smiths were sitting down to dinner, the wind and rain ceased almost as suddenly as they had begun in the early hours, and the heaviness in the air was replaced with something akin to spring, although only a fool would expect it to last. Spring was in no hurry to arrive that year, it seemed.

Jane was ushered outside to play, alternating between haphazardly helping her mam with the washing and chasing the hens with her cousins Ann and Elizabeth, aged four and three respectively, who lived next door in the old schoolhouse. They were a lively wee clan, causing much mischief and drawing exasperated glances from their busy mothers, especially aunt Elizabeth who also had an eight month old son to contend with.

Margaret let out a sigh as Jane ran into her, for the third time, as she was trying to hang up the washing. Sensing her mam's temper Jane scurried away joining her cousins who were looking for beasties in the puddles.

Ann was poking a stick into the muddy water, careful not to splash two pairs of bare feet which were already cold in the damp air. It was Ann's turn to wear the one pair of shoes shared between them all.

"I canna see any." The stick was moved again causing the water to stir up more mud.

"I thinks they're hiding."

Jane crouched down and peered into the murky water. "Nae beetles today."

Elizabeth took charge -as always- and tugged on her sister's sleeve. "Let's find worms round the back."

The bairns left the puddle and skipped towards the side of the shed but Jane tripped on a stone and landed heavily on her bottom. Her wee lip quivered as she looked down and saw a red scratch on her foot as the cold seeped through her thin dress. Sensing their cousin's feelings Elizabeth and Ann quickly pulled Jane up by her hands and Elizabeth's wee arms wrapped themselves around Jane in a tight bosie.

"Come on Jane, you can play wi' the biggest worm," Elizabeth promised with a smile.

Jane returned the smile and the quines went in search of some wriggly playmates. Ann, being the wearer of the shoes, stomped her feet on the muddy ground and three eager faces watched and waited for the soil to move, ready to pounce on an unsuspecting creature. Squeals erupted as little heads broke through into the daylight and were grabbed by grubby fingers. Five worms wriggled and squirmed on dirty palms.

"Look at this one!"

"Mines is tickly!"

"This one's called Jessie!"

Margaret beckoned the quines, so the worms were reluctantly placed back on the ground as they were given a bucket to collect the eggs. They shooed the hens out of the shed and carefully picked up the eggs in their wee hands, then Elizabeth, straight backed and head held high, held the handle tight and walked slowly towards her mother.

"We have one, two, three, five, eight eggs," said Elizabeth. "And nones is broken."

Her mother smiled. "Well done. Here Jane, you take these in to yer mam."

She removed half the eggs and Jane carefully carried them into her kitchen shouting to her mam,

"We hae a hundred eggs for supper," then ran outside again disturbing the hens as they pecked and clucked between little legs. The three bairns ran, jumped and chased the hens, and each other, round and round the yard, enjoying being out having been cooped up inside all morning because of the stormy weather.

Every now and then little Elizabeth would cough. After a particularly long bout of coughing she started to cry which upset her sister Ann who also started to greet, and not knowing what to do, wee Jane joined in and there was an almighty howling and greeting coming from the back yard. Margaret quickly scooped up Jane and Ann together and deposited them on her knee, whilst Elizabeth gathered little Elizabeth in her arms and took her inside, her brow furrowed as her eyes caught Margaret's that mirrored her own worried look. Her wee quine had been coughing a lot the past week and it appeared to be getting worse.

Margaret's ears pricked as she heard the sound of hooves approaching and sure enough the snorting of a pony was followed by a knock on the door. She rose to answer and was greeted by the clerk, Mr MacPherson.

"Afternoon quine, I'm here to drop off the census form. Yer father needs to fill it in, if he's able to read and write, and I'll collect it the morn'."

"Aye, that's fine, I'll see that he gets it. Are you for a cup o' something hot tae ward off the cold?"

Na, na quine, I dinna hae time to stop. There's many a hoose needing visited yet, but thank you. I'll be on my way."

"Right you are, Mr Macpherson. We'll be seeing you the morn'."

Margaret placed the form on the dresser having taken a cursory look at it. She was aware of what was to be written but as the day wore on it slowly dawned on her that perhaps there could be some meaning in it for her daughter, having been denied her father's name on her birth certificate. She had avoided John Cantlie as best she could over the years, her heart sore at his denial and the easy accord between them long since broken. She often wondered if he stole glances at Jane in passing, and if things would always be as they were. As she put some water on to boil, acting as if she was commenting on nothing more significant than the time of day, Margaret stated to her mother,

"Jane's last name on the census form will be Cantlie."

There was a moment of silence as Margaret's words registered in Sarah's mind and her anger flared.

"Is Smith nae good enough for ye, quine? What good can come o' it to separate the bairn from the family name? Folk already hae their opinions and the Cantlies made things clear afore she was born. Will it nae make life harder for Jane?"

Margaret did not answer her mother but she had thrawn-ness in her blood and although she knew her father would have final say she was determined in her convictions that right be done by her bairn.

No more was said but Sarah was troubled. She had been unable to decipher her dreams lately, but she had a feeling of foreboding and felt that some great sadness lay ahead. She turned to the old woman by the hearth who shook her head and passed through the door. It was not a good sign and as she looked upon Jane's wide expressive, blue eyes, full of eagerness, mischief and innocence she could only wonder at what lay ahead for her and wished with all her heart that her dreams would tell her that all would be well.

Jane was fed and ready for bed by the time her granda and George returned home. Luckily the weather had held, and they were dry, so the few extra peat would be saved for another day. The fir candles had been taken from the dresser drawer and lit, providing some light for the evening chores. Sarah had their supper ready and father and son sat down heavily.

John reached into his pocket, "Here Sally. For the pot."

Sarah took the pennies with a smile and put them in the empty pot on the dresser.

Jane ran to her granda and following him giving her a beardie, which always made her skirl, he wanted to hear everything she had done that day, so she sat on his knee and snuggled into him.

"I got a hundred eggs fae the hens and I did all the washing and granny let me wind the clock. Can you hear it tick Granda?"

"I can, Jane. It sounds perfect. Ye must hae made a fine job o' it."

John's eyes closed for a second. "Poor Granda. When I'm four soon I will be a big girl and I can help ye on the farms so you winna be so tired."

John felt an unexpected rush of emotion at his grandbairn's words. His body was indeed weary but her wee, kind heart melted his.

Margaret was anxious to speak to her father about the census, so quickly settled Jane into bed and returned to the kitchen to broach the subject. John was by the hearth, his pipe in hand, glad of a seat after a long day's work and the knowledge that tomorrow was Sunday, a day of rest, to be spent with his family. Sarah sat opposite darning socks, her mind uneasy as she knew what Margaret was about to say, and George was at the table knitting.

Margaret picked up the census form from the dresser and passed it to her father. John shook his head as a wry smile surfaced.

"I can hardly believe it's been ten years since I last filled one in and I must be a vain man indeed, as I dinna relish the thought o' having to write my age as fifty six." As he picked up the pen his head lowered, covering the sad look that passed fleetingly over his eyes as he thought of the names that would not be written on the form. Only two of his eleven bairns now bade in Milton Cottage, the other nine either grown and away or taken from the world as bairns.

Margaret stood in front of John and with a strong sounding voice with an edge of grit in it, which belied the rapid beating of her heart, she stated, "I want Cantlie written as Jane's last name."

Her father's eyes narrowed and his mouth opened as if to speak and closed again just as quickly. Slowly he placed his pipe on the hearth and rubbed his chin causing it to redden slightly as his lips pursed and his head shook from side to side.

She offered no explanation and as a woman with a quiet disposition John was unsurprised that no further words were forthcoming. He knew that as head of his house his will would be done and glancing at his Sally he suspected that she was troubled by the idea.

John snapped, "The Cantlies are oor neighbours and sometimes employers, Margaret. I've had many a day's work over at Keithmore Farm and William Cantlie employed your sister Ann afore she married. I dinna seek work at Clunymore Farm wi' Francis Cantlie being John's father, oot o' respect for you, but young George will be leaving school next month and in need o' steady work. I dinna want him tae be a day labourer like me."

Margaret did not answer and her father sighed.

"John denied the bairn and although we know the Cantlies to be good folk they may not take kindly to the taking o' their name."

Margaret stood tall, "I ken that, Father - but she has a right to her name."

John looked straight into her eyes and his voice softened. "Maybe, but we need tae work and eat."

There was a long silence and John's eyes moved between the worried face of his wife to the determined one of his quine.

John looked at his daughter again and saw the need in her eyes. He recalled asking her to tell him who the father of her bairn was when he found out she was with child. Margaret had always been an open and honest quine with no conniving or selfish traits in her and when she had given him the name, John Cantlie, he had believed her immediately and without question, and it was never spoken of again. Until now.

John had a strong sense of what family meant and he recounted the old Gaelic saying that his own father used to say,

"Cuimhnich air na daoine bhon táinig thu." (Remember those you came from). With a nod of his head he dipped the pen in the ink and deftly and decisively wrote Jane Cantlie, aged three, on the form.

So it could be argued that Jane had two birth certificates. The second, formally written on the census six weeks before her fourth birthday, stating her surname as her father's family name and forever linking her to the Cantlies. Whatever consequences that were to follow, Jane was to carry the name throughout her life.

Parish of Moulach			The undermentioned Houses are situate within the Boundaries of the						
No. of Schedule	Road, Street, &c., and No. or Name of House	HOUSES	Name and Surname of each Person	Relation to Head of Family	Condition	Age of Males / Females	Rank, Profession, or Occupation	Where Born	Whether Blind, or Deaf and Dumb

| No. of Houses ... | 4 | | Total of Males and Females ... | | | | Total of School Children and Windowed Rooms ... | | |

PEAKS AND TROUGHS

T HE FOLLOWING MORNING passed peacefully: church was attended and neighbours caught up with. Margaret went about her daily business with a sense of peace and a thankful heart towards her father. She would bring Jane up to have a quiet acceptance of who she was and she could already see a thrawn streak in her which, if nurtured gently, would perhaps help her to survive what could sometimes be a cruel world.

As much as her kin had been supportive over the years she longed for a home of her own and a good man by her side. The Feeing market, where farm and domestic servants sought work every six months, and wages were bartered over whisky, was to be held in May, so perhaps there would be a prospective husband amongst the new lot of farm hands. Why only the other day a live coal had tumbled from the fire and rolled towards her, a sure sign that marriage was afoot! Margaret was engrossed in her imaginings throughout the rest of the day and it was only when her mother bellowed across the room at her to say the pot was billowing smoke, as Margaret had forgotten to put water in with the tatties to boil, that she snapped out of her dreaming.

The clerk arrived to collect the census form just as the family were sitting down to supper. John handed it to him and Mr MacPherson gave it a quick glance to check it had been filled in correctly. There was a raising of the eyebrows and a questioning look to John but he held his tongue, thanked him and left as quickly as he had arrived. Francis Cantlie was the next house to be visited but he was conscious of the old saying, "It's well that the teeth are before the tongue."

Now the clerk had no malice in him nor propensity for gossip but even he was not immune to it, and by the time he had reached the farm at Coldhome he was fit to burst, which was unfortunate as the wife of the house was a fierce, narrow minded gossip.

So as things would have it, it wasn't long before most folk had heard the news. Now, John Cantlie's name had been whispered when it became known that Margaret was with child but no one knew for sure, and this was not the only illegitimate bairn to be found close by, so tongues had quieted and life had moved on, but now Jane would be known as a Cantlie and learn to write her name as such when school began. The Smiths were poor folk who lived from hand to mouth whereas the Cantlies were land proprietors who had provided work for the Smiths over the years.

But, as is often the way, life, like the river, twists and turns unexpectedly, so it came as some surprise, and perhaps relief, to the Smiths that nothing happened at all. There was no hammering on the door from any Cantlie demanding explanations, or turning heads away when meeting on the road. For a time life just carried on as before except for poor little Elizabeth, who four weeks after the census, aged just three, died in her mother's arms on 8th May. The whooping cough had fractured her tiny ribs and filled her lungs with pneumonia.

Jane's brow furrowed in confusion as she listened to her mam's words.

"Elizabeth has gone my quine. God has taken her to Heaven."

Jane saw the tears on her mam's cheek and wiped them with her wee hand. "Dinna greet Mam, God will take her back tomorrow."

FEAR SOAKED INTO the hearts of families, throughout Mortlach, as the whooping cough spread. The Smiths were not the only ones to know the rawness of grief: its weight shackling the heart and the memories pulling the mind into a black abyss, the cruel unfairness of a bairn suffering and leaving the world long before she should. Little Elizabeth was a child among many who were taken, not by the fairies, but by a world lacking in both knowledge and medicine, such as it was, when Queen Victoria sat on her throne. The medicinal herbs which hung from hooks in kitchens used in the hope of easing the suffering of those who succumbed to disease, with death at its root, did little.

Sarah was bereft. She whispered to the auld wife in the kitchen, " I kent that death was near - my dreams warned me - but so many are ill, young and auld, I hoped and prayed it would not be my kin. What's the use o' dreaming o' the future if I canna stop things fae happening?"

She slumped her head into her hands, "It's a cruel curse and I dinna want it."

The auld wife rested her boneless hand on her quine's shoulder: seen but not felt.

$\mathcal{J}$ANE AND ANN continued to play together each day, as they always had, but sometimes they would forget that Elizabeth was gone and shout for her to come outside. Then one of them would remember that she wasn't there anymore and it felt strange for them. A few weeks after Elizabeth's death Jane was playing outside with a hoop, rolling it along the ground towards Ann, when she saw little Elizabeth peeking around the corner, a wee smile on her face.

The hoop fell as Jane pointed and her eyes sparkled, "Look, Ann - it's Elizabeth."

Ann spun round but no one was there. Her eyebrows squished together as she looked back at Jane. She shook her head slowly and stared at the ground as she whispered, "No."

Jane'e eyes fell on Elizabeth again and she wanted to call out to her but as she peered more closely she realised that she looked like the other people who lived in her home, who were different from her family, and could not speak to her, so she held her tongue and just smiled. Elizabeth gave a wee wave and disappeared leaving Jane with a feeling of comfort as if she had been given a bosie.

Losing Elizabeth was a happening that would forever live with Jane, a loss she would never quite understand, but wee Elizabeth would remain with Jane throughout her life.

THE POOR, CLOSE - knit community that Jane was born into was a place fast changing with the coming of the modern world. Death touched all classes through the high prevalence of disease and poor living conditions but there was a shared sense of togetherness binding folk together, whether through stubbornness, folklore or love: the work got done, bairns were born and the world moved on.

The year end came and brought with it the death of Prince Albert and a grieving Queen Victoria, whilst across the ocean, civil war raged in America. Each week folk gathered round a neighbour's hearth, with the newspaper, sharing the announcements and stories from both near and far.

The Feeing Market had brought new blood to Mortlach in November and young minds were planning, and loins stirring, in the cold winter evenings. Margaret found herself being wooed that winter by one George Scott, a mason, with promises made and the lure of her own cottage, a man by her side, and a father for Jane. It was a time of contentment and hope for Margaret, but although the Cantlies may have held their tongues there were others who took it upon themselves to judge her.

As Margaret was walking past the mill early one January morning two elderly wives were making their way to Keithmore Farm on their way to collect some milk. Margaret braced herself as she knew them of old.

"Well here she is, Miss high and mighty, thinks she can steal a name and hae a Cantlie bairn with nae ring on her finger. The bairn will turn oot a thief like her mother."

Margaret's chin lifted. "Morning to ye both. Is there no new news to be keeping your tongues busy?"

A loud tut was the only answer and Margaret's heart righted itself again as she passed. Mostly she did not answer such folk but sometimes bravery won. She was thankful for George, as surely to be married offered respectability and perhaps the quieting of loose tongues. The air of excitement in Margaret on being courted by him, had spread itself out like a blanket, covering good sense, which would have its own consequences.

THE BLOSSOMING OF snowdrops in February preceded the excitement coursing through Mortlach for the upcoming opening of the railway station at Dufftown, a growing town which attracted skilled workers, and over the years more stores selling food, clothing and hardware opened up alongside bakers, butchers, a bank and post office.

A grand opening was planned on the 21st with everyone being given time off to attend. There were to be speeches and a feast and Jane had been promised that she could go and see for herself the great invention that was called a train. There was what felt like a wedding procession as everyone travelled together, either by pony and trap or on foot, the two and a half miles to Dufftown. Luckily there was no snow on the road although there was a biting wind, but the eagerness to get there quickened the limbs and warmed the hands. Every so often one of Jane's uncles would carry her on their backs to hasten her along, although uncle William struggled sometimes, being overtaken by a bout of coughing.

Sarah watched him anxiously but refused to believe what her dreams had revealed.

Jane revelled in the easy camaraderie of the afternoon, alternating between chatting excitedly with her friend Jessie, the blacksmith's daughter, and galloping like a horse on someone's back.

On arriving in Dufftown Jane had never before seen so many people in one place. She had heard of cities and she knew that Aberdeen was one such place and she imagined it to be like this with hordes of folk and thundering noise. Not one to be scared easily, Jane stood wide eyed and drank in every detail before her. Bagpipes stirred the soul and whipped up the excitement as whisky flowed and the gentry made their speeches. Archibald Brown, the railway station agent, stood tall on a stool as a hush descended on the crowd.

"Ladies and gentlemen, today is a day to be proud. Proud of the hard work in the laying of this railway line and proud of taking our town and the surrounding area into the future. No longer will we be on the sidelines of business but able to trade with the best of them, bringing more employment and more money in pockets. This line is our future. A future filled with prosperity and respect for what we so ably produce in terms of farm produce, wool and whisky."

The crowd clapped and cheered at his words as whisky flowed and backs were slapped. Hope for a better future for all enveloped minds and brought wide grins to faces. Tables laboured under the weight of great platters of cake and food that left Jane awestruck, and she wasn't the only one - granny had suddenly gone very quiet, a look of wonder on her face as her eyes glued themselves to the steam engine. Granda noticed and handed her his glass of whisky which she quickly gulped, causing her to sputter and cough and granda to laugh.

Jane's belly had never been so full or her mind so enthralled, and when the time came for the train to leave a hush descended on the station, before the sound of a slow rumble began to quicken into the clattering of metal, slamming of doors, and shrill whistles, fused with the smell of coal burning and the smarting of eyes from billowing smoke. Shouts and cheers roared in her ears as the mighty metal horse slowly pulled its carriage of gentlefolk on its maiden journey to Keith. Jane cheered along with the crowd and felt nothing but an exhilarating excitement, as her granda hurled her up onto his shoulders to watch the engine disappear from view, although the musical clacking sound lingered for some time, carried by the wind. In later years she would have no recollection of the speeches or the feast but she would forever remember the sight, smell and sound of the steam engine, its magnitude dwarfing her and rendering her granny speechless, which was a rare thing indeed.

That same evening John took down the fiddle from above the box bed and his fingers deftly played a reel, the buoyant, melodious notes bowing to the hearts already lightened by the day's proceedings, lifting feet and skirts in the air as his kin danced to the tunes of fortune. They had witnessed progress that day and a way of life to come, and as Jane birled round with the ghost of a woman long past, she felt the excitement of what might lie ahead.

In the weeks that followed there was nothing but talk of the train and the goods that now arrived and left with haste. The atmosphere was one of hope, and Margaret's romantic heart could see only good things ahead. But come May, talk turned to work, and farm and domestic servants set off to the Feeing market to barter their wages and secure new employment. Margaret, believing herself in a secure position, found herself deserted, her man, George Scott, moving on to pastures new, never to return.

Promises broken, hopes crushed and new life in her womb.

The anger in the Smith house was palpable.

"By God, if I see that loon again I'll string him up!" John paced the floor as he ranted, spewing scorn on the man who had deserted his quine. Margaret was slumped at the table, a feeling of numbness shrouding her mind, broken only by her mother's words, directed at her, as she lashed out with scathing judgement,

"It's nae wonder tae see a fool courting an idiot!"

Tears coursed down Margaret's cheeks. "I ken I have brought shame on ye both again. I thought we were to be married. I thought he was a good man. I thought…"

"How many more excuses do you hae?" her mother bellowed, standing over her daughter, hands gripping the edge of the table, her eyes blazing.

"Sally! Enough." Sarah was quietened. Her husband's tone cutting off her tongue as she too slumped into a chair.

"God has sent us another bairn." John's words hung in the air as his women folk quietly wept.

𝒥ANE TURNED FIVE when the atmosphere in her home was tense and fraught. Unable to understand the feeling she took comfort from the other people who lived alongside them, who sat with her and although could give no words, provided a sense of safety and security as they always had done. Sometimes little Elizabeth visited too and she alone could bring a smile to Jane's sweet face when her mother wept quietly as she sewed.

To rub salt in Margaret's wounds, one Helen Gibb brought a child into the world in June, a quine named Helen, illegitimate but with John Cantlie's name firmly on her birth certificate.

𝒮OME DAYS JANE accompanied her mam to Dufftown, to visit the likes of the fishmonger or post office, excursions she enjoyed. One particular day, on entering the grocers, two women were passing the time of day, and upon seeing Margaret remarked,

"And there's another orraster, a loose woman by any other name, carrying a second bairn to be born on the wrong side o' the blanket."

Their words were loud whispers meant to be heard and their looks hard and condescending. Margaret took Jane's hand and walked with shoulders back, over to the boxes of vegetables.

"Good afternoon, it's a fine, warm day," she said to the women as she passed.

The reply was a tut and a shake of the head as Margaret went about her business of selecting some kale and took it up to the counter.

"Anything else, quine?"

"That's all, thank you, Mr Simpson."

The grocer smiled at Jane as he handed the kale to her mother, "You're getting tae be a big girl, Jane. Will you soon be off tae school?"

Jane grinned, "Aye, and I'm getting my own pair o' shoes so I can walk there every day, even in the snow."

She held up a leg, showing Mr Simpson a wee bare foot, black as the lum. "Granny says she's fed up scrubbing my toes."

Margaret shook her head as the grocer chuckled. "Well that's fine indeed, quine."

Margaret thanked the grocer and bid him good afternoon and left the store smiling again at the gossips on her way out.

Jane was aware that the women had not been kind in some way although she had not understood their words fully, but her mam chatted away to her as if nothing was amiss and they continued on with their chores. It was not to be the last time that such incidents occurred and as Jane grew up over the years her understanding of the words also grew, as did her stubbornness and pride.

The following Sunday brought the weekly visit to kirk for the Smiths, but the minister, being witness to so many of his flock having illegitimate children, was determined to teach a lesson and unfortunately for Jane she was to be the example. Following the first hymn, as hush descended, he left his pulpit and placed a stool at the foot of it, then proceeded to walk up the aisle to where the Smiths were seated. "Come with me, Jane."

The family looked at one another unsure of his tone and Jane herself looked to her mother with questioning eyes. "It's alright, quine, off ye go," Margaret said, but the lightness in her voice belied the fear in her mind.

Jane followed the minister back down the aisle aware of folk watching her.

"Sit on the stool, Jane," the minister said, his voice quiet. So Jane sat down facing the congregation as the minister returned to the pulpit and with a booming thump with his fist on the lectern, the tirade began.

"What you are looking at is SIN," he roared, as he pointed down at Jane. "SIN of the flesh. SIN of weakness. You sit here in the house of God and you MOCK him."

Jane's wee body jumped at the thundering voice but she was unaware that she was the core of his words. She did not know why she was sitting on the stool but when she saw tears running down her mother's face she was frightened and confused.

The minister raised his arm and pointed a gnarled finger as he roared again, "ANN, you are guilty of this sin. MARY, you are guilty of this sin. ISOBEL, you are guilty of this sin. MARGARET, you are guilty of this sin. Not just once, but TWICE. TWICE you have let the Devil into your heart. You sit there with EVIL in your belly."

Margaret's hand instinctively covered her belly, rubbing it as if to reassure her unborn child, but her tears stopped and were replaced with anger as she watched tears trickling down Jane's cheeks. She longed to gather her up and take her outside but it was the way of things to listen to the minister, so she sat, suspended in time, and waited.

Sarah clutched Margaret's hand, squeezing it hard, as she herself fought back both tears and anger. John sat upright, his face unreadable, as he stared at the minister. Quiet sobs could be heard, echoing around the walls of the kirk, as shame was thrust down throats.

Some heads nodded in agreement and eyes burrowed into the quines who were exposed. They may as well have been naked, so vulnerable did the young women feel.

The scorn continued as the minister furiously turned the pages of his bible and bellowed parts of verses,

"...*the lust of the flesh and the lust of the eyes and the boastful pride of life, is not from the Father,*"

"...*the carnal mind is enmity against God.*"

The pages were rapidly turned again.

"*The one who does what is sinful is of the Devil*"

His fist pummelled the wood again as he roared, sweat forming on his lip, spit firing from his mouth and eyes wide. "You must repent and you must give your bastard children unto the Lord for his judgement."

Jane's head lowered but her eyes darted around the kirk and her wee hands covered her ears as the bellowing continued over her head. She found her granny's eyes and held them, as the back of Sarah's hand rose up and lifted her own chin, as she nodded to Jane with a small smile. Jane too lifted her chin and sat still and upright, her eyes never leaving her granny's.

The thunder eventually subsided and with a succession of 'Amens' the minister descended from his place of power, and walked proudly the length of the aisle to wait for his parishioners to bid him farewell at the door. Sarah beckoned Jane and she rose quickly to be enveloped in her granny's skirts. Margaret took her hand and one by one the flock left the kirk.

John led his kin out and for the first time in his life, did not shake the minister's hand.

*

School provided a refuge from the atmosphere at home, a place where Jane shrouded herself in the wonder of letters and learning and absorbed knowledge, as a cloot does water. Her teacher was strict but fair and encouraged Jane in her studies, despite her being a quine. The day was long, seven till four, and she walked to school carrying a peat for the school room with her every morning, as the other children did, to keep the room warm whilst they studied. The passages to be learnt from the scriptures were long and difficult, but Jane met the challenges in her work with enthusiastic commitment, alongside learning her domestic chores. Each day the number of pupils present differed, between six and eighteen, according to who was needed to help at home, or work on a farm to help bring money in for their families. Margaret wanted Jane to attend everyday and learn what she herself had been unable to, and it made her heart sing to see Jane thrive in her learning and accomplish what she had not.

What had begun as a refuge soon became another place where Jane was trapped in an atmosphere she had no understanding of, where the older bairns had listened to their parents' chatterings by the hearth.

"My mam says your name's Smith, nae Cantlie."

"You dinna sit at any Cantlie's hearth," sneered another quine.

"Your mam's an orraster and you dinna hae a father," spat another.

Jane was surrounded by the three older girls outside the school who poked at her chest and laughed. Her heart beat faster and tears threatened as she bit her lip, unsure of their words' meaning, but she felt the cruel sentiment in them and she was unsure what to do. Their own failings and secrets were forgotten as they latched onto Jane's. Thankfully the quines ran off home as Ann and Jessie appeared and took Jane's hands, walking home together.

At that time Jane felt no loss of a father, as she had her granda at home, but these cruel bairns made her feel that her home was wrong, and her mam bad. Margaret caught her daughter running into the yard after school, tears streaming down her cheeks. On hearing the reason she knelt down and instructed her,

"Dinna give yer tears tae the spiteful, that only feeds them. Starve them wi' yer smile instead."

These were words that Jane would strive to adhere to whenever someone chose to be malicious or hurtful. She had observed her mother doing the same and sought to mirror her, but at times this proved too difficult and her tears would flow freely in secret, as she suspected perhaps her mam's did too.

T HE MONTHS PASSED, made somewhat easier by the news that Uncle John and Aunt Elizabeth were expecting another bairn in the summer. Little Elizabeth would never be forgotten but it was seen as a blessing that new life would soon be in their cottage. A little girl, baptised Jane, but to be called Jean, was born at dinner time on 11th August 1862, in Glack of Clunymore, where her parents had moved to, following the loss of Elizabeth.

Margaret's heart both healed and hardened that summer. She came to terms with her situation and accepted her lot for what it was. Shame had been brought to the door but she felt her mother and father's forgiveness in the way they now looked at her. Her second bairn would be loved, same as her first, and she wished the auld gossips sour breath and cold erses. She would protect Jane as best she could till such time as she was able, herself, to deflect torment. Jane had a mind full of energy and wit and she prayed that no person would suppress that.

In the final week of harvest, on 21st September at 9pm, a brother was born to Jane, named James Alexander Innes Smith. Jane was to meet him for the first time the following morning and was struck at how small he was, with a lack of hair on his head and a fearful howling from his lungs. She enquired if her mam had picked him up with the post, which caused some hilarity in later years, when the tale was remembered, as James himself would become a postman.

SARAH

At the age of fifty four, Sarah was hard worn and weather beaten but it did not occur to her to mind. She had both blessings and curses in her life. Known as Sally to no other but John, she knew she had a good man by her side, who calmed her sometimes troubled soul, and together they navigated a tumultuous world. Blessed with eleven bairns, Sarah buried four of them over the course of her life, a piece of her going with each of them, and at times a piece of her mind too, but somehow she managed to claw it back, slightly altered and harder, but there all the same. Encased within the metal, a softness lingered, visible in a sense of humour intertwined with the ability to love fiercely. At times, frustrated with the world around her and those who inhabited it, she lacked the gift of patience and vigorously kicked life up the erse with a quip, either fatal or humorous, depending on the disposition of the victim.

Early one morning, before anyone else had risen from their beds, Sarah took a minute to sit by the freshly lit fire in the hearth. This was her time of day to be spent alone with her thoughts, where she contemplated life and allowed her mind to decipher her dreams.

A woman holding her young bairn, no longer in this world, sat opposite Sarah on John's chair. She smiled at Sarah as she rocked her child and Sarah returned the smile, acknowledging their presence.

"Morning, quine."

No answer came, nor was expected.

"Did you hae secrets like me, I wonder? The awareness of those who have passed and dreams that tell o' the future?"

Sarah sighed and her eyes surveyed her kitchen but her mother was not present.

"When I was a young bairn I told my mother that her unborn loon would not live. She skelpt me - hard - for saying such a wicked thing, but a few days later the child was born and died within the hour. My mother looked at me with such fear that I ran and hid wi' the hens. About a week later she sat me down and told me that her granny had known such things and been burned as a witch for it. She put the fear o' God into me and made me promise never to tell a soul and I never have."

Sarah sighed, "I will lose another bairn, I ken that."

Sarah leant forward and poked the fire, losing her thoughts in the flames.

She feared her secrets could have been seen as an evil thing inside her, and life was difficult enough without being shackled with the Evil Eye.

Folk of the time were not known for their couthiness: often thrawn minds and an air of dourness covered tender hearts like the spikes of a hedgehog. Hunger and poverty, driven by politics, hardened some hearts but in others a strong sense of hope thrived, enabling the ability to nurture both their bairns' and their own dreams. Belief in both the scriptures and folklore was strong in the Smith cottage, as it was throughout Scotland, and the power of fairies and the Evil Eye were feared giving rise to the observation of many superstitious rituals.

She had closely watched her bairns growing up to see if they showed signs of either knowing the future or the seeing of ghosts. Considering she had had eleven bairns she had never noticed any clear signs in them, but she wasn't completely sure about her eldest loon, John. Jane, on the other hand, gave her cause for concern, as the bairn had enough to contend with in life. One day the subject would no doubt be broached but it was a day not to be looked for, and she wasn't to know who might broach it first.

Reprieve

The year that followed James's birth eased into a steady rhythm of school, chores and home life for Jane. Her skin had thickened slightly to the taunts of other bairns, home was calmer and she noticed that her mam's smile was often present. At times, notably the middle of the night, Jane could happily have taken James to the chicken shed and left him there, so she could sleep soundly with her dreams, as before, but following the stern rebuke on making this suggestion to her mother, Jane held her tongue, as well as her lugs.

Her dreams were full of babies, bannocks and books and her house full of both her family and the house people, as she now referred to them. It had never occurred to Jane to talk about the other folk she saw, somehow she sensed it was something personal to her and she didn't know the words with which to tell someone anyway.

She missed having Ann next door to play with. The old school house now lay empty, but Ann wasn't too far away, and both Ann and their friend Jessie went to school with Jane, neither of whom called her names. Jane also had a great ally in Ann, with regards to the noise and inconvenience of having a newborn in the house.

The week had come round for the Smiths to host the reading of the newspaper and Jane was allowed to stay up for slightly longer than usual, as long as she promised to be quiet. The reading of the paper from front to back, every single word pronounced, was a reverent and serious business. The head of the house had the honoured task, so John had to remove his pipe and insert a marble or two in order to read fervently and clearly. Only when the entire paper had been read could anyone be allowed to speak, and there followed much blethering on the weekly events in the shires and the wider world.

It appeared that war was still raging in America and that the number of folk emigrating from Scotland was climbing. The lure of pastures green pulled the young, and not so young, across the oceans to Canada, America and Australia to make their fortune.

Donald, the blacksmith, announced, "I hear John Cantlie's younger brother, James, is about to set sail for Canada."

"Off to make his fortune nae doubt," replied Sarah.

Heads nodded as Isabella, the miller's wife, whispered, "Seemingly Helen Kemp is wi' child and John Cantlie named as the father."

Margaret stood quickly and took Jane by the hand. "Come, Jane, time for bed."

As Jane was ushered under the blanket her mam was smiling, "Maybe now the name calling at school will stop, Jane. Night, night."

Jane returned the smile, "Night night, Mam."

She had no idea how that could be but she hoped her mam was right. Jane cooried down and let her dreams take her.

T HE NEW RAILWAY line opened from Dufftown to Craigellachie, but their celebrations were slightly subdued due to the train crash the previous October, in west Lothian, killing fifteen people. Those who had already feared the coming of the trains bellowed and protested against their safety, but no one could halt progress, and the lines continued to open and the trains continued to venture to virgin towns, delivering both goods and people to the stations. Jane was yet to experience the wonder of travelling in a train but she knew with all heart that it would be the most wonderful adventure.

Come December, Helen Kemp delivered a boy, baptised James, and John Cantlie's name on his birth certificate; his third illegitimate child, that was known about. Just eighteen months between wee James and his half sister Helen, Helen Gibb's child, and no understanding or marriage between John and either of the mothers, as was the case with Margaret. A couple of years previously the Queen had declared that only married men were welcome in the Rifle Corp, as she believed that normal marriage improved a man's marksmanship. Well it looked as if John Cantlie put paid to that remark!

When Jane had been born Margaret had secretly hoped that John would accept Jane as his bairn and perhaps even have married her, but now she felt a fool for such thoughts considering his other illegitimate bairns. Perhaps he had not believed that lying together only once could result in a bairn.

"Surely folk will view John Cantlie differently now, Mother."

"Well, a good mother will warn her quines o' his charm and lack o' intentions to marry."

"Maybe tongues will quieten now and life will be better for Jane."

Sarah sighed. "Their opinions may well change towards him, Margaret, but that disna mean they hae forgiven you for the taking o' his name."

Perhaps things would have been different if Margaret had not had a second illegitimate bairn, even though there had been an understanding with his father. Unfortunately for Jane, if opinions on John altered they did not change towards Jane and her mother. Bairns at school continued their taunts and the fact that John Cantlie had fathered another bairn just added fuel to their fire.

Life for Jane suddenly felt a whole lot worse.

DREAMS

SARAH WAS VIOLENTLY roused, from the repeated knocking three times over and over in her dream, by a piercing scream. Disorientated, she lumbered from her bed, telling John to go back to sleep, as it was probably Jane again, and took herself through the house. James was crying now too, having been woken by his sister, and Margaret was trying to comfort them both. Sarah went to console Jane, leaving her daughter to tend to James. It was the third time in a week that Jane had cried out in her sleep, waking in a terrible state and greeting uncontrollably. She babbled about books and banging noises and house people and wanted neither to go to school, nor stay at home, in the day.

She was a troubled bairn and no one knew quite what to do. Jane refused to speak of her dreams in the daytime and became quiet and withdrawn throughout the tail end of winter. Sarah knew the knocking in her own dreams portended death and she was petrified of who it might be.

A few days later, spring had come early, and Jane was outside collecting the eggs and her granny was sitting on the back step peeling tatties in the sun, when she saw little Elizabeth skipping round the corner. She began to chase the hens and they were flapping and screeching and making a right ruckus. Jane and Sarah started to giggle as they watched Elizabeth flapping her arms in the air, running and jumping. Then with a little wave Elizabeth was gone. Jane waved back and at that moment Sarah realised that Jane had seen Elizabeth.

Sarah slowly put down her peeling knife and called Jane over to her. She took her onto her knee and said,

"I saw Elizabeth too, Jane, and I see folk in the house who canna speak to us. They used to bide here but have now passed away. Folk believe that if a drop of water enters a child's eyes whilst being baptised, it opens the eyes to the seeing of ghosts throughout life."

Jane's wee eyes lit up at her granny's revelation.

Sarah held her breath as she asked, "Do you hae dreams, Jane, that tell ye things?"

Jane's eyebrows knitted together. "I dreamed aboot eating a great muckle cake all to myself last night."

Sarah's breath returned and she hoped that that meant no.

She did not wish to frighten her grandbairn but she had to ensure that she would not reveal her awareness. She had enough troubles in life without being shackled with the Evil Eye or some other superstitious belief.

Secrets were a burden but her mother's long ago words echoed in her ear, and although witches were no longer burned at the stake, the wrath of folk could be just as harmful.

"It's comforting to know they are there, watching o'er us," she continued.

Sarah took Jane's chin in her hand and looked hard into her eyes, "It's best to keep it our secret though as some folk winna understand. Promise me you winna tell a soul. Ever."

Jane looked at her granny and felt a shiver of fear. Her granny had never spoken to her in that way before. She nodded seriously, "I promise, Granny."

"Good girl." Sarah hugged her and the moment of fear passed as Jane smiled,

"Elizabeth is happy and the auld wife in the kitchen disna like how my mam makes porridge."

Sarah laughed, "That auld wife is my mother and when she wis alive she didna like how I made the porridge either."

Jane cooried into her granny, feeling the warmth of her, and she was glad that they shared a sense of awareness that allowed them to sometimes see folk they had loved. Something shifted inside her, and her wee heart fluttered with a shimmer of happiness, almost forgotten.

Little did she know that she had made a promise that would cause her angst throughout her life.

So, LIFE CHANGED again. Slowly, attention shifted away from Jane at school and her dreams settled, allowing her to continue to enjoy both her school work and playing with her brother. Margaret was relieved that her wee quine was happy once more and could see that thrawn streak returning, bouncing around a body full of mirth and eyes full of sparkle. You would sometimes find Jane and Sarah giggling together in the kitchen, for no apparent reason, and for a while at least, contentment lived in Milton Cottage.

The Cockerel Crows

April 1864 brought the sowing of tatties and longer days, but it also brought Jane's uncle William home to Milton Cottage, at the age of twenty six. The doctor, George Menzies, said his consumption had moved on to the next stage, following five years of ill health, and William struggled to work now. He had had periods of remission but his painfully thin, pale appearance told a story of an ill man, grappling with the almost certain call of death. Sarah settled her loon in the box bed in the kitchen so she could tend to him easily, a stone weighing down all of their hearts, as they waited.

Jane was approaching her seventh birthday and continued to bring joy to the cottage. Her quick mind and constant chatter and giggles mingled with her stubborn streak that ran her mother ragged. She was aware that her uncle was ill and was told to be quiet in the home, but often you would find her sitting with her uncle, telling him anecdotes from her school day.

Her granda had taken a knife and cut the leather away from the front of her shoes so her wee toes peeked out, allowing them freedom and space to grow till new shoes became available. Jane would sit on a wee stool and place her feet on the bed beside William and wriggle her toes making them speak. These stories turned the ordinary into the entertaining, and she prised smiles and laughter from him that lifted the spirit and eased the mind, as often only bairns have the ability to do.

James was a toddler now, and wreaking havoc in his own way.

It was a constant battle keeping him away from the spinning wheel and out of the peat basket. He was mothered by Jane who, having forgiven him for sleepless nights in the early days, was both protective and intrigued by him. William too watched him with a melancholy washing over him at the realisation that he would never be a father.

As time trudged on, across the ocean the Ionian islands were ceded to Greece by the United Kingdom and in Britain little boys under the age of ten were no longer sent up chimneys. Slowly the world outside was evolving, but inside Milton Cottage the world was diminishing. William's body was wracked with pain and fever, and it was almost a relief to Sarah when she heard the cockerel crowing at night, a sure sign that death was imminent - and on 7th July in the early hours of the morning, William closed his eyes for the final time.

John was the first to rise that morning, and on seeing his son with life no longer in him, he opened the window and door to let his spirit rise and stopped the clock. Taking a few moments to compose himself he dragged his unwilling feet towards his Sally, perched on the fireside chair, where she had watched over her dying son all night, her eyes blank, her mind impenetrable and her heart shackled.

John knelt in front of his wife, taking her trembling hands in his. No words were spoken as the couple sat once again, lost in the grief of the taking of yet another bairn.

As William had slowly succumbed to death, now the cottage slowly came to life. John and Sarah worked in silence, each knowing what had to be done. A nail was driven into the cheese and the pail of milk was poured away outside. Water was sprinkled over William's clothes as well as the kitchen furniture, and a saucer of salt was placed on his chest, followed by the covering of the mirror with a cloth. John left to fetch the wright to measure and make the coffin, ensuring on his way out that the hens were shut in, as they would not be let out until William was buried.

Sarah tenderly washed William's body as she quietly spoke.

"Ye will be wi' yer brothers now. They will guide ye and look after ye till I join ye all again."

Following the washing and dressing of his body, a fir candle was lit and William watched over, night and day to ward off the evil spirits. This was not as solemn a time as one might think, a gentle humour lingered, pipes were smoked and whisky drunk, and when the final friend and neighbour had looked upon William, the coffin was shut, a tiny piece of the covering sheet having been taken alongside a lock of hair, to be tenderly preserved.

The coffin was carried to its resting place, the bell toller leading the procession, and William was lowered to the ground, the end of his life's journey.

Throughout that week Jane felt a great sadness in her heart but had an understanding beyond her years that William was now free of pain. She heard names mentioned of others who had also passed and it frightened her to have folk disappear from her world. The house was full of family and friends and the house people mingled, unseen, smiling at Jane and sitting with Sarah, offering their presence as comfort.

As is often the way, life follows death, and a child was conceived shortly after the loss of William, another daughter for aunt Elizabeth and uncle John, and a little sister to Ann, John and Jean. Born the following February, the bairn was christened Elizabeth, which in the year 1865 was not unheard of, to name a child the same name as a child lost previously, but it did make Jane wonder what Elizabeth would have thought - honoured or replaced?

Little Elizabeth was often present beside Jane - sometimes in the cottage and other times she would appear skipping along the road beside her. Some of the ghosts that Jane could see remained in one place, like the old man and the young woman with the wee bairn in her home, others she saw fleetingly and never saw again. She commented to her granny,

"I dinna think ye grow old when ye die. I am taller than Elizabeth now."

"Aye, quine, it would seem so." Sarah thought of her lost bairns as she and Jane gathered in the washing. Shaking off the thought she quipped,

"Still, it would be an awful thing if all the ghosts we saw were auld and crabbit."

The two quines laughed as they saw Sarah's mother, hands on hips, making a scowl on her face, which quickly turned to a wee smile.

*

ACROSS THE OCEAN the Civil war ended in America, bringing with it the end of slavery and in Britain the Salvation Army began on the streets of London, helping the poor and the destitute. Locally, John Grant opened the Gelenfarclas distillery, south of Aberlour, providing more work for folk in Speyside. Life was advancing, the wealthy were wearing velvet and silk dresses but the poor were still choking by their lumless hearths.

The following year brought yet more grief, this time for uncle John and his bairns. Aunt Elizabeth's heart, full of disease, gave up the struggle to beat on 13th August, and she died quietly, sitting at the table at four in the afternoon, whilst preparing the evening meal for her family, leaving four bairns, the youngest just eighteen months old, and a heartbroken husband who would never again marry.

Jane was learning too young, what it meant to know and love someone, and then have them taken away. For a while, as she grew up over the years, she wondered if she was somehow unwittingly causing these deaths. So many neighbours and friends, as well as kin, had succumbed to illness and her mind tried to make sense of it. She pondered over trying not to care about folk, so as not to miss them when they left, but found this an impossible task, one which left her feeling worse at having tried.

Her mind reflected like a loch, on a calm summer's day, but it was often disturbed by life's storms, whipping up the water, wrestling with the subconscious and disrupting the natural ebb and flow. There was a loss of innocence that came with the closeness of death, and a time meant for play and imagination was scarred with truth and awareness.

Wee Elizabeth was the only one who had come back to her.

She made a tiny wish in her mind as she whispered to the house people,

"Please dinna leave me."

A seed of fear had been planted, burrowing in her mind, nurtured by every death that touched her, which grew as she too grew, brandishing her forever petrified of who she would lose next.

A Changing World

In the year that Jane turned ten, her brother James started school. Their mother had given him his father's surname, Scott, but he was illegitimate on his birth certificate, same as Jane. Human nature being as it is there was acceptance of this, as it was known that there had been an understanding between Margaret and George Scott, before he abandoned her. James would not suffer the same fate as Jane, with the lashings of cruel tongues, but in later years the consequences would be worse.

James was a quiet bairn, with a temperament like his granda. He was just as content with his own company as he was when surrounded by others, and he followed Jane like a lamb. Two sides of the same coin, Jane's exuberance and stubbornness was balanced by James's placidness and calm nature. Margaret marvelled at how different her bairns were but gave thanks that there were few battles, remembering her own siblings' skirmishes in her childhood. There was a protectiveness in Jane over her brother and her thrawn streak grew over the years especially at school, where she had learned how to stand up for herself.

A loon, full of his own self importance, shouted across the school yard, "Your mother was taken by the fairies and replaced wi' a changeling. That's why she's so wicked."

Jane ran full pelt at him and propelled him into the bramble bushes. She was lucky not to have been seen by the headmaster and Charlie Black clambered undignified out of the bushes, covered in scratches and berry juice, to the sound of laughter from the other school bairns.

THE RECENT 2ND Reform Act resulted in more men folk being allowed to vote but women were making their voices heard. The Suffragette movement sprung up in 1867 in London, but word was spreading, and even the wives of Banff had signed and sent a petition to the Government, demanding a vote. The weekly reading of the newspaper was full of the rights of women, which had caused some ructions and strong words in cottages throughout the country. Women were tired of being supposedly content with their lot, and on hearing their husbands' outrage, at times withheld more than their tongues.

Folk were hearing more and more about the bravery and achievements of women throughout the world. The Edinburgh seven, consisting of seven women, were admitted to university to study medicine, the first in Scotland, and indeed Britain, to do so. Florence Nightingale was a pioneer in the training of nurses and Isabella Fyvie Mayo, living in Aberdeen, was an author. But of course the struggle was not helped by the Queen, who despite being a woman, looked upon womens rights as being, "*mad, wicked folly.*"

So Jane was growing up in a world steeped in tradition and a certain way of doing things, otherwise known as peer pressure from dead folk, now peppered with contemporary ideas and happenings. She had no awareness of wealth, silk clothing or indeed a silver trinket made in Banff, once famous for its silver trade. Her feet were often shoeless, her kitchen floor was made of earth and her bed was sporadically warm, depending on the weather.

WITH JAMES NOW at school, there were no bairns in the cottage throughout the day, and Margaret worked in Dufftown as a domestic servant, so Sarah found herself alone with her chores. She felt older than her sixty years - life had worn her soul despite the tenderness of a good family, and there was a need in her for some lightness. Her tenth bairn - George, Jane's uncle, who had been more like a brother to Jane, there being only nine years between them - had been out working as a farm labourer for some years now and following the Feeing market the previous year in 1868, found himself working on a farm in Keith. News from him was sporadic, despite the postal service, George not being a lover of the pen, so it came as something of a surprise when a letter arrived the following May.

Dear Mother and Father,

I am not one for the letter writing but I think o' ye often. I hope all is well in Milton Cottage. I am writing wi' happy news for ye. I have met a lass, Margaret. She is a farm servant here and we are to be married in June. She is with child so ye will have another grandbairn later in the year. We would like it if ye could manage tae come to the wedding. It's to be on the 12th June here in Keith. I hope we will see ye then,

Your son, George.

There was much excitement in Milton Cottage and John surprised them all by announcing that they would go by train. With fewer mouths to feed there was a little money to spare and it would be an adventure for them all.

It was impossible to tell who was the most excited, waiting on Dufftown platform on 12th June, everyone dressed in their Sunday best. It had been seven years since the memorable, grand opening of the line but they had never had the chance, or occasion, to step onto a train and travel the eleven miles to Keith. Jane remembered the wonder of that day but the thought of actually being able to sit in a carriage made her tremble with anticipation, and as the engine pulled into the station she thought she may burst with excitement.

There was much hustle and bustle climbing onto the carriage

and finding themselves seats. "Careful, Sally, mind the step. Come away bairns, quickly now, sit doon there wi' yer mother."

John shepherded his kin as if he had travelled on a train every day of his life.

Sarah and John sat side by side, the bairns opposite, with Margaret, the window between them, allowing them to see out. When the whistle blew and the wheels began to turn there was a wee squeal from someone's lips and an intake of breath from another. As the train gathered momentum Sarah was slightly alarmed by the pace, and feared for their safety, but only the words, "Michty me," fell from her lips as she gripped onto John's hand.

The landscape poured away and the rhythmic melody of the wheels sang to them as they pointed and exclaimed,

"Look - a deer!"

"Oh me, the loch is beautiful."

"Mam, Mam, look, look, a castle!" Two bairns jumped up and down as the train whisked them through the countryside revealing sights never before seen.

Margaret watched her bairns' faces, their eyes vivid and their smiles wide. They climbed up through the enchanting countryside and down into Keith approximately thirty eight minutes later, astonishment and fascination in their minds. John marvelled at the wonder of it all and felt a sense of fulfilment that he had been able to take his family on such an adventure that would surely be remembered for a lifetime.

The wedding that followed was a small and simple affair but nonetheless enjoyable. Young George and his bride Margaret were a picture of happiness and the Smiths were proud of their lad and glad to see him wed and settled. So it was with a joyous heart that Sarah and John slept that night, dreaming of journeys and weddings and bairns to come, whereas Jane and James took forever to sleep, too excited with the day's happenings and not wanting the day to end.

Just two months later, the world welcomed a new bairn, a quine, to be called Sarah, after her granny, to be followed by another quine, Lilia, two years later, completing George's wee family.

Affiliation

As Jane progressed into her teenage years her understanding of the folk around her increased, alongside that of the outside world. Her father's other bairns now attended school, but it was known that they sat at the Cantlies' hearth. They were often seen out with their father or visiting their granda, Francis Cantlie who, to her, was a neighbour and nothing more, although he had always been kind towards Jane, enquiring about her schooling on meeting her out and about. It hurt her heart to see her half siblings, Helen and James, accepted as Cantlies and spending time with them.

Jane whispered to little Elizabeth, "I'm nae wanted as a Cantlie. They talk tae me in passing but they dinna see me. Ye'll think me daft but sometimes I imagine sitting wi' my father eating dinner or walking wi' him across the fields, blethering away. Why aren't I good enough, Elizabeth?"

A tear escaped and sat for a second just below her eye, before slowly trickling downwards, alerting Jane to its presence. Jane wiped it away quickly, as anger replaced hurt, and she ran with Elizabeth, the wind blowing her hair and carrying away her sadness.

Margaret's heart had hardened over the years and John knew it whenever their paths crossed. Walking with Jane one day they met John Cantlie on the road,

"Morning to ye both." John doffed his cap and glanced fleetingly at Jane.

Margaret's face was expressionless. "Morning."

Jane waited, as she always did, for more words to be forthcoming, but her father walked on by. Her heart constricted and her tongue spat, "Maybe if you were more polite he would stop and speak."

"Dinna you blame me for his lack o' interest."

Margaret's voice softened as she saw the hurt on Jane's face. "Be content wi' the family you hae."

Jane said nothing and the two walked on. She felt no sense of loss of a father as such, her granda filling any crevice that may have existed in her young life, but Jane did feel the loss of acceptance.

She carried the name Cantlie but lived the life of a Smith, bringing a sense of not belonging fully to either: a lamb in another lamb's skin.

𝒥OHN CANTLIE WORKED at Keithmore farm, some 300 acres, his uncle William being the wealthy proprietor as well as manager of the bank in Dufftown. He was known to be a genial and likeable character and his son James, John's younger cousin, studied medicine and would go on in life to be a famous surgeon, pioneer of First Aid and a Sir.

John's brother James, who had emigrated to Canada, also made a name for himself as a businessman and Governor, faring better in life than John with regards to worldly achievements. As to whether John was content with his lot, in his mid-thirties, no wife or farm of his own, and a reputation for the women, only he could answer. Perhaps he lacked ambition and the want of a permanent woman in his bed; or maybe life had gone as he had pursued it: little responsibility, a reliable wage and no one to answer to.

Whatever the truth, John Cantlie, aged thirty eight, in the year 1872, married one Mary Richardson and became overseer at Earnfold farm, the same year that William Miller died, the Scottish author of the bedtime rhyme, Wee Willie Winkie, sung to him by his mother, as a bairn.

John's newfound happiness was shattered the following July however, when his niece, Jessie Elizabeth, aged just two, died from Scarlet fever and nine days later her mother, Janet, John's sister, followed her wee bairn to Heaven, having succumbed to the same disease, at the age of twenty nine. Robert, no longer a husband and father, lost and broken with no one left.

Yet again Mortlach lived in the grip of fear, powerless, as they watched folk around them being taken too soon. The seed of fear in Jane burrowed deeper, its roots spreading.

As the world shifted and altered, so too did Jane. She had been both nurtured and anguished in life, tenderness shown and loss experienced. Her spine was straight, her heart compassionate, and she soaked in the comfort the house people brought. When the time came to leave school and look for employment, Margaret instructed Jane that they would visit Dufftown to secure work for her.

"The MacDonell family are looking for a quine to work as a general servant. I have arranged for ye tae meet wi' Mrs MacDonell on Tuesday. She will want tae ken that ye can cook well and keep a house in order, so make sure ye tell her everything ye are capable o' doing. And dinna be asking too many questions, she's looking for a servant - nae a soldier fae the Spanish Inquisition."

"Aye, Mother."

There was little consultation with Jane on the matter, it was a case of going where you were put and no questions asked, and Jane at the age of fifteen didn't think to question what had always been. There would be no further education for her - she had had more years at school than most, but she could read and write well and no more was required. That being the case, Jane found herself earning a wage, six pounds a year, to clean, sew, darn, prepare food and fetch and carry messages, from sunrise till evening, six days a week.

$\mathcal{M}$ILTON COTTAGE WAS quieter now with Jane out working. Sarah missed the constant blethering and shared awareness of the house folk. There was a close bond between them - closer she suspected than that between Jane and Margaret - and Sarah was aware that Jane struggled to carry the Cantlie name. She had feared the consequences when the census had been filled in. Margaret only saw the righting of an injustice, but she wondered… if history were to repeat itself would she burden the bairn with her father's name. It had been many a year since Jane cried over her situation and the wicked words of other folk, but sometimes her eyes betrayed the happy smile and revealed a wounded heart.

One particularly bonny June Sunday, Jane and Sarah took themselves off for a walk up to Auchindoun castle, an old Iron age fort derelict since 1725. They followed the path by the river, sheltering from the sun in the canopies of the trees, and for a while their tongues were silent as they listened to the sound of the water flowing by on its journey north. The River Fiddoch flowed from Genfiddich forest skirting the old Glenfiddich hunting lodge and thrusting its way past the castle, where it turned sharply westwards, meeting Bell's Burn and continuing on to Dufftown.

It was a bonny walk, the surrounding hills basking in the sun and the old ruins of the castle telling their own stories. Turning around at the top they could see over the valley, their homeland a scene of beauty, holding the lives of hardworking country folk in its palm. Behind them the mountain Ben Rinnes sheltered the parish of Inveravon from the cold northerly winds. As they breathed in the warm, fresh air and felt the sun on their backs, Sarah turned to Jane.

"When yer heart is suffering, take yerself oot and look upon the hills that surround us. Their height envelops and comforts us, like a bosie. Let the wind lift yer spirit and let the sun be a balm tae the scars on yer heart. Ye are never alone as long as ye are amongst hills. Life can be cruel and unfair, and at times feel unbearable, especially when ye carry a secret, but remember those ye come fae and draw on their strength. They walk aside us everyday, and you and I are lucky to be able to see them. Some think it's the Evil Eye so we keep quiet aboot it, but the child should not be blamed for the minister's shaky hand."

Jane nodded but remained quiet. As she looked upon the hills she indeed felt their comfort but she vowed to herself, *I will not be hurt by any man or have bairns be spurned. I will never marry.*

Many times in her life to come, you would find Jane outside absorbing the comfort of nature, both in times of need and in times of thanks. Her love of hills would remain with her till her dying day.

Servant Life

THE MACDONNELLS WERE a highly educated and wealthy family, in need of a quine to help with the day to day running of the house. Situated on Fife Street in Dufftown, theirs was a grand house close to Mortlach Distillery, and a short walk from the clock tower and jail, which all four main roads led to. The clock itself was transported from Banff, fame at its root, as Jimmy MacPherson, having lived a life of robbery, was hung from the clock tower in Banff in 1700.

Mr MacDonnell - a feuar, and a magistrate of police - was not yet forty, with a wife ten years his senior and three offspring. The two eldest were loons, away studying in Aberdeen, and the youngest, Annie, still attended school. The previous servant, Constance, had left to marry her lad and now bade in Elgin.

On arriving in the morning, Jane was presented with her uniform, a black dress, stiff white apron and cap, and she was instructed that it was her responsibility to keep it clean and in good condition. As Mrs MacDonnell ran through the list of duties that she would be required to undertake, Jane couldn't help but marvel at the house and its contents. There was an atmosphere of prosperity about the place. The first thing she noticed was the wooden floor throughout the downstairs and the array of large heavy furniture. There were paintings on the walls and matching crockery in the kitchen, which was separate from the living room. Upstairs each bedroom held only one bed, a decadence Jane had never before imagined.

There was also an awareness coursing through her as she turned and saw a young loon standing by the window, looking out towards the river. Perhaps the ghost of a lost MacDonnell son, she would never know. As she followed her employer through the door Jane paused to see the loon turn from the window and she nodded to him with a small smile, as he doffed an imaginary cap and sent forth a wink.

It would be Jane's responsibility to cook and clean for the family, amongst other general duties, and although her mother and granny had taught her all they could in terms of cooking, it was a daunting task, especially later when she was faced with a joint of beef to be roasted. Jane set to work, her first task being to make soup for dinner, which she could do quite easily, followed by the scrubbing of the floors, including upstairs. In her hurry, Jane knocked over her bucket of dirty water soaking some garments strewn on the bedroom floor belonging to Mr MacDonnell, in her distress Jane bundled the clothing under her apron and quickly hurried unseen down the stairs, passing the young loon seen earlier, who raised his eyebrows and grinned. Jane snapped,

"Thank goodness you canna talk as I'm sure you would clipe and get me into trouble." Arriving in the kitchen, she rinsed them and hung them out to dry, praying no one would see. It was a day where her fingers were clumsy and her mind boggled, and when she finally managed to roast the beef and was lifting it from the pot, she watched in horror as she lost her grip and the beef promptly fell and lolloped across the floor, coming to rest under the table.

For a second Jane froze, but sense took over and she sprung into action, scooping up the joint and pitching it onto a plate. A quick rub down with her fingers to remove any debris, she stepped back to see to the vegetables, when Mrs MacDonnell walked through the door. Jane spied the loon, laughing, and although she was mortified, it was a struggle to keep from laughing herself, and she was glad that he was there to lighten her distress. She was just thankful that the floor was not earthen, as that really would have been disastrous.

Eventually Jane settled into a routine, and although the work was hard and the day long, her employers were fair, if a little stern. She counted herself lucky, as she knew of others who worked for strict, dour folk, with nothing but harsh words on their tongues, who were never satisfied and always criticising.

Often sent out and about for one thing or another, Jane became acquainted with other folk who lived or worked there. Each Friday she was required to visit the fishmonger as Mr MacDonnell, being a creature of habit, liked to have a certain meal on a certain day. The fishmonger, unbeknownst to Jane, was an awful man for charging folk different prices, but one morning Jane was fortunate to be there at the same time as another quine, also employed as a domestic servant in the town, who knew of his swindling ways. As Jane entered the store another lass followed behind and the two were met with a formidable scene.

A quine was standing, hand on hips, chin high, and barking, "And you can take what I have given you and be grateful. You winna make a fool out o' Elsie McDonald."

Mr Robertson, on seeing new customers entering, held his tongue but on turning to leave Elsie added, "And I will stay here whilst ye serve these two quines to make sure you dinna overcharge them either."

Jane suppressed a smile and purchased her fish for far less than she had the previous week. The other quine, slightly shy, timidly asked for what she wanted and the three servants left the shop together triumphantly, leaving a disgruntled man behind his counter. That was to be the beginning of a lifelong friendship between Jane, Elsie and Eliza.

Mrs MacDonnell was partial to the drinking of tea, a relatively new habit, adopted initially by the wealthy due to its cost, but now enjoyed by most, as it was more affordable. One particular afternoon Jane was offered some to try, and was pleasantly surprised by the mild taste of it compared to bitter coffee, and found herself taking quite a liking to it. Eliza, on hearing this, told Jane that the grocer's wife offered the reading of tea leaves, believing herself to have the same ability that Gypsies were known for. Seemingly she could tell you what type of person you would marry or if you were headed for a gruesome death. Her readings were quite popular with both the gentry and the working class: folk were always keen to know what lay ahead, as long as it was favourable of course. No one was quite sure what the clergy thought about this so voices were hushed when talking of it.

Jane was full of the gossip regarding the grocer's wife, on her return home, but was quite perturbed when her granny harshly told her,

"Dinna you be meddling in such things. Nae good can come fae knowing what lies ahead, and those who believe it are ignorant fools!"

Reflection, 1877

Margaret was sitting, absorbed in her sewing, her folks either side of the hearth, each employed in their evening chores, the scent of her father's pipe mingling with that of the peat fire. Jane had just returned from Dufftown and James, now a farm labourer at Coldhome, was at the table regaling his sister with a story from his day. The past five years had seen Jane grow into a woman approaching twenty, as strong of spirit as ever, thrawn, compassionate and quick to smile, but with the ever present fear of losing folk, so she returned each evening to the bosom of her family, reassuring herself that all were well and calming her worried heart.

She was quite beautiful, though none had said it, as to do so would feed the sin of overpraising. The combination of dark curls and blue eyes was striking, but she was oblivious to her attractiveness. She held strong to her promise to herself of never marrying, though she held it close so as not to attract comment from her kin.

John set aside his pipe and retrieved his fiddle from above the box bed. It had belonged to his father and John had learnt to play by ear, as a young loon, having a natural talent for it.

The haunting sound of a slow air meandered through the smog of the fire, John's melancholy seeping into the soul of the fiddle. His eyes were lightly closed and his fingers danced of their own accord, lamenting with the notes, and mournful in their depression of the strings. Tongues were stilled and eyes looked over uncertainly, as the cottage was enveloped in an atmosphere of unexpected sorrow.

John's mind journeyed through his seventy three years of life, drifting past the good and pausing at the sadness. He saw the faces of his bairns lost, and his life as a pauper, the struggle to feed his family and the lack of shoes on their feet. Sally's haunted look as another bairn was taken, looking to him for answers that he could not give. He felt the weight of his kins' sufferings, and with no words with which to express it, he allowed the soulful music to convey the sentiment of his heart.

As the final notes melted away Sarah gently touched John's hand, nodding to the ghosts of John's mother and father, standing by his side. She looked into his eyes, conveying her understanding and love and said,

"Now for pity's sake play something cheery and we will dance aroon' as if it were a wedding."

T HE FOLLOWING MORNING brought with it a blast of fresh air from an easterly wind, which pushed its way through the cracks and crevices of the cottage, clearing away remnants of sadness and replacing the air with a sense of spring and hope. John had left for his day's work with James, his mind again settled and Jane was on her way to Dufftown, having moved on from the MacDonnells, Jane was now employed by a family with young bairns. Her general duties were similar as before but with the added work of having little legs under her feet. Their mother seemed to have no clue as to how to look after them, the house was permanently in chaos and full of noise and Jane was forever chasing the bairns outside so as she could get on with her duties. It was a happy home though, despite the disorder, and Jane found that her days passed quickly, as did any fleeting thought of having children of her own!

She quite liked her daily life in Dufftown, the hustle and bustle, with the growing number of shops and trade, thanks to the railway and the established woollen mill. Dufftown was a thriving town with many incomers, so her days were no longer affected with old gossip, although some had long memories, and her life, for the time being, was settled.

MILTON COTTAGE FELT very quiet and far removed from the noise of Dufftown, when she returned in the evenings, and she knew that James might well be living away soon, depending on what work he found at the upcoming Feeing market. As quiet as he was, he lacked no confidence, and had proved himself a hard worker, so Jane was sure that he would manage fine in the world.

News had reached her ears that she had a new half sibling in the world - another person to be added to the list of folk that she had no relationship with. Her father had been married five years and this was his first legitimate child with his wife, Mary. The bairn was named Mary Jane, which did cause a momentary piercing of her heart, as no sibling would usually be baptised with the same name, out with death. It wounded her, but, as her granny once advised, a walk in the hills soothed her mind and was a balm to her bruised heart.

As wee Elizabeth skipped alongside her Jane lamented, "I am to be forever invisible, Elizabeth."

She supposed that more bairns might follow but she was well aware that things would likely never change, so continued as she had always done, with her head held high and her feelings concealed. A part of her felt an affinity with the world's first human cannonball, that had just been shot into the air in London, catapulted, disorientated and desperate to navigate safely to the end.

MARGARET NOW HAD employment in a house in Botriphnie, near Glackmuck, working for a retired farmer and his wife. She often contemplated life on her walk to work, and although she had been spurned and deserted in life, her romantic notions had never really disappeared, nestling quietly in the far corners of her mind. There was a part of her that still desired the warm company of a man and a hearth of her own. She had observed her parents' marriage over the years and was conscious of their strong bond, and Maragret longed to experience such a relationship for herself.

One Willie Balgown, ploughman at Midthird, had of late often been in her company, by happenstance or otherwise she could not say, and she was afraid to question it, having been so wrong in the past. Their paths seemed to cross with regularity and their conversation was easy, with no awkwardness in it, but Margaret was wary. She was past forty and Willie might just be a genial man with no intentions towards her whatsoever. She would not make a fool of herself or indeed be made a fool of, so she continued about her work and life as she had done those past twenty years, and tried to suppress any hope of attachment. Surely romance was for young quines.

News that John Cantlie, married these past five years, was a father again, caused Margaret to pause and wonder - if things had been different, perhaps they would have married and had a large brood of bairns, none of whom, born on the wrong side of the blanket. She allowed her mind to travel back to when her and John were young…

Reap What You Sow, 1856

AUGUST WAS A time for harvest to begin. All hands were required to help, from the youngest to the oldest, with school being abandoned for a few weeks. Prayers were sent to ask for fair weather to aid the bringing in of the crops and there was an air of excitement to be had throughout Mortlach. It had been a long, bonny summer bringing with it the expectation of a decent crop, but too good a crop was seen as a bad omen, so mixed in with the excitement there was always a general wariness and some would say, dourness to the soul. No one would want to be accused of being overly cheery or proud! Long hours were worked with extra hands being hired in from other counties and the farmers provided much broth, bannocks and beer, throughout the days, to sustain the workers.

Summer had also provided the warm, light evenings for daring dalliances.

Being a small, tight knit community, everyone knew everyone else's business and not much happened without someone noticing. The minister was listened to and superstition observed within the staunch folklore beliefs. Which one was most feared was anyone's guess - the lure of the Evil Eye and the power of the fairies appeared to have equal standing. Yet, neither stopped both sexes from flirting and seducing one another.

*J*OHN CANTLIE WAS, in the year 1856, a young twenty one year old chiel labouring on his uncle William's farm, Keithmore. He was considered handsome, 5'11" in standing, with a broad stature and dark, wavy hair which peeped out from under his cap, below which sat mischievous brown eyes, a straight nose and a curved, smallish mouth. It was said that he had a look of his mother.

He displayed a likeable personality, although there was a touch of arrogance there, and despite having the reputation of a hard worker he could also be found blethering happily away to the female servants as if there was no work to be done at all. Although he had an air of ease about him there was also the presence of pain lurking behind the mirth, the result of having lost his mother five years previously.

The eldest of seven children to Francis and Mary Cantlie, John had farming blood in him, was well educated, but as yet lacked the impetus of achievement. His father was a feuar and the proprietor of Clunymore Farm, John's childhood home. He had known a good standard of living and although aware of how poor some folk were in Mortlach, he had never known hunger in his belly.

There was the awareness that as the eldest son there was a degree of expectancy that he would achieve much in life, marry well and earn respect from his community. Sometimes this pressure was best eased with a few drams and a dalliance with a willing quine that had caught his eye. The summer brought with it less layers of clothing for all and the loosening of more than just collars.

*M*ARGARET SMITH WAS, at this harvest time, a twenty year old quine, and unbeknownst to herself, very becoming. She was fair of hair with large, deep blue eyes and a generous mouth that was quick to form a smile on seeing you, but her tongue was often still. She went about her day as a domestic servant with quick efficiency, which was at odds with a mind which was prone to daydreaming, and a romantic heart that lay within her.

She enjoyed, as other quines her age did, carrying out the rituals to see who a future spouse would be. On hearing the first crow of the cockerel, she spun herself round three times, anti-clockwise, and looked for a hair under her heel, the colour of which was to be her husband's. She was disappointed in her findings as fair was not a colour she admired. It was too close to her own and her vanity would have preferred it to have been darker.

She possessed a dogged determination, like her mother, that had often caused words between them but her father always calmed the waters, in his own quiet way, without offending either party, which was a feat in itself. Hers was a happy, if poor, home. The fifth of eleven bairns, crowded together in their cottage, life had often meant hunger and cold beds, but where the bellies may have been empty at times, the minds were offered wisdom and the hearts tended.

$\mathcal{J}$OHN AND MARGARET had grown up together. Their paths crossing often in the countryside where they lived, although they had attended different schools. John had gone to the parish school, and did well there, whereas Margaret had been taught in the side school next to her cottage, in Milton itself, and had struggled with her learning, despite Mr Stuart's best efforts. All the letters seemed jumbled to her and throughout her life she struggled to read and write.

Occasionally John Cantlie stopped to speak with her and offered a compliment. She took both his time and his compliment with flirtatious grace, if such a thing existed. Up until that summer things between them were as they had always been, an easy accord brought about through familiarity over the years of childhood. What brought about the change was not clear. The circumstance of the harvest, being in close proximity over long days and perhaps an unacknowledged mutual attraction somehow manifested into a new way of feeling.

On what was expected to be the last day of cutting, Margaret set to work with a sickle, working alongside the men with scythes. Some days she had worked behind the men raking and gathering but it had become routine now to work alongside John Cantlie. No words had been uttered but both had naturally converged at the same point each day and Margaret realised that she looked forward to being by his side.

"Morning, Margaret," a wide grin greeted her and two eyes penetrated.

"Morning. Will the weather hold dae ye think?" she asked, as the sickle cut swiftly leaving a pile to be gathered behind her. Her heart missed a beat.

"Aye, here's hoping." Those eyes spoke again.

The line worked in sync, like a hive full of bees, but little conversation flowed as their energy went into cutting, their backs protesting at the relentless bending and twisting. The occasional curse was sent forth as a scythe misbehaved or a muscle screamed. The day wore on and the few clouds that had been gathering were blown east as nature decided to be kind, and the weather remained dry, but not too warm. As the last bundle of barley was tied into a sheave, and the sheaves gathered into stooks to dry, folk sighed with relief.

Margaret felt a rush of disappointment at the thought of no longer working alongside John each day. Although she would not miss the back breaking work, she would miss his company and the easy accord between them. Her friend Jean had noticed the looks between them and warned Margaret, "Oh Margaret, he's a handsome chiel but he's always.... Oh I dinna ken the word, but if he was a quine I would call him flighty. I fear ye canna trust him."

Margaret was mortified that anyone had noticed her behaviour and spluttered, "We're friends and nothing more, Jean."

Jean did not reply, and merely nodded.

What Margaret had not confided was that she had grown to have feelings for John and he had a way of looking at her that she did not have the words for - but she liked it.

T HREE WEEKS PASSED and the stooks were dry so the day came for folk to load them onto the carts and transport them to the sheds. Margaret sat at the table, her breakfast in front of her, but her mind was not on her porridge. Her brothers were bickering over something or other and her mother was scolding them, but all Margaret's thoughts belonged to John Cantlie. The evening would bring the end of the harvest and the celebrations that followed would involve much dancing with a feast and whisky to be enjoyed, and Margaret secretly hoped that she would be in John's company for most of it.

"Hurry up, quine. Stop yer daydreaming and finish yer porridge. It's after five and the barley is waitin'."

Margaret spooned the last of her breakfast into her mouth and hurriedly followed her mother outside as George followed on behind, dragging his nine year old feet with him. Their father and brothers were ahead walking alongside the Mcbains, and the party made their way to Keithmore Farm.

It was hard work for both folk and horses as the carts were loaded and the sheds filled. It was the job of the younger loons to bring the workers food and beer to sustain them but with it being the last day of what was a good harvest, there was mounting excitement of the ceilidh and feast to be had in the evening.

The last shed was filled as the clock hands approached five o'clock, and tired bones and relieved minds sat themselves down, or lay on the ground, bathing in the warmth of the sun. Bairns ran in the bare fields as tables were laid with a feast for all, and whisky and beer began to flow down dry throats.

Little rest seemed to be needed with the knowledge that the harvest was now over and the hard work done, so once the music commenced feet began dancing and quines were birled round.

Sarah danced with young George, her husband playing his fiddle, and as the evening wore on and the whisky flowed, the folk of Mortlach soaked in the joy of a good harvest and the company of good folk. The floor of the barn crooned with the reels and jigs, and sighed with the slow waltzes.

A hand stretched out to invite, "Would ye like tae dance, Margaret?"

Margaret nodded and took the hand as she rose, and was led to the floor. As they danced she was acutely aware of the feel of his hand holding hers, as his other hand on her back pulled her into him firmly, its warmth seeping through her dress. John's eyes never left hers and as the last notes died away he whispered in Margaret's ear, "Shall we go oot and get some fresh air?"

The wide door of the barn was open and folk were coming and going the whole evening so no one appeared to notice John Cantlie and Margaret Smith leaving together to take in the evening air.

Margaret's normally quiet tongue found its voice. "We could tak a walk along the river. It's been weeks since we've seen the other side o' a field."

"Aye, ye are right. If we hop o'er the dyke we can join the wee path that taks ye doon tae the riverbank."

They turned as if heading to the tables of food but a convenient shed allowed them to skirt around the back, unseen. John climbed over the stone dyke and taking Margaret's hand helped her over to the other side. As she landed gently, their hands remained together and the two ambled slowly along the path, the sun low in the sky, till they reached the edge of the river where the trees stood tall and the long grass brushed against legs.

"It's been a fine summer, working alongside ye," John uttered as his hand slid around Margaret's waist and he pulled her in for a kiss which began slowly, tentatively, and grew in passion with every breath of the light breeze. Lips moved to kiss a neck, whispering, "Ye are so bonny."

Margaret's breath caught in her throat with his kisses and she allowed herself to be lowered onto the bank, sinking into the grass, as buttons were somehow undone and skirts lifted in wonder. As the light breeze rose, the grass moved rhythmically in a dance, and fingers clutched at its roots. The proud tree above, its September leaves turning in colour, gently swayed with the breeze and mimicked the grass below, as nature followed its natural path in the seasons. The air crooned and moaned as it moved, its energy heightening with every breath.

The breeze eased itself into a wind and the leaves, ready to fall, shivered and trembled as the grass was finally freed from its roots, and the leaves succumbed to the wind, as they were plucked from the branch and scattered in the air.

As nature sighed and the wind ceased, returning to nothing more than a flutter, it already held the awareness of new buds that spring would bring.

COME DECEMBER SARAH'S dreams began to make sense and her entire being was jolted as realisation dawned one morning on hearing Margaret retch outside in the yard. She flung open the door.

"Ye are with child!"

Margaret froze and stared at her mother. "Na, na - that's nae possible."

"Ye are with child. I ken it." Sarah looked at her lass with a mixture of anger and angst.

Margaret lowered herself onto the cold step, her mouth agape and her head shaking. "Na, na - I canna be," she stuttered.

Sarah's anger subsided as she looked upon her quine's shocked face. "Tell me, Margaret, did someone force themselves upon ye?"

Margaret's dishevelled mind grasped at her memories and she shook her head slowly.

"Oh, Mother, what will I do?" Her head fell into her hands and she wept.

Only the other week a quine had been denounced at kirk over the shame of carrying a child outwith wedlock and the thought sent a sliver of fear down Margaret's spine. It had been different with her sister Ann, who had had an understanding with Findlater when she was expecting a child, and they had formally married in church in January.

Sarah's anger flared again. "Whose bairn is it?"

Margaret stood up and paced the yard. "It canna be true." Denial flowed through her veins but Sarah, her own body held up by the wall, retorted,

"Ye ken it to be true. If ye have lain wi' a man ye can hae a child."

Margaret's tears started again and her mother's anger scattered in the breeze as she moved forward and held her quine.

"Yer father will need answers, lass."

Mother and daughter stood together in the yard, one thinking o' the shame and the other of having one more mouth to feed.

IT WAS A long working day for Margaret knowing that she would have to face her father that evening. Sarah decided the best course of action was to tell John herself, in private. No temper was feared, but this was a shameful situation all the same and she was unsure as to how he would react. Life was easier with the oldest offspring out working, some having left home, but there were still seven bellies to fill.

WHEN JOHN RETURNED that evening Sarah beckoned him out to the yard, taking a lamp with her and hanging it on the hook on the shed. As calmly as she was able, she revealed the news to her husband.

"Margaret is with child."

John's stomach clenched and a spark of anger passed through his eyes. He clutched Sarah by the elbows.

"But she's nae courting. Was she forced upon?"

"Nay."

John's hands fell by his side and Sarah leant her head on his chest. They stood under the light of the lamp which gently swayed in the breeze, as arms entwined and each comforted the other.

"I will think on it, Sally," were all the words John spoke and walked back to the kitchen where he took his seat by the fire and lit his pipe.

T HE FAMILY WERE busy with their evening chores, the two youngest bairns in bed. Margaret was sitting at the table supposedly knitting but dropping more stitches than she was catching. Her father had not looked at her since walking in.

John smoked his pipe in silence for what felt like an age, little expression on his face. Sarah seated herself opposite him busying herself with some mending and waited, the clock hands moving as if dredging through mud. When he was finished John leant down and gently tapped the pipe against the hearth, emptying the used tobacco. He sent the remaining bairns to bed and turned to face his daughter.

"A name, Margaret?" were the words he spoke, and as he looked into the eyes of his daughter whom had always been a kind and obedient child, she uttered the name.

"John Cantlie".

John nodded, said nothing and left his hearth to walk the mile to Clunymore Farm.

Francis Cantlie listened with a somewhat shocked expression to what John had to say and called for his son to come through.

John thrust his chin out and crossed his arms. "It's nothing to do wi' me."

Just as John Smith chose to believe his daughter, so too did Frances choose to believe his son.

"There's yer answer," Francis said.

"You will deny the bairn then?" John enquired of Francis' son.

John Cantlie, his voice strong, but avoiding looking into his eyes, said, "Aye."

On hearing the answer John replied, "The shame lies not just with Margaret then," and left the way he had come.

On his return Sarah and Margaret questioned him with their eyes and he shook his head. Sarah's head lowered. The colour drained from Margaret's face as the realisation hit that her bairn was to be denied. Her hand instinctively touched her belly and her father quietly spoke.

"Any bairn coming into this home will be taken care o' and love shown to it. The Cantlies have made their position clear and no more is to be said on the matter."

And that was that.

1877

MARGARET SHOOK THE memories from her mind and continued on to her work. It did no good to think of the past. John had always been over fond of women and what was done was done.

SARAH HAD ALWAYS been restless, and perhaps searching for something that had eluded her, a feeling that followed her like her shadow, that she was unable to shake off. Her bairns were all grown and some of her grandbairns too, and John continued to seek work each day, although unable to do so for quite so long. His body, like hers, was showing signs of age, and the long years of hard work caused the bones to creak and moan. Sarah was often short of breath with the bronchitis that had ailed her the past three years, but her dreams portrayed a wedding, which lightened her heart, and she wondered if it would be Jane. Sarah worried for her still, and wanted to see her settled and happy, but she noticed how she batted loons away, with a sharp comment, softened with humour, and wondered what kind of lad it would take to capture her heart.

MAY BROUGHT WITH it a birthday for Jane and a new abode for James. He had secured work as a farm labourer at Glencorrie, staying there to work and coming home to visit every couple of weeks. The atmosphere changed again in the cottage, with his absence, and he was missed, but there was an air of excitement in him when he left to make his own way in the world, and his kin were glad for him. John schooled him on life living on a farm and reminded him, quite tersely,

"Mind yer manners with the quines, and behave in a gentlemanly manner. Ye will not bring shame on this family or yersel'."

Respectful in his manner, James replied, "Aye, Granda."

"If ye stay away from quines and whisky for a few years, ye will do just fine."

A flush crept up the loon's cheeks as John chuckled.

James adjusted to his new life quite quickly. Being the youngest farm hand he was often the butt of jokes and teased about the young milk maid, but he took it in good jest and got on with his work, but as time went by he was not sure if farming was the life for him, but until something changed, he would carried on in his own steady way.

T HE SEASONS CHANGED and the folk of Mortlach journeyed on, some skipping, others stooped. A mild autumn afternoon found three auld men, converging by the Mill, sitting on the low dyke, each with his pipe. Alex, the miller, was between Francis Cantlie and John. Each having known the other for over fifty years, there was an easy accord between them and a disgruntled acceptance of old age.

Francis, at eighty, was the oldest of the three, but sprightly, his body having been less battered by physical work. There was height in him yet, and he lacked the stoop that ailed John. Alex was stocky in stature with a belly that portrayed a liking for beer, but his quiet voice belied his size, unlike John whose voice was powerful, though his body was gnarled with arthritis. There lay approximately half a dozen hairs on each man's head, desperately holding on, under the refuge of caps, and they sat mainly in silence for a while, the scent of their pipes mingling in the air around them, the low sun on their backs.

John commented on the busyness of Auchindoun in recent times.

"Hae you noticed how many loons travel by bicycle now? Stepping out yer own front door is a danger in itself, the speed they go past."

Two heads nodded in agreement and John continued,

"I can see the attraction, and would probably have enjoyed having one in my younger years, but I dinna think I would be able to balance on such a contraption now, and anyway my hair would surely be blown into my eyes."

The chuckles lingered as talk turned to the politics of the day and the latest news in the week's newspaper. Some gentleman had returned from America and was reported to have commented on the invention, over there, of earmuffs, to keep the ears warm in winter. Alex looked over at Francis taking in the the large lugs residing on each side of his head and said, "Thon muckle lugs must have scooped up a fair amount o' wind o'er the years, would you like me to order you a pair?"

Francis harrumphed and a low rumble of a laugh escaped John's lips.

The wee Edmundston bairns toddled past with their mother, who bade at Bridgend cottage, next to Francis, and the conversation moved on to family. There was a general consensus that bairns brought as much angst and frustration as they did gladness, and that all seemed to know better than their elders, no matter what they were telt. Francis commented,

"We all married thrawn quines so I suppose it's nae surprise that our bairns dinna listen tae us."

"Aye, there's that. My Isabella always seemed to ken the right words when dealing with our bairns."

Both Francis and Alex were widowers and felt the loss keenly. Francis' head cocked to one side.

"I wonder what Mary would think sometimes."

John looked upon his cottage. "Jane is my most thrawn grandbairn but the biggest hearted."

Alex slowly rose and tapped his pipe against the dyke, and remarked,

"She's also the spit of her granny."

Two tongues said, "Aye," and the men ambled their way back to their own hearths, in the knowledge that Alex was not referring to Sarah.

A Time For Contentment

As winter approached Jane became aware of a shift in the cottage's atmosphere, so subtle but there all the same. It was not a change that she could name, or indeed give the term good or bad to, but the house people appeared more frequently, and she was aware of their presence, right by her, more than they had ever been. It did not trouble her, but it intrigued her, and when she mentioned it to granny, Sarah said that she had not been aware of any change.

Margaret, having protected her heart for over a year now, had finally succumbed to Willie Balgown's attention, who had stated that he intended to marry her, sooner rather than later. But Margaret was still wary and put forward the proposal that they would marry in the summer, giving him plenty of time to change his mind and move away if he so desired. If, come July, he felt the same way, she would consent to be his wife. Her words were stern and serious, belying the soaring joy in her heart that he wished to marry her, and Willie solemnly agreed to her request, then winked and pulled her to him, trying his best to convey the love in his heart.

Sarah saw the lightness in Margaret's step, a tune never far from her lips, and she was glad that at last, her quine had found happiness.

"Well, quine, life has finally turned."

"Aye, I must admit I wisna sure that it would. I thought I was to be an auld maid like Annie along the road."

Her smile faltered for a second and Sarah took her hand.

"Willie will marry ye, Margaret. I know it."

Margaret saw the earnest look in her mother's eyes and chose to believe her. She may have thought that all was a secret, but the whole of Auchindoun and half of Botriphnie knew that she and Willie were courting, at the grand ages of forty two and forty nine.

Jane observed her mother's happiness and was glad for her, but was concerned that she might move away, although she kept that to herself. Jane had little wanderlust in her but she suspected that her mother might have, as she had often complained at having never been further than a few miles from Auchindoun, her entire life.

John too was grateful for his quine's delight in life, of all his bairns she was most like him in character, and they had always had a quiet alliance. Her own hearth was long overdue but by God he would miss her.

That evening, as neighbours gathered, John picked up his fiddle and filled every crevice of his home with the spirited sound of reels and jigs, his feet tapping to the beat, and friends and kin singing and dancing with enthusiasm.

"Play another one, John." Alex puffed as the last reel finished and he sat heavily on the chair, having birled Jane around the kitchen. "But make it a slow one - auld Annie here is in need o' a romantic waltz."

The room chuckled and auld Annie, - no one quite knowing just how old she actually was, including herself - retorted, "Aye, maybe Alex, but ma bed's cold at night, are ye offering tae warm it fir me?"

Whisky was sputtered and a neck turned red as the laughter in the cottage rose.

Another took the fiddle from John and as the melody mingled in the warmth of the air Sarah and John danced together, the years falling away. The fire and candles provided light and warmth to the assembled bodies, the December wind howling outside, its own version of crooning.

T HE LAST SATURDAY of the year arrived gently that morning. A beautiful, calm day, with the sun in its full glory, low in the sky. Only John and Sarah were in the cottage, sitting either side of the hearth, which they were prone to do in the daytime, now they were older. Sarah was wrapped in her shawl, her body trying to ward off flu.

She looked upon the man she had shared her life with and quietly told her tale.

*

A FTERWARDS, THE COUPLE sat together, contentment in their hearts and Sarah realised she had found what it was she had been chasing all of her life.

"I dreamt last night of Jane, sitting at a table, by her own hearth, a man by her side and a brood o' bairns."

"I'm right glad to hear it, quine."

Sarah looked at the man who had been her husband for fifty years and she smiled a smile which conveyed the whole of her heart, and he returned the smile, the same sentiment in his eyes for his Sally. Sarah then closed her eyes, the smile still on her face, and drifted into her final dream.

Farewell

THE STILLNESS IN the cottage hung in the air, its soundlessness deafening to the inhabitants, desperate for it to be shattered. Two chairs sat outside the door, lying in wait. A lock of hair and corner of the winding sheet was carefully taken from Sarah, and her body was carried out, the coffin gently placed on the chairs and covered with plaid. As the bearers lifted the coffin, the chairs were deliberately overturned, to be left there till sunset, and the procession began.

John was first with his son, John, their steps heavy and solemn. The others followed, some arm in arm, others set slightly apart. Margaret linked arms with Jane, who was accompanied, unseen, by little Elizabeth. The bell tolled as they made their way to the kirk, and above, a dove circled in the air, the symbol of the Spirit. The cold, January air was sharp in the lungs, but the low sun in front of them pulled the unwilling feet.

As the minister's words drifted over their heads, in the breeze, the coffin was lowered to the low, keening sound of grief, where knees buckled and shackled hearts broke.

THE MOURNERS PARTOOK of a meal and whisky, friends and neighbours offering both food and compassion. Stories were remembered and retold, Sarah's wit and heart lauded, her thrawn spirit smiled upon.

"Father, do ye mind the time when Mother had a slight disagreement wi' auld Mr Roberts?"

John chuckled. "Aye, lad, it was the talk o' Auchindoun."

The room smiled and young John continued, "I was aboot six at the time and had been playing outside when he staggered along the road after drinking illicit whisky, and on a Sunday too, and for whatever reason, decided that I was up tae no good. I was so terrified o' his bellowing and cursing that I scrambled up the old oak tree by the mill, and luckily he was too drunk to climb after me. Mother came outside after hearing the commotion and promptly went back in again and returned wi' a bucket o water and threw it o'er him, then hauled him by the lug away fae the tree, saying, "Ye will not be coorse tae my bairn." I watched fae the tree and she kept hold o' his lug all the way tae his cottage, him stumbling all o'er the place."

Archie added, "Aye, and when she got there she handed him o'er to his wife. The least said aboot her the better! I think every man in Mortlach felt a bit sorry for Ian Roberts. She was enough tae drive any man tae drink."

The room laughed.

"He came back the following day, shame faced, wi' a couple o' rabbits for the pot and a wee carved horse for John. Sally, never one tae hold a grudge, took him in and fed him bannocks."

And so the stories continued and as folk lamented, John was proud to hear their words, and shared a few of his own, recounting stories of his Sally, although his tongue lost its ability to speak at times, and the unfinished sentences hovered in the air. His children talked of mischief and scoldings, tight bosies and kissed cheeks. There was soft laughter and the shaking of heads, and as the last neighbour left, the cottage was imbued with a tender quietness.

T HE WEEK FOLLOWING the funeral, Jane bade farewell to her employers in Dufftown, having thankfully secured work, albeit very low paid, with Elspet Grant, biding in Bridgend Cottage, just a minute's walk away from home. Jane could not bear to be far from her granda, her fear of losing folk at its height, possessing her mind and terrifying her heart. The loss of her granny had a profound effect on Jane, the foundations of her life were fractured and the bond they shared, unique only to them, untethered.

Jane whispered to the ghost of the quine with the bairn, "My secret feels heavy now somehow. I am alone in it, yet the fear o' sharing it is too great to consider. There is such a yearning in me for my granny, that I feel it ache."

She raised her eyes to the roof. "I will keep our secret, Granny."

Elspet was unmarried and working, so is in need of someone to look after her bairns and home. There would be less money coming in but they would manage, and Jane would ensure that her granda was cared for. Still working when he could himself, John was angry with Jane for giving up her work when he was quite well and able to look after himself. Margaret shared the sentiment but a part of her was glad that Jane would be close by during the day, for her father. The arrangements had all been made before Jane informed anyone of her plans, so what was done was done.

As each of Sarah's kin travelled their own road of grief, each was unconsciously oblivious to the other, it being impossible to comfort someone, whose road was theirs alone. The house people lingered with Jane, but as time went on she felt no comfort from them, turning from them when they appeared. Her heart and mind hardened and her grief manifested into anger.

𝕵OHN FELT AT a loss within the cottage, and attempted to gain more daily work, just to keep busy and prevent his mind from thinking too much, but his body was not fit and he struggled. As much as folk sympathised with him they could not afford to pay a man for doing little, so fewer were willing to offer him work. His son, John, was aware of this, and asked his father to help on his wee croft in Glack of Clunymore, a few days a week, paying what he could. It was an arrangement that suited them both, the father felt needed, and the son felt he had done right by his father and enjoyed his company. Jane was also glad: when he was at Glack she worried less, and between her and Margaret's wages they got by well enough.

The evenings were strange for many a night. John sat in his usual chair by the hearth, and Margaret and Jane theirs, but Sarah's lay empty, no one willing to occupy it. To sit in her chair would be like wearing her shoes, too personal and intimate and wrong somehow. Jane noticed too how no ghosts chose to sit there either. A part of her willed her granny to appear alongside the house people, but another part of her was terrified that she would appear, as she was not sure she would cope with seeing her, and would be unable to explain any outcry to her mother or granda.

Margaret, like her father, was bereft, but she was also glad that her mother no longer suffered. Her bronchitis had made it so hard for Sarah to breathe, and watching her struggle and cough had been difficult. For three years she had watched her mother decline, and although rarely mentioned, her mother always brushing off any concerns, the memories of those lost previously were in their minds and it had felt like a waiting game.

John had, in some ways, been the most prepared. Sally had let him know in her own gentle way what to expect, but of course, the flu had come unexpectedly and that was that, so the end had been a shock. He had no words for his loss and a part of him had gone with her, but at the same time his heart was glad that he had shared his life with someone so uniquely good and fiercely loving. He could have chosen no one else to have by his side for fifty years.

Both Margaret and her father were concerned for Jane. Her manner was brusque, her temper short, and the spark in her eyes had dulled, her natural good humour no longer visible. There was a perpetual air of slow burning fury about her, which was so far removed from their Jane, that it was akin to living with a stranger.

Jane herself felt very little, except perhaps fear, the wall she had built around her served to protect her heart, but what she had not yet realised was that walls stopped all the good in life from entering, as well as the bad.

As winter ended and spring began even James came home less frequently, the atmosphere in his childhood home strange to him, and Jane's easy nature, gone. One Jessie Ann had just been born to John and Mary Cantlie, another half sibling to Jane, a happening that did not register in her mind, such as it was.

One evening, on returning home, John and Margaret having not yet arrived, Jane walked into the kitchen to find little Elizabeth playing with another little girl, and Sarah's mother sitting by the hearth in Sarah's chair. A well of emotion rose up in Jane and she screamed at her great granny,

"Get out of that chair!"

Clawing and scrabbling at her, her fingers failing to catch the air, Jane bawled,

"Out! out, ye auld besom."

Great granny remained seated but held out her arms. Jane fell to her knees, her head on the chair and sobbed the tears left unshed for all these months. The mournful cries were heard by the cottage walls, its fabric absorbing every painful tear.

Eventually the greeting calmed, to become intermittent gasps of air, and Jane was left spent. When she looked up her great granny was still there, Jane's head on her lap and little Elizabeth was kneeling beside her, her wee arms around Jane's shoulders.

Slowly the anguish left her body and Jane allowed herself to be comforted, a final tear rolling silently down her cheek. And that's how Margaret found her daughter.

A Wedding

As summer gradually presented itself, the sun lightened more than just the sky. There was a general feeling of relief, as if following thunder, and Milton Cottage was filled with an atmosphere of excitement. Willie Balgown had proved himself worthy, and Margaret was caught up in the thrill of becoming a bride, alongside the eagerly awaited anticipation of a home of her own. She would be moving to Glass, about five miles away, as Willie had secured work as an overseer on a farm there. Jane was thankful that it was fairly close but would miss her mother dearly.

The run up to the wedding followed the usual traditional preparations, and even though Margaret thought herself too old for such things, a part of her was secretly delighted, and she felt like a young quine again.

"Stand still, Margaret, I need tae tie the blindfold."

Margaret did as she was told, a feeling of apprehension in her mind as her sister Ann placed a stick in her hand.

"Now, ye ken what to do. There are three bowls in front o' ye on the hearth and ye must point yer stick where ye think the bowl wi' the pure water is."

Margaret took a breath and imagined being able to see the bowls. One empty, one with dirty water and one with pure water.

She moved her arm towards the left, to the delight of Ann and her friends, as it pointed at the right bowl. Three times the bowls were moved position, and three times she had to point her stick. Whichever bowl she pointed to twice marked the outcome of the courtship. The dirty water portrayed a dishonourable marriage; the empty bowl, no marriage at all; and the pure water an honourable marriage.

Elspet squealed like a quine half her age. "You've done it, Margaret. That's twice now you've found the bowl wi' the pure water!"

Margaret breathed a sigh of relief as the quines congratulated her. She had always held strong beliefs in old traditions and it reassured her that things were as they should be.

Her kist was full of the pillows, sheets and blankets made over the years in preparation of a wedding, and her sister Ann had accompanied her to Dufftown to purchase a dress from the tailor's shop. The Saturday before the banns were read in kirk, Willie arrived in Milton Cottage to partake in a feast with Margaret's family. Much fuss was made of them both, with whisky drunk and music played. It was the first time John had picked up his fiddle since losing Sarah, and the cottage seemed to sigh in repose as the music once again caressed the crevices and contours of its walls.

The night before the wedding Willie's friends arrived at his dwelling, filled a large tub with water and performed the feet washing ceremony. One removed his shoes and socks and plunged his feet into the tub, vigorously rubbing them, whilst another was just as quickly clarting them in soot, all the while laughing and jesting and drinking whisky. Willie was long past being a loon but the whole shenanigans caused much hilarity, and it was good to feel light hearted. He had waited a long time for Margaret's heart, and at half a century old, couldn't quite believe his luck.

T HE MORNING OF the 19th of July broke with the cockerel's crow, and the sun rose, as it was inclined to, beckoning folk from their dreams. Margaret and Jane set quickly to work, preparing the breakfast meal for the guests who would be arriving early. One started on the making of porridge, the other the curds and cream. They even had some tea, kindly given by Margaret's employer, Mrs Reid.

Ann arrived to help Margaret with her dress.

" Oh, Ann, what if it disna fit? Mrs Reid has been plying me wi' scones for months saying I'm too thin, and that no husband wants tae sleep wi' a skeleton."

"I have noticed you're rounder than ye used tae be but ye ken the rules - the dress canna be cut."

Jane glowered at Ann and tried to reassure her worried mother,

"Look, Mam, the folds can be stretched a little if need be. That's not against tradition. Step into it and we'll make it fit just fine."

Margaret gingerly followed her quine's instructions and there were sighs of relief all round when it went up and over her hips, and fastened as it was intended.

Following breakfast both Margaret and Willie set out from their separate abodes, each leading their wedding party and accompanied by pipers and the firing of pistols, meeting at the kirk, where they were married by the minister. Following much congratulations from all and paying the minister his fee of sixpence, the party then proceeded to the barn for the celebrations.

A feast was prepared and it was the bridegroom's task to serve the guests. Three courses followed by puddings were offered, and there was an abundance of ale and whisky, all neighbours and friends bringing something by way of a gift. Following the meal the tables were cleared to make space for the dance and fiddlers.

It was a day to remember and Margaret was as happy as the day her bairns' were born. Jane and James observed their mother's joy and had a grand time dancing with everyone. James was now a tall, strapping lad of seventeen and although still quiet in nature, confidently swung the quines around the room to the sound of the fiddler's reels, and occasionally his granda would take up his fiddle and join in. Sarah was missed but Margaret's jubilation made John smile, and he was glad to see it.

So, SUDDENLY MILTON Cottage had only two inhabitants, one young, one old, and the character of the dwelling changed again. Where once it had housed a couple with eleven bairns, almost fifty years had passed, and there was a gentle quietness hugging the walls now, memories had soaked into the fabric, and the minds were comforted by their presence.

Not long after the wedding, the two were sitting having their supper, blethering about their day, when John suddenly said,

"Your granny told me about the house folk. It took her nearly fifty years to tell me, said she was scared as to how I might react. As if anything could have stopped me loving her! Hadn't told a living soul till she saw it in you. She thought I should know, so that you wouldn't feel alone in it." Jane looked at her Granda and nodded but no words came.

"I feel her with me, Jane, but if you see her, please dinna tell me." Again Jane nodded and the two continued to eat their supper.

TURBULENCE

THE SUMMER WAS a bonny one and Jane continued to work along the road at Bridgend, her charges being somewhat better behaved than her last, and she was kept busy with her chores. Neither herself nor her granda had mentioned again his knowing of her awareness. It took a while for the news to sink in for Jane but out walking one Sunday, her granny having joined her, Jane turned to her.

"I dinna understand why ye told him. Ye made me promise that I wouldn't tell a living soul and I remember how scared I felt. Still do. I dinna need anyone else to ken."

The two walked through the woodland, the sound of creatures scurrying and birds singing filling the summer air.

"My awareness is a part o' me and I am not ashamed o' it, in fact I find it comforting, but you made me see how others might react and it terrifies me to be made an outcast or feared by others."

Jane could not discern the look on her granny's face, a touch of sadness perhaps, but for what reason, Jane had no way of knowing.

SOON HARVEST WAS upon them and Jane looked forward to a change in her routine, as all hands were required to help. It was hard work, but she enjoyed the long days outside, and the banter that went with it. Many a quine and loon enjoyed the general flirting that accompanied harvest time and although Jane was not immune to it, she kept her words light hearted and did not give any man cause to think she was interested in romance.

On 23rd September, harvest was nearing completion and the weather was holding. Francis Cantlie at this time had become sub postmaster, in the wee post office in Milton itself, and on receiving a telegram from Keith, he left the post office and walked along the road to the Smiths' cottage. It was with a heavy heart that he handed John the telegram with the terrible words,

Deeply regret to inform you
George Smith killed in quarry accident

John sat down heavily as Francis handed him a whisky.

"I'm sorry, John. It's nae right when our bairns go afore us."

John looked up at Francis, a feeling of nausea rising in his stomach. "My fifth bairn to be lost."

"Aye, I ken."

John stared at his whisky. "Thirty one in years, wi' two wee quines."

Francis shook his head and sighed as John continued, "I'm glad Sally's nae here to suffer the loss o' another bairn. She's only been gone nine months and I don't ken if I can grieve any more than I already am."

Francis sat with John for a while and then left to fetch John's son from Hillhead Croft and when Jane returned that evening she found the two of them by the hearth, sitting quietly, and her granny by her granda's side.

It was a shock to see her granny and Jane's heart missed a beat, a barrage of emotion coursing through her, from disbelief and sadness, to joy and love. It took a moment for her to realise that anything was wrong, so caught up in seeing her and trying to process it.

So Jane's world was shattered yet again. The uncle that was more like a brother, taken from her, enraging the inner fear of death even more, and thickening the wall around her heart.

T HE REST OF the year passed in somewhat of a daze for all the Smiths, but the sun still rose and set, and folk continued to live and work. The weekly newspaper told of the world's happenings and folk were amazed that two men, Joseph Swan and Thomas Edison, had invented the light bulb. No one could quite imagine a life without candles.

There was much gossip about the newlyweds, Peter Geddes, a farm servant of Glack of Clunymore, and Ann Nicol, domestic servant, at Clunybeg, he being twenty six years her junior, but as much as folk speculated, they were glad of happy news.

John settled into a life that revolved around his family and daily work. His old friend, Alex, the miller, had died some months before Sarah, and he missed their conversations and banter. Francis was still along the road and showed no signs of slowing down in life, which gave John hope, as his body rattled and groaned with age. Like an old plough, the beam and braces were no longer strong, and the handles were worn, but the wheels still turned, and although slow, managed to furrow the land.

Stooped and old as he was, John had a presence about him that went before his quiet tongue, and unbeknownst to him he was a well respected and liked man. His sorrows were no worse than any others of the time, all shared the experience of loss, but they also shared the closeness of community, and outsiders had commented on the wit and character of the country folk in the shires, and it was precisely that, that allowed them to get on and progress through life, combined with a thrawn need to better the world for their offspring.

Jane marvelled at how her granda seemed to cope with life. She was in awe of his open outlook and ability to always see the better side of things. She had chosen to stay and work in Auchindoun because he needed her, but as time went by she admitted to herself that it was because she needed him.

Margaret's life in Glass was more than she had hoped for. William was doing well, and for the first time in her life she had spare money. With no little ones to look after and none expected, due to her age, life was easier, and some would say much deserved. She revelled in having her own cottage to look after and a good man to share it with, and oh how she loved living somewhere new. They hadn't gone far but it was far enough to be different, and she felt a new lease of life within her that showed in her eyes.

James was working as a farm hand and had grown into a steady chiel, his quiet, confident manner marking him as a man of understated authority, which she was sure would stand him in good stead in later years. Jane had lost some of her spark, but Margaret prayed often that it would return shortly, and restore happiness to Jane's bruised heart. Full of her own romance, she believed that marriage would be the best thing for Jane, and she would be saying so on her next visit.

T HE YEAR 1881 brought with it two births, a romance and a conception. The first birth was that of John Cantlie's daughter, Williamina, born on 17th April, to which Jane merely sighed and carried on with her day. Her father, now at the age of forty six, ran his own farm, Bakebare, paying twenty four pounds a year for the privilege.

The second birth happened in Ayrshire and was of no consequence to anyone at the time, other than the bairn's family. The child was a loon, christened Alexander Fleming, and he would go on in 1928 to discover penicillin, saving the lives of many millions. Little Elizabeth would have been one of them, had she been born much later.

The romance concerned James, Jane's wee brother, still a farm servant at the time, and that of one Ann Ramsay, a domestic servant. Just eighteen years of age and quiet as a dormouse, James was smitten and the feeling appeared to be mutual. He was back living in Milton as he had work on a nearby farm, and there was a bit of life about the cottage again which both granda and Jane enjoyed. Jane too had moved to a new place of work, and was working for a family about a mile away. John had encouraged her to go further afield and live her own life but she refused, although she was slightly less anxious these days.

Now aged twenty four, Jane was adept at the work of a domestic servant, and although quite proficient at caring for bairns, had no wish to have her own and risk the grief that went with losing them. She ignored the tiny seed of want that grew within her, too scared to love another and have them ripped away. She could not comprehend how her granda managed to live with having lost his wife of over fifty years, knowing the bond they had shared, and their shared loss of five bairns.

It was her mother who sat Jane down and explained to her that she understood her reticence but that if she herself had given up on life she would not be happy today. She told Jane,

"Walls stop all life, nae just the bad. Good comes wi' bad and if you canna feel either there's nae point in living ava. Aye, it's traumatic losing a loved one, and a part o' ye may well die wi' them, but not to hae known their love would be far worse. Your granda will die one day and we will grieve, but we will be glad that we have known and loved him, and he us. Dinna hide from the world, Jane - go oot and live your life, and know the joy o' your own bairns."

Jane looked at her mother and noticed how the house people had gathered around her as if in agreement. She supposed she could be more amiable the next time a chiel deigned to speak to her, and her mother smiled and retorted, "Well, Jane, dry shoes winna catch fish!"

Some time later Margaret revealed to Jane that she was with child, and that she and Willie were delighted as they never thought it was possible. Something again shifted in Jane when she saw her mother's happiness, and she allowed herself to wonder what motherhood would actually be like. Her fear of losing folk was still there and perhaps always would be, but she could see the wisdom in her mother's words, and for the first time since being a bairn Jane dared to dream, and wonder at life again.

NEW BEGINNINGS

MARGARET ANN BALGOWN was born on 26th June 1882 in Glenlivet. Her father kissed her forty six year old mother with relief and thanks, and cradled his first and only child in his arms. Margaret sighed with contentment in the knowledge that this child would not have the word illegitimate on her birth certificate, but her father's name instead, and Margaret stated as a married woman.

Little Margaret, known as Maggie, was to bring them much joy, and both Margaret and Willie settled into a happy, contented life.

Just one month later, on Sunday the 24th July, James and Ann married in Mortlach church, a strapping nineteen year old lad, and a bonny twenty one year old quine, heavily pregnant with their first child, James Alexander Scott, who would be born the very next day, at ten to eleven in the morning. Not quite the wedding night they had expected!

So James had a sister and a son, born within a month of each other, both healthy and both legitimate, but within three years one of them would have a different surname.

JANE'S MIND POSITIONED itself somewhere between calm and fearful, a new ebullient self emerged over the following year, one that mirrored a good part of her childhood, and by letting down her guard, the wall she had built around her heart began to crumble. It was not an easy thing for Jane to do: letting herself feel emotion again and allowing expectations to rise, caused her trepidation, but she wanted more in life, and no matter what she did or did not do, she could not control who lived or died.

Sitting alone early one morning Jane talked to her granny. "I think I would like a family o' my own but it scares me. I dinna think I could cope wi' losing a bairn."

John encouraged her to visit folk more, go for walks and spend time with friends her own age. He didn't want to be cosseted, and anyway he was always out and about keeping himself busy and earning where he could. His heart was glad to see his wee Jane with a spring in her step again, and a twinkle in her eye, her quick wit wakened the sleepiness of the cottage and her laughter echoed in its beams. He couldn't see the house people but he knew they were there and he imagined them smiling alongside him at the change in Jane.

John Cantlie fathered another bairn, Margaret Grant Cantlie, his fourth legitimate child with his wife, and his seventh and final bairn, that was known about. Jane, now twenty six, no longer ached with the injustice of never having been accepted, but there lingered an old yearning for acknowledgment, buried deep in her heart, that would live there till her dying day. With a sigh in her breast she held her head high and vowed that if she was ever blessed with a child she would make it known how much the bairn was wanted and needed.

ELSIE, WHO STILL worked in Dufftown as a domestic servant, persuaded Jane to try and find work in Dufftown again as there was so much more life there, and being a bit flighty Elsie enjoyed the attentions of the tailor and the butcher's son. Both were quite taken with Elsie but she couldn't make up her mind which one she liked best, so decided that she would go and see the grocer's wife and have her tea leaves read. She asked Jane to accompany her and although she remembered her granny warning her of such things, she couldn't see the harm, so agreed to go.

Jessie MacKenzie, sat at the little table in her back room of the shop. She was a woman in her fifties who attempted to keep herself smart, especially as she helped her husband serve in the store, but somehow she was always in disarray. Her grey hair had a mind of its own and refused to keep still in a bun. Wild tendrils flew around her round face, somewhat fiercely, with every bob of her excitable head, and her hands, which appeared too small for her body, were forever jerking and gesticulating unnecessarily, as if they were hens disturbed by a fox. The roundness of her form, imprisoned in its corset, screamed for release, yet she had the daintiest, quietest feet that appeared to float across a room, and her movements were soundless.

Her voice alternated between the gentle sound of a soothing melody, to the booming crescendo of a fog horn, depending on the recipient of her conversation. Her husband was accustomed to the latter. She had borne six loons but none, as yet, had procured a wife, much to her consternation, and she consulted the tea leaves every morning looking for answers as to who would marry her darlings, and when she would be made a granny.

Elsie and Jane were invited to sit at the table and tea was poured into two delicate cups. Elsie drank her tea quickly and handed her cup back to Jessie, who promptly turned it upside down and back again, emptying it of the remnants of liquid and turned it three times anti clockwise, leaving behind a gathering of tea leaves, both scattered and clumped, awaiting the telling of their secrets. Jessie slowly turned the cup and many "Oohs" and "Aye, ayes" were muttered as she proceeded to tell Elsie,

"I can see two marriages ahead, in quick succession, and a journey on a train."

Elsie's eyes widened. "Two marriages? Am I tae marry both the tailor and the butcher's son?"

Jessie shook her head, "The leaves canna tell me names, Elsie."

"Well if I dinna like the first husband I will surely like the second."

There was a ripple of laughter and Jessie turned to Jane, "Would you like a reading, quine?"

To her surprise Jane found her tongue answering, "Aye, why not?"

The cup was taken and turned the same as the first and Jane waited as Jessie's eyes focused and her expression softened.

"I see new beginnings and a chance meeting."

"Ooh, Jane, perhaps ye will meet a rich merchant and be whisked away to a new life."

"Wheest, Elsie, stop yer blethering and listen to Jessie."

The cup was turned again and Jessie glanced quickly at Jane. "Ye have a secret."

Elsie launched in again, "Do ye have a secret lover? I hope it's nae auld Mr Yule in Auchindoun, who lacks both teeth and good hygiene, and is always complaining he has nae wife."

The mirth lingered as the two quines paid Jessie and bade her goodbye, venturing out into the street, Elsie talking ten to the dozen and speculating, whilst Jane tried to hide how perturbed she was over the hidden secret comment. She had thought the reading of tea leaves a mere imaginative pastime but perhaps her granny had been right.

It had intrigued her though, and she wondered at what it all meant. She would not return to Jessie again, fearful that her secret would be exposed, but over the years Jane herself would become prolific at reading tea leaves.

FOLLOWING ELSIE'S ADVICE Jane secured work with a family in Dufftown. The Morrice family lived at 47 Castle street and consisted of David, a veterinary surgeon, his wife Christina, and their six children, the youngest being eleven. It was a change not having to look after young bairns and her work took on a housekeeping role, which meant she was often to be found in one store or another purchasing food or household items. Jane had to admit that the bustle of Dufftown did excite her, and it was good to blether with folk as she went about her business, but she was always home in the evenings in time for supper with her granda.

Five of the six offspring were at school each day, including the eldest daughter, Mary Ann, who was eighteen. Jane could not imagine being able to attend school instead of going out to work, at such an age. The eldest, Alasdair, was a tailor, and on meeting Jane for the first time he seemed flustered, and left the room in a great hurry with the excuse of having much work to do.

Both parents were quite genial, almost gregarious, and exceptionally well dressed. Christina often led the way in Dufftown fashion, purchasing the popular magazine *Myra's Journal of Dress and Fashion,* printed monthly, detailing the latest trends from across Europe. Jane marvelled at how her mistress both dressed and spoke, an ardent believer in women's rights, she was very outspoken on the subject, and regularly read *The Women's Penny Paper* and attended Suffrage meetings. Sometimes when Jane stopped her work for a cup of tea she would read some of these magazines, which she found fascinating, but not for the likes of her, she surmised.

There appeared to be the ghost of a young chiel, in his twenties, always appearing in the back bedroom. His presence was both expected and acknowledged by Jane, being used to having those that have passed, around her. He seemed quieter in his ways than others she had seen. Some were obviously mischievous or decidedly crotchety, and Jane liked to blether away to whomever was there, not requiring an answer, and always careful that no one was nearby to hear.

He had a way of cocking his head to the side, when spoken to, as if listening intently, and there were times that she wished he could speak to her, as she suspected that she would have liked him very much.

Alasdair often appeared nervous in meeting Jane, but one particularly dreich, winter's evening, he offered to see her home in his father's buggy. She gladly accepted, eager to be home and see to granda's supper, so the two set off in the dark, and lo and behold Alasdair found his tongue. Having just the moon for light, his nervous face was hidden, and he spoke freely, and eloquently to Jane, on several subjects, taking her quite by surprise.

Often, over the course of that winter, Jane would be escorted home, their conversations light hearted and Jane began to look forward to these times together. Alasdair was younger than herself, but a small part of her wondered if this could be more than friendship, although she would never dare to mention it. She followed her mother's advice on being more amiable towards a chiel, and was conscious of not allowing her tongue to offer a quip, however natural it seemed.

One afternoon, whilst tidying, she came across a little book about tea cup reading, and pored over the symbols and their meaning, committing them to memory and practising each day with her mid morning cup of tea. Occasionally she would read David and Christine's cups before washing the breakfast dishes, and noticed that something she had seen in the leaves, like a journey or a special occasion, would turn out to be true. It fascinated her, although she did worry that she would see death, so once having learned the symbols she rarely read her own leaves, just those of others.

Elsie had quite quickly fallen for a carpenter, boarding in the town, and Jane and their friend Eliza were taken by surprise when it was announced that Elsie was to be married and moving to Aberdeen the following month. She had decided that neither the tailor nor the butcher's son were for her, and were never again mentioned. Eliza wondered if husband number two would be found just as quickly, remembering the tale of the tea leaf reading, and having been married for several years, fleetingly imagined a second for herself, but decided that the risk was too great. The quines would miss Elsie with her constant blethering and flightiness, but wished her well and decided that whatever happened in her life she would come through it a'right.

Jane had confided in Eliza about the friendship with Alasdair and how much she enjoyed his company. She asked Eliza, "How do you ken if you have found the right man?"

Her friend took her hand and said,

"Jane, when you find the right man you will ken it fully and completely."

This left Jane slightly flummoxed, as she could see Alasdair was a good man but she most certainly did not know if he was someone she would marry.

He was no longer taking her home as often, as his work kept him busy and spring was on its way. He had kissed her several times which was quite enjoyable, but there was no understanding between them, and she really wasn't sure what to think, so she decided not to think about it at all and see what happened.

A Chance Meeting

Not long after the Feeing market in May, Christine asked Jane to deliver a parcel to Mrs Stuart, an auld wife and a widow, who lived further along the street at number seventy three. Christine declared that Mrs Stuart had taken an avid interest in the Suffrage movement and wished to know more, but was not fit enough to attend any meetings, so she had put together some pamphlets, articles and the minutes of the last local meeting, for her to read. With a hint of summer in the air, Jane set off, a lightness in her step and a small smile on her face, little Elizabeth skipping alongside her.

She had just become an aunt again: James had a son named Peter, born on the 7th June in Auchindoun, but James himself was away working in Elgin, having left farming life and acquired a position as a postman. Jane knew that once his wife Ann had recovered from the birth the family would be moving to join him, and she would miss them greatly. But today the sun was shining and she would not let melancholy thoughts spoil the day, so she continued on her way, delivering the parcel with a cheery smile and made her way back along the street to the centre of town and entered the hardware shop to purchase some laundry soap.

Jane approached the counter and just as she was about to ask for what she needed, a stocky, red haired man bounded into the store as if his erse was on fire, and began reading off a list of items he wished to purchase, completely ignoring the fact that

Jane was present and clearly first in line. Jane felt the rising of anger surging up from the soles of her feet at his impudence and her tongue lashed out,

"Well, you were born far fae the house o' good manners, and if ye think that ye can storm in here and completely ignore the fact that I was first and start barking yer orders tae Mr Fraser here, well ye can think again. Yer mother waited for yer birth, so ye can hold yer tongue and wait yer turn. Your business is no more important than mine."

Two pairs of eyes met, two thrawn souls collided, and two hearts missed a beat. And that was how Jane first met Alexander Farquharson.

ALEXANDER FARQUHARSON

ALEXANDER, KNOWN AS Alec, was in his thirty fourth year and was at that time a farm manager in Corran, Aberlour. Standing at five foot ten he was broad in shoulders with a girth used to physical work, red of hair with grey eyes, which appeared either brimming with mirth or full of challenge, depending on the seer and the time of day.

When Jane had finished tearing a strip off Alec he was bemused, furious and smitten, in that order, over a period of five seconds. He looked upon this feisty, extremely bonny quine, and realised that somehow life would never quite be the same again. It was not a feeling he had experienced before, but by God he liked it, and feared it, simultaneously. His heart beat faster and his tongue wanted to retaliate, but all that happened was a wide grin from lug to lug, and a look in his eyes, so sincere, that Jane herself stopped short, her tongue still, and her mind stirred, with a thirst to know who stood before her.

Mr Fraser cleared his throat which had the effect of returning some normality to the place. Alec proffered his arm, inviting Jane to go ahead of him. "I apologise for my rudeness. I have yet tae eat dinner and I am told that my usual amiable self becomes lost on an empty stomach. Please make yer purchase and I will wait my turn."

Jane was gracious in her reply, but somewhat perturbed and off balance, "Thank ye. I accept yer apology."

She faced Mr Fraser. "Just some laundry soap, please." As she made her purchase she was conscious of the man standing behind her and a feeling of eager anticipation passed through her. With a smile on her lips she purchased her soap and left the shop without looking back.

Alec felt a sense of panic when the intriguing quine left the store and without thinking, he hurriedly passed his list to Mr Fraser. "I'll collect these supplies later."

The merchant chuckled knowingly and would later tell his wife how Alec Farquharson had acquired more than some farm supplies that day, and had lost his heart in the process.

Outside Alec scoured the road, left and right, seeing nothing but ponies and traps, loons and auld wives. Dismay flowed through his veins as he frantically searched, but to no avail. The spirited quine who had affected him so, was nowhere to be found and Alec returned to the store a despondent man.

Now, on seeing Alec's face, Hector Fraser chuckled once more but took pity on the man. He had known Alec for a while and had been in his company when taking a dram with George Farquharson, Alec's cousin, who bade in Dufftown. He decided to give fate a helping hand.

"I suggest ye might want tae pay the veterinary surgeon a visit to enquire about a bull that is off its food."

Understanding the confused look on Alec's face Hector also added, "I hear that the housekeeper there is a bonny quine who takes umbrage wi' rude men."

Alec grinned, and as he left the store for the second time, Hector shouted, "For pity's sake - hae yer dinner first!"

Later that afternoon Jane was in the middle of washing the Morrices clothes, haphazardly, as her mind was elsewhere, thinking about the infuriatingly handsome man she had met earlier, when she heard someone knocking on the door. She tutted with exasperation at the interruption, wanting to both finish her washing and get it outside, and work out what it was about the man that had affected her so. Drying her hands on her pinny Jane proceeded to open the door and looked straight into the eyes of the very same man on her mind. Speechless for once in her life, Jane's mouth opened and stayed that way, whilst a cap was doffed and a voice stated,

"Alec Farquharson. I apologise in advance if our bairns inherit my temperament, but if the quines inherit yours, God help the loons."

Jane snorted in a very unladylike fashion and two mouths laughed, as two pairs of eyes lit up and something akin to desire was born.

THAT VERY SAME evening on leaving Castle street Jane told Alasdair that she valued his friendship but that there could be nothing more between them, and she hoped that they could remain amiable with one another. He wasn't the least put out at all which was both a relief to her and simultaneously a dent to her ego!

She had realised on meeting Alec, what was missing with Alasdair, and that spark had ignited a fire, which brought to mind a warning from her mother, "Kindle not a fire which you can't put out."

Answers and Questions

Meanwhile in Elgin, James was sorting the parcels to be delivered and noticed the name George Scott, 'mason' written on a label. He stopped short, his hand going up to his chest, and wondered how many masons in the world went by that name, and which one of them was his father. His mother had never spoken to James about his father, merely stating that they had been abandoned and that was that. Many questions had gone unanswered for them both, and James had given up on ever finding out the answers. He may well have passed him on the road, oblivious, having no idea of his father's physical appearance or indeed if he was still alive, but having no time to ponder he continued with his work and set off on his deliveries.

It had started to rain quite heavily and James had donned his cape, supplied as part of his blue cloth uniform, the collar up and his hat pulled low, covering the majority of his face. He was glad of the rain that day as his uniform provided anonymity.

When James knocked on George Scott's door he felt a mixture of trepidation, excitement and fear, of what or whom he might encounter. He waited, sheltering under the porch, his heart fast in his chest. The door was opened by a middle aged woman with a young bairn clinging on to her pinny.

"Afternoon, I hae a parcel here for George Scott, needs

signing for."

"Thank you, lad. It's a coorse day," the woman replied as she took the pen from James.

"It is that." James bent down, making a fuss of the wee loon, his heart hammering as he said, "You're about the same age as my oldest loon."

The lad buried his face in his granny's pinny and James stood up again. "He's a shy one."

The wife handed James his form and took the parcel. "Aye, and he's three already. Time passes at an awful rate. Before you ken it you'll be like me, married for twenty six years wi' a handful o' grandbairns."

James managed to stutter, "Nae doubt."

He turned to leave as a man hurried up the path, home for his dinner, and there was a brief meeting of the eyes. George Scott gave a slight nod as he passed, and entered his house.

The few yards walk back down the path to his buggy felt like a hundred miles, as time stood still for James. With a tightness forming in his chest, his hand covering his mouth, shock engulfed James like the mouth of a fox on a chick.

The form had been signed, Mrs George Scott, married these past twenty six years, five years before James was born, and with a grandchild the double of James's own first wee loon.

So James had his questions answered and two things happened next.

James travelled to Glenlivet the following Sunday, leaving his wife and bairns at home. His mother was glad to see him and ushered him into the house, full of questions and depositing his wee sister Maggie on his knee.

James looked at his mother and sighed, "I have news, Mother."

Margaret, sensing his tone, turned to her husband and Willie rose. "Come, Maggie, we'll go ootside and see the horses."

Margaret put her hand on her son's arm. "What's wrong, James?"

"I dinna quite know how to say it."

Margaret straightened her shoulders. "Best just to come oot wi' it, loon."

James rubbed the back of his neck and lowered his eyes but his voice was steady. "I delivered a parcel to George Scott." He looked up at his mother as her eyebrows rose.

"Oh."

James could not decipher any other emotion in his mother's eyes and continued, "I met his wife o' twenty six years."

Margaret was both silent and still and James waited, unsure of what to do or say. "I'm sorry if I have upset ye Mother."

Margaret patted his hand, a small smile forming on her face, "I'm nae upset, loon, at least not fir myself. I came to terms wi' him abandoning us years ago, but it's good to finally ken why."

James stood up and paced the floor. "Are ye nae angry, Mother?" His voice boomed. " I've carried that devil's name my whole life!"

Margaret rose and faced her son taking him by the shoulders. "Ye have a right to yer anger, James, but you also have a right to yer name."

"A man should be proud o' his name. I will never use it again."

Margaret paled. She had felt little emotion with regards to herself, on hearing the news of the man who had abandoned her – indeed, a small part of her was even relieved, as she realised that George, already being married on their meeting, had never been hers to lose, but her heart was sad for James who had carried his name for twenty one years. She felt unsettled within herself for putting that on her son, but as with Jane, she had always felt strongly that they should know where they came from, and had a right to their surnames. Her mother had not agreed with her, at the time, claiming no good could come of it, but Margaret had been adamant.

Regret, doubt and guilt, fought against truth, pride and sureness, each emotion grappling with the other, pulling Margaret this way and that, her mind trying to straighten her thoughts, as the combs did wool.

"I'm sorry, loon."

James's anger evaporated as the two again sat down, each with their own thoughts. From that day forward James Scott became James Smith, and his wife, Mrs Smith. He held his head higher than it had ever been, and the name George Scott was never again mentioned.

Until her dying day Margaret would never be able to decide if she had done right by her bairns or not.

BECOMING ACQUAINTED

OVERSEEING THE SHEEP shearing and hay making, as well as the general running of the farm, kept Alec busy from morn' till night. The 1884 January storms that had come across the Atlantic battering Scotland, had caused many a tree to fall and farm sheds collapse, which five months on, still involved repair work for many hands. This had been the reason for the visit to the hardware store that fateful day.

He had certainly had dalliances with quines over the years but none had changed his opinion on marriage, although one or two had tried, and he had believed himself a confirmed bachelor until the moment Jane Cantlie ploughed into his life and churned the thoughts in his head to butter.

Following the unexpected appearance of Alec on the doorstep, Jane's mind too was sent into excited disarray, but where she had always felt fear around the corner there was something about Alec that calmed a part of her, bringing with it a sense of lingering awareness that he was what was needed in her life.

Fortunately the day following their first meeting landed on a Sunday, which allowed Alec to call on Jane in Milton, where they strolled up to *The Giant's Chair,* a large rock gouged by the River Dullan in spate, over many years, forming the appearance of a large seat. A fine summer's day, and Alec offered Jane his arm as they walked together, talking animatedly, an easy, light hearted banter between them, and a shimmer of sparks in the air.

"So, who is Alexander farquharson?"

"Well now, let me see. I am the second o' twelve children, and I was born on 14th April 1850 in Lumsden, Auchindoir, to James Farquharson and Marjory Duncan, known as May. My elder sister died when I was fifteen and my father three years later. I am thirty four in years and stand at five foot ten. I hae all my teeth and my hair is not dyed."

Alec's tone was light but Jane knew that much hardship would have followed his losses and she nodded for him to continue. What Alec had withheld was the fact that he had gone to bed many a night on an empty stomach so that his five wee sisters between the ages of two and seven could eat.

"Fifteen years have passed and my brothers and sisters are grown now, wi' their own families. I have always worked on farms, going where the work is, and am now a farm manager at Corran as ye ken."

Jane's wit surfaced as she teased, "And what about this impatience o' yours? I have heard it say that red hair prickles the sensitive brain, stirring up bouts o' irritation or fury."

A loud laugh emanated from Alec, "Well, quine, perhaps that is true, but I can assure ye that I am quite amiable on a full stomach, although I will admit to being a cantankerous bull when it is empty, and have been prone to kicking an erse or two, usually an incompetent farm hand's."

"Hmm. I'm nae sure if I want to be in the company o' a cantankerous bull who is prone to kicking erses."

Alec stopped and looked at Jane face on, a spark of humour passing over his eyes, "Well I promise to ensure that I am always well fed on meeting ye."

Jane saw the same spark that lit her own mind and realised that whatever lay ahead, life would involve Alec Farquharson.

Alec had never lifted a hand to anyone, nor offered cruel words or sentiments. He possessed both humility and respect, and his humour and big heart doused his moments of frustration with quiet equilibrium. In the past he had thrived on being busy, his mind happy to be occupied with farm life and with no urge in him to marry, but as he listened to this feisty, warm hearted quine his way of thinking unravelled as easily as wool.

After walking for about an hour Jane was mid sentence when Alec suddenly stopped, put his arm around her waist and kissed her deeply and passionately, enraging a fire that would forever burn, and the rest, as they say, is history.

COURTING WAS NOT to be an easy affair, living ten miles apart, both working long hours, and Jane devoted to her granda, the day only had twenty four hours in it, and time would not be on their side. So the couple took to letter writing.

JANE AND ALEC

IT MADE JOHN smile to see Jane's hand forever busy, scratching ink on paper, and her tongue a constant flow of words, relating tales of Alec in Aberlour. Old and becoming frail, it reminded him of his youth and his own courtship with Sally, and on meeting Alec he could see how well matched he and Jane were. Both headstrong and quick humoured, there would be clashes, but only a fool would miss how smitten they both were. It was a relief to him to see Jane with a man who clearly cared for her, and he hoped he would live to see her married and settled, so he could depart this world at peace.

Margaret too was fair delighted to see that Jane had indeed gone fishing and caught herself a fine salmon to boot, a comment made in Alec's presence, causing his face to turn the colour of his hair. Jane was black affronted at her normally quiet mother, but the look in Margaret's eye caused all three to giggle, one from embarrassment, one with pride and one with love.

Jane had felt a great sadness for her brother on hearing the news about his father, and writing to Alec helped her to put into words some of how she felt about her own situation of having been born illegitimate. She found it very easy to talk on paper, and her letters were long, covering everything from local news to innermost thoughts, interspersed with humour and banter. Alec's replies were shorter but with similar personal disclosures and funny anecdotes of farm life.

Over the next six months Jane and Alec grew to know one another through their letter writing, meeting every Sunday in Milton and coordinating short visits in Dufftown during the week, when Alec was collecting supplies or on some other farm business.

They talked of a future together and the hope of bairns to come, but Alec was under no illusion as to how much Jane needed to be with her granda every day. John was now eighty and plagued with the physical ailments of age. A long, hard life consisting of physical labour and living in a cottage where smoke and soot filled the lungs, had taken its toll, not to mention the emotional batterings of his losses over the years.

My Dearest Jane,

The arrival of yer letter today helped warm my core, frozen by the north wind and snow which have not ceased these past twa days. As much as I embrace the countryside there are times I wish I worked in a mill or some such place indoors. It appears we are in fir another harsh winter but thankfully there is plenty o' food for the animals and the bulls are in good order, so will hopefully fetch a good price at the next stock sale in Keith. There will be a dram in it for me if they sell for more than twenty five pounds.

The farm is to lose twa farm hands come spring. They are off tae America, lured by the promise of land, good money and bonny weather. Good luck tae them but I couldna leave my kin behind.

My sister, Christina, is looking fir a new position and I saw an advert in the newspaper for a good, plain cook in Elgin. Do you think that would be of interest to her?

Peter, the young loon taken on as a farm hand in November might be better suited for the cook's position as he has not the temperament for beasts. I can understand a chiel being wary o' a bull but he squeals when a chicken clucks at him. How can I train him to look after animals if he is feart o' them all? I fear I have used up my lifetimes worth o' patience and my already receding hair is in danger of disappearing all together.

With that in mind I would like to be married afore I am bald so I will say it in writing so you have proof of my intentions incase my words on Sunday were not believed. I will climb Ben Rinnes and shout across the hills my feelings for you my darling quine, and I will give ye some Deller's Essence for deafness so you may hear my words.

It is late and my bed is calling, so till next we meet, Jane.

Forever Yours,

Alec.

Dearest Alec,

How I enjoyed seeing you on Sunday and my heart rejoices in your heartfelt words. I feel as you do and I am glad of your patience knowing that I am loath to leave my granda. Thank you again for the sack of peat. Granda feels the cold more now and it is good to have a decent fire going during this harsh winter. Plenty of soup seems the best way to keep chests warm but I do fear for the auld and the bairns in Mortlach.

The trains are managing to get through so at least Dufftown has plenty o' supplies. Mr Fraser will be glad tae be able to purchase more of Lockyer's Sulphur Hair Restorer, having seen him in the street, his cap blown off and the snow wetting his locks, causing the hair dye to run doon his cheeks in black streaks. The bottle claims to deepen grey to a perfectly natural shade but obviously the manufacturer is unaware that Mr Fraser's hair was a light brown colour. Mrs Fraser must get an awful fright in the morning on opening her eyes thinking a stranger to be in her bed, (or maybe she is disappointed!)

In answer to your question - NO - do not inform your sister of the advert for a good, plain cook as she will be highly insulted. Folk requiring such have nae use fir tastebuds and a quine daring to add a bit o' garlic or other common herb to a pot would not be tolerated by such a family.

Better to inform her that Pratt and Keith in Aberdeen are looking fir a quine tae help sort the furs to be sold at "modern prices." If the wages are in line with modern prices she will be rich indeed!

I had a letter fae mother on Tuesday to say that she would visit when the weather improves. It has been three months since I have seen her and wee Maggie will be growing fast. I fear she will see a difference in granda though as he seems to lose strength daily. His humour still bides though and he dared to read out the instructions in last week's paper on how to make a good cup o' tea, emphasising tae me the part where it said water had to be free o' smoke and fresh boiled!!

With regards to young Peter, perhaps suggest a position in a bakers or tailors shop and for yourself a dose of Pepper's Quinine and Iron Tonic for great mental strength which claims to "repair the ravages caused by overtaxing the brain," to restore your calm and amiable humour. I fear if you do not you will kick something and break a toe.

Till I see you again,
Goodnight my darling,
Your loving Jane.

Sarah sat by John watching Jane's hand flitter across the page as she wrote to her loon, and she too shared her husband's gladness. Sarah was ever present in the cottage now, and Jane took great comfort from her presence. It had been hard at first seeing her, but she was used to her granny being there now and it brought a smile, and sometimes a tear, to see her sitting alongside John, her hand on his. Jane kept her promise and never told her granda when his Sally was nearby, but a part of her was terrified of what the constant presence may mean. The thought of losing her granda was too much for Jane to bear: even though she was aware that he was now an old man, he was the only father she had ever known and she could not bear to lose him.

Jane had grown to feel very deeply for Alec over those first six months, and although her heart soared when he talked of a future for them both, a part of her held tight to the fear of loss in her,

"Oh Granny, I am petrified o' marrying and having bairns in case they are taken from me. I canna decide if it is better to know a family o' my own and lose them, or to face a life without one. Both would be a loss to my heart and it's a question I dinna ken the answer to."

It left her in a state of perpetual swithering, one minute elated at the thought of being a wife and mother, and the next haunted by imagining losing a bairn or living life as a widow.

Although Jane did not voice this concern with Alec he could see the fear in her eyes when she talked of her granda's health and she would change the subject when he talked of when they should marry. He was sure of his feelings and knew they were reciprocated, so he needed to find a way of reassuring Jane. He suggested to her that because he held a good job in Aberlour it would make sense if they married and lived there, and have John come and live with them. Jane needed no time to think about it as she knew that her granda would never leave his family home of over fifty years, full of the memories of Sarah and their bairns.

She herself felt an added fear - by leaving Milton Cottage, would she also be leaving behind her granny? Some ghosts, like wee Elizabeth, seemed to be able to go where they pleased, but Jane had only ever seen her granny inside the cottage and she was not prepared to lose her presence. She would not tell Alec of her awareness of those who had passed. She understood why Sarah had kept it a secret from her husband, the fear of how Alec might react was too great a risk, no matter how much she knew she was loved, and having been on the receiving end of folks tongues as an illegitimate bairn was enough in a lifetime, without adding fuel to the fire and giving folk something else to be cruel about.

At such times, when thinking became too difficult, Jane closed her book of thoughts and got on with life, pretending her fears did not exist. For a while she allowed herself to revel in the emotions of being in love, and the harsh winter which brought low temperatures caused the loosening of frocks, in the name of keeping warm.

A s 1885 DAWNED, it dragged with it the continuing severe winter. The previous January had seen fierce storms raging through Britain, and this one brought extreme cold, and the illnesses that go with it. Not a soul in Scotland felt warm that season, families huddled together for warmth and the peat smouldered in the hearth, barely drying the wet outer clothing and rarely reaching the chests or toes of the young or old.

It was a time of excitement for some: the very young played and slid on the ice; the young frolicked as usual; the middle aged did a mixture of both; and the old smiled knowingly, through the chattering of what teeth they had left.

THE GROUSE DANCE

As the water in the rivers lowered and the buds started to appear, spring beckoned with its promise of new life, and the inhabitants of Mortlach awoke from the slumber of winter. Old joints, stiffened from the cold, began to ease with glimpses of a warmer sun, farmers turned from calving, to lambing and sowing, and the minds of folk lightened alongside the days. The grouse rose at dawn to dance and sing, their red eyebrows raised and their chests puffed out.

This was Margaret's favourite time of year, although she was beginning to feel her age: she was enthralled with the miracle of a third bairn but run ragged at the age of forty eight with the constant activity of a toddler. Little Maggie was a fiery one, much like Jane at that age, but oh, how Margaret rejoiced in her married life, with her own hearth. She did wish, though, that her mother could have met her new grandbairn and seen for herself, Margaret settled and happy.

On visiting her father one afternoon, Margaret was saddened by the change that confronted her, some time having passed since her last visit. Her sister Ann had told her that he was failing but it was a shock to see him frail, his lungs causing him at times to fight for breath. The second shock was on seeing Jane, the terror in her eyes thinly veiled with false smiles and blithe words.

Margaret sat down soundlessly as she watched Jane scurry aimlessly from one task to the next, fussing round John like a moth to a flame. Thankful that wee Maggie had been left with her aunt, Margaret sent Jane outside for some air so she could sit alone with her father. He was in good spirits, just tired these days he said, but still managed to potter about and get wee jobs done about the place, and he wanted to know all of Margaret's news. They had a fine blether between themselves and when she could see that he was needing to snooze she held his hand and sat with him until he fell asleep. Covering him with a blanket Margaret went outside in search of Jane and found her by the dyke looking out onto the hills.

Standing alongside her, Margaret gently spoke.

"He's failing, Jane, but he's nae at death's door yet. There's spirit there still and you need to take stock and calm yer sel'. He's had a long life and misses yer granny, and when the time comes we'll hae to let him go, as hard as that will be. He's a father to us both, I ken that, and you have looked after him well, but now you must look after yer sel' especially wi a bairn coming."

There was a sharp intake of breath as Jane looked at her mother with wide eyes, her hand instinctively going to her belly. Margaret smiled at her daughter.

"Alec is a good man, Jane. Does he ken?"

Jane shook her head. "I didn't really ken myself till now. I have been so busy worrying aboot granda that time has just gone by. How did you ken?"

"There's something about how a quine carries herself when with child, and a look in the eyes that is only present at that time."

Jane sat on the dyke, her tongue quiet, her mind dazed.

"Oh my quine, what a fine mother you will be."

Jane smiled for the first time, her hand still on her belly and instead of panic and dread in her heart she felt a sense of something akin to happiness.

As Sunday approached Jane was looking forward to seeing Alec, and having had a few days to fully acknowledge her condition she was both keen and apprehensive of sharing her news. She was sure of his feelings and intentions but wary all the same because of her mother's experience. Beyond that, Jane had dared not think at all.

When Alec arrived Jane suggested a walk, leaving her granda to his afternoon sleep. It had been a dreich morning but the sun was trying to make an appearance as they walked hand in hand along the river bank. Alec had been worried for Jane as she was clearly concerned for her granda, but she told him of her mother's visit which had calmed her mind to a certain extent. Alec was glad to hear it and was about to talk further when Jane stopped and turned to face him, a look on her face which he could not discern.

"I am with child, Alec."

They each held the other's gaze, Jane's heart missing a beat, as a slow smile spread across Alec's face, his eyes crinkling as he picked Jane up and whirled her around, laughing as he did so.

"Oh, ma quine," were all the words spoken, and the only words needed to be heard, the emotion in them enough to reassure Jane that this was indeed serendipitous.

Before Jane could fill her head with worries of what lay ahead Alec's words tumbled out, as he spoke of marriage and jobs and cottages and John, and how they would make it all happen. But the most precious words that Jane heard were that no child of theirs would be born illegitimate.

$\mathcal{J}$ANE WAS UNSURE as to when the bairn would be born, having been absorbed with both her granda and Alec, but she thought maybe the end of September. May was fast approaching and there was much to be decided, but no one ever married in May, it not being the custom of the time, so the earliest it could be would be June, and Jane only hoped that the bairn growing inside her would not be too big by then. First Jane and Alec needed to tell John that they were to be married and that a bairn would be coming later in the year. It was not customary to tell family till all the arrangements had been made but Jane wanted her granda to know as it affected him and she hoped that the news would bring him gladness.

John was overjoyed but not the least surprised, and he upped and hugged Jane with the agility of a man twenty years younger, the news putting some life back into his old bones. When the congratulations were passed John made a point of telling Jane that on marrying Alec she would be moving to her own cottage and that there were plenty of folk around to help him if needed. Alec saw the fear in Jane's eyes and reiterated his idea of John coming to live with them but John would have none of it. Milton Cottage was his home and that was that.

"This is your time, Jane, and I will not have you changing any plans for me. If you want to do right by me then go and live your life, lass, and be as happy as is possible."

T HAT EVENING JANE sat by the hearth of the only home she had ever known. Cantlie in name and Smith in heart. She gazed upon the room and its other inhabitants, long gone from this earth, their presence ever comforting and, she had come to realise, needed.

Yes, she needed them.

She knew not why she was able to see them, but they communicated with her in their own way without words, and Jane felt their wisdom, even from those who were cantankerous in nature. They had made her laugh with their expressions and gesticulations, and sat with her when she grieved. Their smiles had offered agreement and support, and their presence, strength. Jane had no number for how many folk that no longer lived, she had seen. Every cottage visited and every road walked, she had met someone in another form. Before she could even talk Jane had played with bairns from another time, and sharing her awareness with her granny had been such a special and unique time for them both.

"How can I leave ye behind?"

Wee Elizabeth, who visited Jane often, was the only one she saw in many places. Some seemed stuck in one place, in a room or a garden, and she suspected that was the case in Milton Cottage. She looked at the old man knitting at the table, no idea of his name, but she loved him, having known him her entire life. The bairnie that never grew up, being rocked by its mother, she loved them too. Her crotchety great granny, who was very particular about the making of porridge, she loved her, and her granny Sarah, the only one she had known in life, she loved her the most.

"How can I leave ye behind?"

$\mathcal{J}$ANE DID WHAT she always did when thinking became too hard - closed her feelings away inside, and let life carry on. Meanwhile, Alec had been offered a small cottage to rent in Carron, Aberlour as part of the married man's fee as a farm manager. It was available to rent in mid June, so the wedding date was set for Saturday the twentieth. Jane exclaimed and oohed and aahed in all the right places, but her heart was torn. If only she could have cut herself in two then one part could have lived happily with Alec in Carron, and the other in Milton Cottage.

John could see that all was not well with Jane and when pressed she said that she was finding it difficult to contemplate leaving her childhood home. It made no sense to him that she was not excited to start her own life in Aberlour, and something in Jane just snapped and she roared,

"For pity's sake, Granda, have you forgotten what and who I can see? Leaving them here is the same as them dying. I will lose them, and when you are gone I won't be visiting here and they will be lost to me forever. I can't grieve for so many all at once, and I canna bear to never see their faces again."

Tears coursed down Jane's face as she slumped on to the kitchen table.

John sat in silence, till Jane's tears subsided. His eyes searched the kitchen of his home but he could not see what Jane could, not even a flicker of light or a shadow. He had asked Jane not to tell him if his Sally ever appeared but of course he had wondered at times.

"Tell me about the folk that live among us."

So Jane described them - their age, appearance and their personalities that were evident to her. She told him of the folk who were always present and those who came and went, like wee Elizabeth. John marvelled at how it could be and he hesitantly asked who was with them that night. Jane turned her head and said that the old man was in the chair by the hearth but neither the wife with the bairn nor her great granny were present.

"And my Sally?"

Jane paused for a second and said, "She is sitting beside you."

John lowered his head, hiding his tear filled eyes and his hand reached out and rested on the empty chair beside him.

The two of them sat in silence for a while and Jane noticed that her great granny had appeared by the door. John cleared his throat and asked,

"Do you think they might go wi' you to Aberlour?"

Jane shook her head, "I dinna think they can."

John touched her hand and said. "You could ask them."

Jane turned to the old man at the hearth and he shook his head. She looked over at her great granny and was stunned to see her nod. Very slowly Jane lifted her eyes to her granny, who smiled and nodded, and tears of relief and happiness rolled down two cheeks.

MARRIAGE

MAY BROUGHT WITH it a birthday and excitement for Jane, as she finally allowed herself to revel in her wedding preparations. Her mother and Eliza had accompanied her to Dufftown to choose a wedding dress which would encompass her growing abdomen, mindful that no cutting or sewing alterations could be made on the wedding day. Undergarments and shoes were also purchased, following the tradition of nothing but new clothing, so as to ward off bad luck.

The kist in her room was full of the linen she needed in her new home, including feather bedding and pillows. It was to be sent to Jane's new home a few days before the wedding, unlocked, as to lock or bind it in any way could portend a difficult life. Family and friends had been formally invited in person and the minister, who was always the last to know, was invited when all the arrangements were made, as to do so earlier would have been bad luck indeed.

John looked on as Jane bustled and organised, and relief unfurled within him at seeing his wee quine happy. Knowing that she would be cared for by Alec allowed John to relax and give in to the tiredness in his bones. It became more and more difficult to catch his breath and sleep did not come easily at night, so he had taken to sleeping in his chair by the fire. Having not wanted to know in the past if Sally was present, he now took great comfort in knowing that she was by him, and he would imagine her sitting opposite him on her own chair by the hearth. He knew that Jane worried about him but he tried as best he could to put her at ease. He was old and infirm now and that was just the way of things.

On the Saturday night three weeks before the wedding, Alec visited the session clerk to hand him his own and Jane's names for proclamation of banns of marriage, known as the laying doon of pawns. This was called 'Beuckin Nicht' and the banns were to be read out on three consecutive Sundays preceding the wedding. This having been done, Jane and Alec's friends were expected to rub shoulders with them on meeting, in the hope of 'catching' marriage for themselves. Some carried out this action more whole heartedly than others!

The bride's ale had been brewing for weeks and neighbours were busy baking and preparing food for the marriage feast. It became obvious that John would not be fit to attend and Jane was deeply saddened. Family and neighbours took it in turns to call in and sit with John and feed him soup when he felt up to it. Beckoning her over the day before the wedding she sat down by her granda's chair at the hearth.

"I am not long for this world, quine. I canna watch ye be married, but I will be there in spirit."

Jane's eyes filled with tears. "Oh, Granda, I ken it, but I canna bear it."

John took her hand. "Ye have found yersel' a good man in Alec, and it puts me at ease knowing ye will be looked after."

John was taken by a bout of coughing before being able to continue. "Promise me ye will be the happiest bride. I will be here in the morning to see ye off and I will imagine the whole procession and the service, and it will make me happy tae do so."

Jane swallowed hard. "I promise, Granda."

T HE MORNING OF the wedding arrived, as did Margaret and Eliza to help with the wedding breakfast and to dress Jane.

Margaret was busy making the curds and cream when she stopped for a moment to look at her quine and she gently spoke.

"My bonny quine, ye hae become a woman o' substance, possessing an abundance o' compassion and an inner strength that I think ye are unaware o'. I'm sorry yer life as a bairn wis hard, and I wish ye all o' life's happiness."

Jane's tongue was unable to speak at her mother's outpouring of such words. She was not used to such openness or praise. Her hand clutched her mother's and with a nod of her head her tongue allowed her to whisper, "Thank ye, Mother."

T HERE WAS MUCH hilarity and excitement, as well as relief, when the wedding dress was able to be adjusted to fit and Jane glowed with happiness, surrounded by those she loved. A knock on the door heralded the arrival of the sens, two men who had been sent by Alec to fetch his bride, as was the way of the time. The old ritual was played out with the familiar words:

" Does Jane bide here?"   (Does Jane live here?)

"Aye, faht de ye wint wee ir?" (Yes, what do you want with her?)

"We wint ir for Alec." (We want her for Alec.)

"Bit ye winna get ir." (But you won't get her.)

"But we'll tack ir." (But we'll take her.)

"Will ye come in, in taste a moofu o' a dram till we see aboot it?" (Will you come in and take a mouthful of whisky and we will see about it?)

So the sens entered the cottage to take possession of the bride and following a dram escorted her to church. Before leaving, Jane ran over and kissed her granda on the cheek and he kissed her back, a look of understanding between them.

The wedding party made their way to the church accompanied by the playing of stirring bagpipes and the firing of guns and pistols. Old shoes were thrown behind them as the whisky flowed, and tongues were full of banter and mirth, and Jane laughed to see the ghosts of the past dance on the road, wee Elizabeth birling around her father, Jane's uncle John, as he walked with Jane.

Alec led his own procession in a similar fashion, and his brothers James and George who had both married quines named Jane, joked to Alec that the Janes in this world got the best husbands.

The bride was led into the kirk and placed beside her groom at the bride stool, a pew used for those who were to be married. Eliza Black stood by Jane, and George Glass by Alec, their chosen best maid and best man, and the two were joined in marriage by the minister, James Cruickshank.

Jane shed the lamb skin and became a Farquharson, a name to be proud of that fit her absolutely.

Margaret, her husband Willie beside her and their wee Maggie on his knee, had a tear in her eye as she listened to her eldest child say her vows. Her thrawn, witty, sensitive wee quine had become a strong and loving woman. Her humour would carry her through life and she prayed that Jane's home with Alec would be full of warmth, understanding and bairns. Willie noticed the tears on Margaret's cheek and whispered in her ear,

"Gie yersel' a shak woman - it's meant to be a happy occasion." This caused Margaret inadvertently to snort and little Maggie to giggle. Alec's mother, May, also felt similar feelings having watched her son take the place of his father and put aside his own needs.

And so it was on Saturday the 20th June 1885, Jane Cantlie married Alexander Farquharson in Mortlach church, two folk who never thought they would marry, two minds that sparked and two hearts that welded.

188_5_. MARRIAGES in the _Parish_ of _____ in the _County of Banff_

(Page 5.)

No.	When, Where, and How Married.	Signature of Parties. Rank or Profession, whether Single or Widowed, and Relationship (if any).	Age.	Usual Residence.	Surname and Rank or Profession of Father. Name, and Maiden Surname of Mother.	If a regular Marriage, Signatures of officiating Minister and Witnesses. If irregular, Date of Conviction, Decree of Declarator, or Sheriff's Warrant.	When & Where Registered, and Signature of Registrar.
9	188_5_ on the _____ day of _____ at the Church _____		26				188_5_ At _____ Registrar
10	188_5_ on the _____ day of _____ at _____		30				188_5_ At _____ Registrar
		(1)	(2)	M	(3)	(4)	(5)

_____ Registrar

Two Ends and a Beginning

F IVE DAYS AFTER the wedding on a mild evening, the window in the kitchen of Milton Cottage was opened to allow John's spirit to rise, and the clock stopped at nine o'clock. The milk was poured away and a nail thrust into the cheese, as fir candles were lit in the shattering silence, and tears flowed soundlessly.

Jane settled into Carron in the way that the tide ebbs and flows. Some days her feelings rose up to catch her unawares, and on others they receded, pulling her back to calmer waters. The growing life inside her wriggled and pushed, reminding Jane to be excited and to look ahead. Her days were now filled with knitting and sewing in preparation for the bairn's arrival, but she missed the familiar faces of Milton, not yet having grown to know her neighbours well.

She missed too the ghosts of her childhood home and she grieved them as she did her granda, knowing she would never live among them again and now that her granda was gone she would no longer visit them and they, too, were lost to her.

At times she would find her mind wandering, carrying her back to Milton Cottage to sit among her lost loved ones. She would visualise the ghost of the old man, his white hair and beard, his stooped back and his kind eyes, sitting knitting by the hearth; the young mother cradling her bairn, rocking her gently, a quiet smile on her bonny face.

Jane's heart, torn in two by both losses; but the thought of her coming bairn, sewing the pieces together stitch by stitch.

Her granny was present often, which came as such a relief to Jane, and she chatted to her about the excitement of her coming bairn. Great granny visited too sometimes, always with a wary look in her eye which Jane could never quite decipher.

ℒETTERS FROM ELSIE in Aberdeen kept her entertained, as she was forever in one scrape or another, Elsie being Elsie, and Eliza visited, as did her mother with words of advice on not eating pickles whilst with child, otherwise the bairn would have a sour disposition!

Alec arrived home one evening with a letter from his brother, Robert, in Glasgow. "Happy news, Jane. Robert has married thon widow, Margaret, he was courting."

Jane shuddered and her words came quickly, "But it's bad luck to hae two members o' a family marrying in the same year!"

Her husband tried to allay her fears. "Och quine, it only matters if ye bide in the same place."

"That's nae true and ye ken it, Alec." Jane's hand rubbed her belly, seeking comfort from her unborn child.

"Dinna be worrying, Jane - look what's ahead o' us," he said, as he too placed a hand on her belly.

But that was exactly what Jane was worried about and when Alec left the room, for the first time in years, she read her tea leaves.

Jane slowly turned her cup and looked upon the scattered leaves apprehensively. She saw the wavy symbol portending change and challenge, and lines that spoke of travel. Jane was unsure what to make of it as the coming bairn would indeed be change and challenge, and travel could mean a visit somewhere, but her feeling of foreboding remained, so she was none the wiser.

ABERLOUR, A FEW miles away, had a different feel to it from both Dufftown and Auchindoun. Here, folk talked of distilleries and whisky as much as farms, but being slightly bigger than Dufftown it had a sense of important bustle about it that both Jane and Alec liked. The most refreshing thing was that Jane did not bump into folk there who looked at her with disdain, having no knowledge of her background.

Their cottage was small but habitable, rented to Alec as part of his farm manager's contract and supplied with peat, oatmeal, milk and tatties throughout the year. But just as Jane was settling into her new abode everything changed, just as she had feared.

Fairies At Work

ALEC SET OFF for work as usual, a spring in his step and a belly full of porridge. The world was just beginning to stir and the high pitched chirp and whining of the swallow could be heard, and the bird was soon swooping and diving, its agility surprising to the onlooker. Alec was glad that the working day was now ten hours instead of fifteen as he was keen to get home to Jane and was eager for the arrival of their bairn. He marvelled at the change a little over a year had brought to his life, having thought himself content before, he now realised how much more could be gained from life and counted himself very fortunate indeed.

Alec arrived at the farm just as the sun was rising and set to work, overseeing the farmhands and discussing the day's activities with his employer. All was going as expected until mid morning when the head cattleman came running to Alec with a look of fear in his eyes. "Two cattle, shot-a-dead Alec! I searched for fairy darts but found none."

Now Alec was what you would call a cynical man but he respected the beliefs of others. He had been raised to fear the power of fairies and witches and had been spooked enough times as a child to encourage that fear, but the older he had become the less he feared them, and although he would never have announced it, his beliefs had somewhat changed.

Alec spoke matter of factly. "I'll come and hae a look, George."

The two men set off at pace and climbed the gate into the field where the herd were grazing.

"I fear for the herd, Alec. If it's nae fairies it's an awful disease."

"Well let's just see." Alec answered, as he checked each cow in turn. "Nae sign o'frothing at the mouth and their eyes are clear. There's nae obvious signs o' disease."

Having worked around animals his whole life and listened to the veterinary surgeon speak on animal diseases, he was more inclined to believe that the sudden death of an animal was more likely to be through natural illness than any evil doing.

As he turned to leave the field a cow suddenly bellowed and keeled over. The cattleman was shaking and looking about the place, fear apparent on his face. Alec was startled and bewildered but no fear showed in his expression.

"Prepare a draught for the herd while I go and speak to Mr Stewart," he ordered, as he set off in search of his employer to convey the bad news.

David Stewart was a man in his seventieth year, narrow of mind and set in his ways, whose carnaptious nature revealed itself frequently. Alec approached him.

"Three o' the herd have died suddenly and I dinna ken why. Shall I fetch the veterinary surgeon?"

"Nae need for that expense. It's obviously a disease brought by the fairies so a sacrificial killing o' a pig needs to be carried oot straight away, and it's ashes spread over the byre and farm buildings."

Alec may have acquiesced but Mr Stewart continued, "Cover one o' the herd in tar, set it alight and let it run till it drops dead."

This was an old practice, believed to cure a herd of disease and Alec was shocked.

"Nae need for that surely, it's cruel and unnecessary. We can try various draughts and seek the advice o' the veterinary surgeon."

The old man walked up to Alec and stopped but an inch from his face, his voice low and threatening.

"Ye will do as I order, and ye will also bury one o' the dead cows in the neighbouring farm so as to transfer the disease to them. I am taking nae chances, so all three acts will rid this farm o' this evil. Do it or leave, and dinna return."

Alec's temper rose up from his feet, as quick as a spark from the fire.

"Keep your work, you cruel, gypit, narrow minded fool. I winna lower myself to carry oot such foolery."

The fist came from nowhere, surprising Alec at its speed, and he was too slow to dodge it as it caught him on his left cheek. The force behind it was not strong, being the age Mr Stewart was, and did not cause Alec to waver on his feet. He would not hit the man back but he did kick the milk churns as he strode away, causing them to fall over, spilling their contents and he was left with the words in his ears.

"You have twa days to get oot o' your cottage and I'll mak sure every farmer around kens that you bring disease to a farm. You'll be lucky to ever work again."

Alec stopped dead in his tracks as the farmer turned away. He ran the few steps between them and kicked him so hard up the erse that he fell head first into the pile of dung, steaming nicely in the early summer sun.

ALEC COULD NOT return home with the news of having no work, not to mention no home, so took it upon himself to go straight to Charleston of Aberlour in the hope of securing employment immediately. He knew his name was good and hoped that that would be enough, before rumours surfaced which may hinder his chances. Being August folk were only a couple of months into their six month contracts secured at the May Feeing market, so he knew he would not be offered a managers post, which would mean less money, but less was better than none with a bairn coming.

He tried three farms to no avail and the working day was nearing its end when he arrived at Hatton farm and found the proprietor at home, a fair man whom Alec had worked for, a few years past. Saying as little as possible as to why he was seeking work, only that there had been a difference of opinion, Alec looked Ian Ross in the eye and waited for an answer.

*J*ANE HAD FALLEN asleep waiting for Alec to return for his supper and woke with a start on hearing the cottage door open. He looked exhausted, and slumped into the chair by the hearth, removing his boots wearily before telling Jane the whole sorry tale.

Jane's emotions went from sympathy to anger to distress as she listened, but not a word did she utter till Alec had finished, scared that she would say something that she would regret. She could feel her bairn wriggling, heightening the significance of the situation.

"Twa days, Alec? Twa days tae find a new place to bide?"

Alec looked at Jane's distraught face and his chest tightened. "I hae work, and I will go and see George, in Aberlour, first thing to ask if we can bide wi' him and Rose, till we sort out a house."

"But we haven't seen them since he was best man at our wedding. They winna want us."

"They're good folk, Jane, they'll help us. Ian Ross had no cottages to spare but come the next Feeing market in November things will be different."

Jane nodded, a feeling of numbness in her mind and heaviness in her heart.

"I'm sorry, ma quine, I will make it right."

Jane looked at her husband and saw the shame and regret in his eyes as a tear escaped her eye.

*T*WO CARTS WERE filled with their belongings and made their way to Aberlour under the watchful eye of Alec's old employer who had come to make sure they left that day, as he had ordered. Alec held his tongue with difficulty, looking straight ahead as he told the mare to walk on. Jane said nothing but gave the farmer such a look of disgust, whilst holding her belly, that he had the decency to look away first.

George and Rose welcomed Jane and Alec, offering them the use of their upstairs room, empty at that time as no bairns had yet arrived, although they had been married the past four years. As tired as Jane was she noted the disapproving look from Rose which belied the welcoming words, and her heart sank once again.

Alec started at Hatton Farm the following day, as a farm labourer, determined to keep his head down and work hard in order to provide for his family. Jane arranged their essential belongings as best she could in their room, the majority of their furniture having been sent to her mother to be stored there, until such time as they had a home of their own again.

A few days later on the 18th August - in the wee hours of that Tuesday morning - Jane commenced her accouchement, a labour that was to last until eight o'clock that evening, causing much distress and worry as the bairn was not expected for another month. Alec had to remind himself to breathe as he waited anxiously throughout the day, Jane's screams scorching his heart as she herself pushed their son into the world, small and wiry with a strong set of lungs and a head of red hair.

Rose and Eliza were both present alongside Margaret, who had arrived in the afternoon to help her daughter, and when the time came she passed the bairn to Jane as her own mother, Sarah, had done for Margaret. Jane drank in her son's features, so like his father, and gave thanks that they had both survived. The loon was to be called James, after Alec's father, and as Jane cradled her precious bairn in the minutes before being sained, so as to ward off the fairies, she was aware of her granny sitting on one side of her bed and her great granny on the other. An immense feeling of joy passed through her and for a time, all was right with the world.

Alec was called into the room as the women folk made the preparations for saining and he was overcome with his emotions which were a combination of relief, pride and awe as he looked upon his wife and bairn. Their son, with eyes like his mother's, and his own colouring - what would become of him in life? Both made a silent pledge to love and protect James, and no matter what trials lay ahead, theirs would be a happy home.

Three weeks later on the 7th of September Jane and Alec registered James's birth and two heads were held high, as there would never be any question of his surname or any need to change it.

*

T HE MONTHS THAT followed were not as difficult as Jane had feared. Being a mother suited her, and James was not a fractious bairn, making her daily routine easier. Rose had softened somewhat to having lodgers and often offered to help with James, and Jane could see the longing in Rose's eyes when she held him. One morning following breakfast Jane turned to Rose.

"Pass me yer cup and I'll read your tea leaves."

Rose was both surprised and excited as she handed her cup to Jane and she marveled at the way Jane held and turned the cup, an intent look upon her face.

"I see a thimble which means changes at home."

Rose's excitement faltered. "What changes, Jane? Nothing bad I hope."

Jane scrutinised the leaves again and slowly a smile appeared on her lips as she held the cup up for Rose to see. "See this, Rose? A circle wi' two dots inside means a baby is coming."

Rose's hand went to her chest and she whispered, "So I'm nae barren?"

Jane shook her head and Rose burst into a bout of greeting and hugged her so tight that Jane feared she would never breathe again.

COME NOVEMBER, PRIOR to the Feeing market, Alec was offered the words, "Will ye bide?" by his employer. Answering, "Aye," secured his contract for six months and it came with a wee cottage. Alec knew that the past incident would mean that it was unlikely he would ever be wanted as a manager again, unless he moved away from Banffshire, but neither himself nor Jane wished to move far, so they would make the best of things.

The week that the Farquharsons once again moved into their own home coincided with the birth of William Smith, another son for Jane's brother, and the first with Smith on his birth certificate instead of Scott. The Smith's were settled in Elgin and brother and sister wrote regularly, each keeping the other up to date with their lives and coming together when they could at their mother's home to visit their wee sister Maggie.

SPIRITS

It was fine indeed having a home of their own again and although not as comfortable as the one in Carron, Jane made it as warm and homely as possible. Being on the outskirts of Aberlour it was possible to walk there for provisions and to visit folk that Jane slowly began to become acquainted with. James was a healthy loon and his first year brought Jane and Alec much happiness. Jane took in folk's mending and sewing to supplement Alec's wage and together they made a good life for themselves.

There were no house people in the cottage other than her usual visitors, but out the back in the small garden a young loon of about four years of age was often to be seen running and playing, and it made Jane smile to see little Elizabeth joining him sometimes and chasing one another, laughter in their eyes.

Jane sometimes wished she could share her awareness with Alec but a lump of fear rose in her throat whenever she thought of speaking. Her promise to her granny was held firm in her, and memories of being both taunted and shunned, growing up, were never very far away, feeding her fear of folk knowing her secret.

As she watched her bairn grow, Jane's fear of losing her loved ones grew with him and she confided in the only folk that she could speak to about such things.

"I watch Alec wi' James on his knee, speaking and playing wi' him, and my heart both rises with pride and squeezes with fear at the same time, and my breath halts. The thought o' losing either one o' them terrifies my soul. I ken I'm nae a bairn anymore and I understand that folk die for all sorts o' reasons, but I just canna accept it. It's a part o' life that petrifies me."

Her great granny sat by Jane, her hand on Jane's arm and a soft smile on her face. Jane leaned in to her, soaking in comfort.

1886 BROUGHT WITH IT more change. The May Feeing market bartered lower wages for some and Alec found himself having to move his family again, this time to Tomindongle, Knockando, west of Aberlour across the River Spey. David Stewart's rumours had done some damage but his neighbours knew him well so, ironically, obtaining work nearer to Corran was easier than elsewhere.

Just as members of Parliament in Westminster were debating home rule for Scotland, under a new Prime Minister, Edward Smith Stanley, so too was Jane debating with Alec the necessity for moving.

The two sparked and locked horns. Jane stood, hands on hips, her chin defiant.

"I dinna want tae leave. We are settled here and I have grown tae love Aberlour."

Alec's brow knitted together. "I ken that and I feel the same, but if more bairns come we will struggle wi' money. I'm trying tae look ahead, quine, and do best by our family."

Jane paced the floor, her voice rising. "But we ken folk here now and I dinna want tae start again."

Alec sighed heavily and folded his arms across his chest. "Jane! I have taken the work in Tomindongle. It is done. We have to leave here in twa weeks."

Jane slumped into a chair, all fight gone within her.

Alec took her hand. "It'll be fine, quine."

TWO WEEKS LATER the Farquharson's packed up their belongings and Jane blew a kiss to the wee loon in the garden.

T HE ONE BENEFIT of being in Knockando was that it was closer to her mother in Glenlivet and wee Maggie, now four, but it was yet another draughty cottage with a hearth that billowed out more smoke than went up the lum, and James - who was now walking - was forever filthy between the dirt floor and the stack of peat in the basket.

There were two house people, a man and woman of middle age, who seemed to prowl in the cottage. Jane had known disgruntled ghosts but none who emanated perpetual discontent and she disliked the atmosphere in the cottage when they appeared. Their restless movements and solemn faces unnerved her and she found it hard to be relaxed when they were present. For the first time in her life she derived no comfort from her awareness and she noticed that neither her granny nor great granny appeared when the others were present, which was worrying to her.

Jane was astounded one evening when Alec suddenly asked, "Do ye think this cottage has a strange feel aboot it?"

Her stomach quivered, and she could see the two inhabitants lurking by the door. "Aye, there's an unusual atmosphere at times. I dinna like it much."

Alec shook himself. "It faces north, so doesn't get much light, which is probably why."

Jane breathed slowly. It was the right time to tell Alec of her awareness but her promise to her granny would not allow the words to come.

*

J ANE TRIED TO enjoy her new abode and as much as she loved the surrounding countryside her heart just wasn't in it, and she lost some of her new found spark. Come the end of the year she vowed to try harder to settle and she deliberately avoided reading her tea leaves just in case life had mischief on its mind.

January brought frost which did nothing to help those consumed with whooping cough or stiff joints but it also brought another nephew for Jane, one George Smith being born on the 19th, a fourth son for James and Ann.

ALEC WAS WORKING hard and trying his best not to kick any erses. The pay was better in Knockando and they were managing to put a little by, which reassured him that they had done the right thing by moving. He had lost count how many times he had moved for work, as that was how life was, but Jane had always been used to one place and he knew that she found it difficult.

As May approached Alec grew anxious that he would not be kept on at the farm as he knew that he could not ask Jane to move again, so the only alternative would be him working away, which did not appeal to him at all. Having waited a long time in life before marrying and fathering a bairn he was in no hurry to leave them behind. For once luck was on their side and Alec was indeed asked to bide, which was just as well as Jane discovered that she was with child again.

Jane was delighted to have life growing in her for a second time and for a while contentment lived in her heart, as summer brought long, warm days and wee James was able to toddle and play outside. Watching him chase the hens reminded her of her own childhood with her cousins Ann and Elizabeth. Ann, like herself, had her own bairns now and of course little Elizabeth had never grown, and was a constant shimmer of light living in Jane's consciousness.

News arrived at Jane's door on 17th August informing her of Francis Cantlie's death the day before, at his home in Milton. Jane was quiet on hearing the news, not quite sure of her feelings, as Francis had never been a granda to her, just a kindly neighbour, but she had lived by him for many years and had been fond of him. She would not attend the funeral but she would lay flowers on his grave the next time she visited Mortlach kirkyard.

The months passed and the year ended as it had begun, exceptionally cold. The wind howled and the windows rattled as Jane's accouchement began, but her time was fraught, as the house people prowled ever closer. Alexander, a second son, was born at the stroke of one on the 19th December and as he was handed to Jane she held tight to her loon, her mind filled with foreboding. "Hurry Mother, we need tae be sained."

Margaret heard the panic in Jane's voice. "Dinna worry, quine. It will be done quickly. We winna let the fairies near."

Jane's eyes glued themselves to the two ghosts loitering nearby and although they were not fairies she feared for her child. Neither her granny nor great granny were present and she mourned their absence at this precious time, and she kept a careful eye on the house people, anxious in case they came too close to her bairn. They prowled the room but did not approach. Of course she could say none of this, but it took away the pleasure of seeing her bairn for the first time.

Those first few days were marred as Jane clung to wee Alexander, too scared to let him out of her sight. The house was never empty, folk took their turn in watching over Jane and her bairn to ward off the fairies till the baptism, but Margaret noticed that her daughter was overly anxious and was worried for her. She had seen some women sink into a dark mood following accouchement and she prayed that Jane's mind would not be overcome.

The Tuesday following the New Year saw Alexander baptised and Jane breathed a sigh of relief. The house people had never approached the bairn and hopefully never would, but Jane was unsure as to what harm they could do and it worried her. As the weeks passed her granny and great granny visited more often which allowed Jane to relax and eventually her mind calmed as she convinced herself that although discontent, the house people were unable to be wicked.

WINTER CONTINUED TO blow the north easterly wind into the cottage and the two windows rattled as the door groaned as if feeling the cold seep into its fibre. James girned and Jane kept him wrapped up as best she could as they huddled around the hearth. Although the fire was well stocked no heat seemed to emanate, especially when the house people were present and she wondered at their discontent. Perhaps they were victims of a murder or had taken their own lives, disallowing their burial within the kirk yard walls. She would never know, but she did not like her home.

Alexander was a fractious bairn. Little milk had come for Jane so feeding him involved the preparation of glass bottles filled with mare or cow's milk. When he was just a month old Jane had new life growing in her again but she was not to realise this until calving began in March.

Divulgence

 $\mathcal{J}$ ANE WAITED UNTIL the Sunday before speaking to Alec so as there would be time to talk properly. It was a fretful week as her mind went over the words she needed to say and she worried about how he would react to her confession. Following dinner she put both bairns down for a nap and she took a breath. "Sit down, Alec. I need tae speak with ye."

Alec could see the serious look on Jane's face and was unsure of what was to come. Jane took a long breath and held her hands together to stop them from shaking as her heart beat so rapidly that it caused pain in her chest.

Her voice was soft as she began her tale. "Please listen and dinna speak till I'm finished."

Alec nodded and she continued.

"When I was a bairn I played with bairns that no others could see. I saw folk in my home that no one else saw, and I told no one. I called them the house people and I liked tae see them and they comforted me growing up. When I was five my granny realised that I could see others and she admitted to me that she was aware o' them too, but that it was to be oor secret as folk might not understand and think us possessing the Evil Eye. She explained that they were folk fae the past who had once bade in our home or who were related to us. My whole life I have been aware o' them in every dwelling I have entered or road I have walked. They dinna speak but I see their expressions and I am able to know them. Some are quiet and couthie, others boisterous or cantankerous but I have never been afraid o' them, till now."

Alec's face was pale but he remained silent and nodded to Jane to continue.

"There are two house people here that I fear, one man and one woman. For whatever reason, they are discontented and I worry for our bairns. I blame them for the cold in the cottage and for my lack of milk, and they prowl in the corners with their faces tormented. My granny and great granny visit here but never when the others are present and I am unsure what that means.

We need to leave here, Alec, I am with child and I fear for it."

ALEC SAID NOT a word. His eyes were unsure and concerned but slowly a memory surfaced in his mind and his eyes softened.

"John, your granda, took me aside a few weeks afore he died and told me, quite forcibly, that there may come a day when you tell me something unbelievable which I may even fear, but to believe it totally and completely, as you know not how to lie. He also said that it had saddened him that Sarah had not confided in him till her dying day. He made me promise to swear that I would believe you and love you for it. At the time, Jane, I thought it was the ramblings of an auld, dying man but now I think he might have been referring tae this."

Jane grasped Alec's hand.

"Yes, Granda knew o' my awareness and in the end my telling him that Granny was near brought him comfort. It is not the child's fault if the minister lets the baptismal water run into the bairn's eye."

"Dinna worry, ma quine. I understand, and we will leave as soon as we are able."

"Oh, Alec, ye have nae idea how comforting those words are tae me."

Alec took her hand. "I wish ye had told me afore."

"I promised my granny I would never tell a soul. I have always been petrified o' the consequences."

"Aye, I can believe it. It will be our secret Jane. I dinna want ye persecuted, I ken how cruel folk can be."

CHARLESTON OF ABERLOUR

T HE REST OF 1888 proved to be far less convoluted as life's path uncoiled and straightened, allowing change to occur. A letter from Rose in Aberlour mentioned in passing that the distillery was looking for workers, being the golden age of whisky, work was plentiful. Jane was excited at the prospect.

"Think on it, Alec. I ken it would be a big change but it would be steady work and a house is provided so we could stay there long term."

"I have only ever known farming, quine, I dinna ken if I am cut oot for it."

"Do ye think ye could give it a go?"

"Well, a man needs steady work wi' a growing family and I ken it's better money. I just dinna ken if I could work indoors. I have always been ootside and as much as it's hard in the winter I enjoy the seasons and being oot wi' the animals."

Jane held her breath.

"I will make enquiries, quine."

T WO DAYS LATER, having met with the distillery foreman, Alec walked into the cottage and told Jane, "Well, you are looking at a maltman. We hae a house in Charleston as of next month."

The smile spread across Jane's face. "Oh, Alec, that's good news indeed."

T HE FARQUHARSONS MOVED into 121 High Street, Charleston of Aberlour, on a dreich, wet day but nothing could dampen their spirits when they saw their new abode. Situated at the west end of the town near the end of the long high street, it was a tall, proud, granite building. Neither had lived in such a home. Both had previously dwelt in small, thatched roofed cottages with floors made of earth in the heart of the countryside. For the first time in both their lives they had a home with a wooden floor, and a front as well as a back door, which led onto a garden. They shared the main doors and garden with the McKenzie family above, as the building was made up of two apartments and part of a terrace, but it was modern with a proper lum that wouldn't billow smoke, and with a yearly rent of four pounds and fifteen shillings they could afford it, and hopefully put some money by now and again.

Although it consisted of only two rooms, each was a decent size, with a window, and Alec would section off a corner of the main room to house their bed, whilst the other room would hold the bairn's beds. It looked over towards a handful of cottages and the rolling hills behind, and the kirk was but a minute's walk away, as was the distillery.

Jane moved through her home and garden, looking to find whom she would share her new abode with and smiled when she entered what would be the bairn's room and there was a young woman about her own age, who nodded to Jane and smiled back.

It was perfect.

Jane's mood soared and she flitted around like a butterfly, soaking in the warmth from the atmosphere as well as the fire. Alec too noticed the difference in the feel of the house and was glad that Jane was happy and content. His head still reeled from Jane's revelations but he could see that she was the same kind and loving quine that he had married, who was a good mother, and that was all that mattered. He had asked the odd question now and again, curious to know who lived among them, and at first he felt awkward that he was maybe being watched, but over time he became accustomed to the idea, but he would occasionally ask Jane if someone was in the room, especially if he was about to pull her to him for a kiss.

𝔍ANE'S AUNT ANN also bade in Charleston. Married to Findlater Coutts, a mason, they lived on the same street, at number thirty four. Five years older than Jane's mother, Ann had left home before Jane was born so they had never lived together, but now, living so close by, Ann was a regular visitor and the two women grew quite close. Ann had a similar sense of humour to her late mother Sarah, and often had Jane in fits of laughter over some story or other.

So it was a happy home that Marjory was born into on 20th September at five o'clock in the morning, named after Alec's mother, and with a look of her too. Jane's heart swelled on meeting her and with just nine months between Marjory and her brother, Alexander, Jane was becoming used to her bairns arriving early. Thanks was given for yet another healthy bairn and Jane was relieved when her milk came in, in abundance, to feed her tiny quine.

𝔏IVING IN CHARLESTON brought Jane a sense of peace that she had not experienced since she was a very young quine. A combination of a good marriage, three healthy bairns and a thriving town, served to both calm her heart and excite her mind. She revelled in her happiness and her heart, although forever scarred, had recovered as much as it was able, from the loss of her granda. She often saw her granny but oh how dearly she would have loved to glimpse her granda again, just once. But it was not to be.

The lush, fertile valley of the River Spey gave its pure, soft water in abundance, for man to produce the world's finest single malt whiskies. The 1880s saw the emergence of a booming trade thanks to the ever growing rail network and France's misfortune of their vineyards being devastated by the phylloxera plague. This caused many an empty cellar as no wine or brandy was able to be produced and Scotland seized the opportunity to offer the French, Scotch whisky. Known in Gaelic as uisge beatha (water of life), whisky had soothed and celebrated folk for many a year, more often than not illegally, and some claimed there was no better use for barley.

Alec had taken to distillery work in a way that surprised them both. He found it both interesting and rewarding. The owner, Mr James Fleming, son of a local farmer, founded Aberlour distillery in1879 and when it came to the whisky that he produced he referred to his family motto '*Let the deed show*' - in other words, the proof of how good it was, was in the drinking. Very much a community man, Fleming employed local folk and bought local barley, providing work for many in the area, and by 1886, he and his workers were producing eighty thousand gallons of whisky a year and had two thousand casks maturing in the warehouses. Unlike other distilleries who relied on steam to power their machines, the continuous flow of the Lour Burn provided enough power to drive the machines all year round. It was dangerous work though, as often the mill would overheat, and with so much dry barley, fire was always a possibility.

Mr Fleming was keen to employ locals and encouraged his workers to allow their older bairns to spend time working in the distillery, learning how whisky was made. Both James and Alexander had done so, with James keen to know the workings of the machinery but unsure if he wanted to pursue life as a distillery worker and Alexander had enjoyed working alongside his father but stated that he preferred farm work. Both enjoyed the grand fairs though, alongside their siblings, that were held for the local community on the distillery grounds in April, May and

November. Food and games were on offer and schools closed for the afternoon as folk flocked to the fair to enjoy the event.

Aberlour had a strong sense of community where folk came together in both times of celebration and times of need, which soothed Jane's heart and enabled her and her family to live contentedly there.

Taking a walk over the old packhorse bridge and out into the countryside Jane commented to Alec, "Here I am known only as Jane Farquharson. Cantlie is on our bairns' birth certificates and will be on their marriage certificates, as my maiden name, but I hae a sense o' release, Alec, to be accepted here."

"Dae ye hold any bitterness towards the Cantlies, Jane?"

"Nae, but there's a whisper o' sadness perhaps, over what might hae been."

"But ye are happy here, quine?"

"Aye, Alec, I have never been happier."

ℱOREVER MINDFUL OF her kin, Jane wrote often to her brother, James, still working in Elgin as a postman, and he too corresponded with regularity. As the country hunkered down in the wrath of winter a letter arrived with his latest news.

Dear Jane,

A shorter letter today just to let you ken that a quine was delivered to us on 4th December. We have named her Anna Bella and she is a bonny lass, the spit o' her mother. Ann is well and fair delighted to have a quine, after having four loons. I'm nay sure if I ken how to be a father to a quine but I will do my very best. I have written to mother to let her ken and Ann will maybe drop you a line herself in the coming weeks.

Your brother, James.

Jane's eyes closed and she breathed a slow sigh of relief to know that all were well, and she was delighted that a longed for quine had been bestowed on them. As she rose to put the letter on the dresser a knock on the door revealed aunty Ann, so the two sat down to a cup of tea.

"It's grand news indeed, Jane, and Anna Bella is a bonny name. Yer mother will be delighted tae be a granny again, too."

"That she will. She would love nothing more than to have a hundred grand bairns but she forgets that she's nae the one who has to birth them!"

Ann chuckled, as she took an envelope out of her pocket. "I received a letter yesterday fae my auld friend, Lottie, ye ken the one who bides in London? She put a cutting oot o' a magazine in it. Maybe if I send it to yer mother she will be thankful that her bairns have any family o' their own at all."

Ann spread the cutting on the table, "This is fae a magazine called *Tit-Bits* in which they posed the question *Why are you single?* Lottie says that following the change in law in 1882 which stated that married women could keep some of their own wages and inheritance, attitudes towards marriage are changing but for those looking to marry there are fewer men than women in the country so pickings are limited. Listen to these replies to the question, *Why are you single?*"

'Because I am like the Rifle Volunteer: always ready, but not yet wanted.'
Miss Anne Thompson, 24 Belmont St, Oldham.

'Because I do not care to enlarge my menagerie of pets, and I find the animal man less docile than a dog, less affectionate than a cat and less amusing than a monkey.'
Miss Sparrow, 9 Manor Place, Paddington."

Jane snorted. "That's a bit harsh, Ann, I feel that quine may have been scorned in the past. Perhaps my mother wrote it before she married."

Ann laughed and carried on.

" 'I am now only a dairy maid. If I married I should be wife, mother, nurse, housekeeper, chambermaid, seamstress, laundress, dairy maid and scrub generally.'

That is very true, Jane, but oh goodness listen to this one written in Cockney:

'Dear Mister TitBits - beein a cook with forteen pund 5/10 savins in the bank I natterally looks downon perleesmen, solejeers an setterar, so I ham waiting fur a erle or a dook or sumthin of that sort to purpose fur my 'and and 'art, an that's why I am single.'

(Dear Mister TitBits - being a cook with fourteen pound 5/10 savings in the bank I naturally look down on policemen, soldiers etcetera, so I am waiting for an earl or a duke or something of that sort to propose for my hand and heart, and that is why I am single.)

Miss Anne Newton, Warwick Cottages, Yiewsley, West Drayton, Middlesex.'"

As the two women laughed, James careered into the room, having been playing outside in the garden, covered in mud from head to foot, carrying a muckle, fat worm in his wee hand. He threw it at two year old Alexander who picked it off his thigh and threw it back, and so they continued, skirling and giggling till their mother shooed them both outside and told them to stay there.

Another few months and James would be at school, leaving his brother and wee Marjory at home, but Jane was apprehensive, her protective instinct wanting to keep her wee loon close by, but she swallowed away her fears as she had always done and lifted her quine up onto her knee and sang the rhyme "One, two buckle my shoe…"

The year 1890 provided a link between Edinburgh and Fife by way of the Forth Rail Bridge. It was to be the longest bridge of its time in Britain with the greatest cantilever span in the world, expanding the rail network and replacing a centuries old ferry. Jane was reading about it in the local paper when she felt the first kicks of new life inside her, a sensation which caused a flutter of excitement, quickly followed by the worry of protecting and feeding another bairn. She berated herself for such thoughts, when she was blessed with healthy bairns and a hard working husband, but her fear of losing folk close to her rose up as she remembered her childhood and the losses others had suffered. There were moments when she was seized with panic at the thought of being widowed, losing a good man whom she loved dearly, or one of their bairns being taken by disease. At these times Jane both embraced and feared life in equal measure.

Jane left her three bairns with her friend and neighbour, Isabella, and took herself outside, and strolled over the ancient packhorse bridge where the land opened up, revealing the hills and trees and the rumbling of the Lour Burn crashing into the River Spey. Little Elizabeth appeared alongside her, skipping between trees, a wide smile on her wee face.

"My wee Marjory has the same smile as ye, quine. In a year ye will be the same age."

Elizabeth cocked her head and faded away as Jane paused to take in the view.

"I wonder where ye go, Elizabeth. Do ye hover unseen between two worlds or do ye visit other folk?"

She continued on her way, breathing in the fresh, country air and surrounding herself in nature till her mind soothed itself, and her heart, beat as it should.

T HE MONTHS PASSED and as Jane turned thirty three she watched her bairns playing in the garden and noticed wee Elizabeth running and skipping alongside them. She observed them to see if anyone interacted with Elizabeth, her heart in her mouth as she did so, unsure as to how she would react if one of them could see their long departed cousin. Elizabeth was always a frequent visitor but Jane had never been sure if her bairns were aware of her.

Wee Marjory was sitting on the ground playing with a rag doll, made by her granny, and Elizabeth went and sat by her, her hand on Marjory's. Jane knew how possessive her quine was of that doll and when Elizabeth touched it Marjory did not react or look towards Elizabeth, leaving Jane to think that Marjory was not aware of her. After a few minutes Elizabeth jumped up and started to chase the loons, turning and running towards them as if to give chase again but they continued to play with each other oblivious of another's presence. Jane was relieved, but a small part of her felt that it was sad that her bairns would never know the comfort of those who had passed.

T HE SUN WAS beginning to rise on 21st July, just as the fox was about to pounce on the partridge, and Jane pushed her fourth bairn into the world. A cry announced her arrival to her father and Alec breathed a sigh of relief, yet again. The house people gathered around as the others prepared for the saining, and Jane looked upon her tiny quine, her mind absorbing the features of her newborn as her heart overflowed once more.

A few weeks later the bairn was baptised Jane, and the Farquharsons settled down to life with four bairns under five, with surely more to follow.

A final loon for James Smith was born that October, named Ernest, but tragedy awaited the family in Elgin. Till then Jane and her brother continued to bring up their respective broods with the same degree of love and kindness shown to them as bairns.

A Win and Two Losses

THE FOLLOWING MARCH of 1891 brought with it a beautiful, calm day and perfect pitch conditions for Scotland's final match in the Rugby Home Nations Championship, and they did not disappoint. Securing a win on the 7th against England, added to their previous wins over Wales and Ireland, resulting in Scotland lifting the championship trophy, alongside both the Triple Crown and Calcutta Cup for the first time in the series history, winning convincingly with fourteen tries in three games.

Local newspapers throughout Scotland were full of the victory and folk were elated, lifting the spirits within, as the hands lifted the spirit known as whisky. Aberlour distillery sold a few more barrels that spring! Willie Neilson had scored the first try against England, and Alec, following several drams with James, his neighbour, declared,

"If I am blessed wi' another loon I'll name him Willie. Jane winna mind as his mother is also called Jane."

James nodded reverently, the whisky adding a sense of grandeur to the conversation. "She'll like that, Alec - a son named after a famous loon. My own loon is Willie, as ye ken, so he'll be famous as weel."

"Oh aye, he will that, James. Fame will follow them both."

"I'll drink tae that. Sláinte mháth!"

"Sláinte mháth!"

As the weeks passed and the April showers came and went, Jane received a telegram from her brother,

Sorry to inform - wee Ernest died 1st May, Bronchitis.
James

Jane held tight to her bairns, disbelief numbing her thoughts. Another bairn taken long before he should have been, at just six months old. She could only imagine the depth of grief being felt in Elgin, and tears coursed down her cheeks as she put pen to paper to write to James and Ann, her mind berating a cruel world.

Her own fear, often buried, rose to the surface and suffocated her thoughts, opening the old wounds within her heart, bleeding fear throughout her body.

My dearest James and Ann,

I have no words for your terrible, cruel loss. The world makes no sense at these times and I fear I can say nothing that will offer you comfort. You gave Ernest care and kindness in his short life, as you do all your bairns, and I hope that in time his memory will draw a smile instead of a tear. Know that our love and thoughts are with you and we will visit soon.

Your loving sister, Jane.

Folk, as folk must, continued to breathe and move through life, only the eyes betraying the smiles and words, as they tried to make sense of the loss of an innocent bairn.

Margaret mourned her grandbairn, but she did not berate the world as Jane did. Throughout life both had held their heads high, with thrawn minds and scarred hearts, but Margaret allowed life to flow, whereas Jane appeared to hold her mind against the current, to thwart danger, more so since becoming a mother. Margaret admired the strength that it took to do that but Jane would one day have to let go of her bairns and allow them to go out into the world on their own, and that was a different kind of strength altogether.

T HE SUN ROSE, bringing summer with it once again and wee Jane turned one, and surprised them all with her first steps. James had started at Charleston school and was thriving there much to Jane's relief and delight and Jane herself took in sewing and mending to supplement Alec's earnings, whilst looking after her other bairns. It was a busy life and the house was neither quiet nor empty, between the giggles and squabbles of the bairns, to the presence of the house people. They were far from rich, huddled into their two-roomed abode, but bellies were always full and there were some spare pennies at the end of the week which were saved for visiting family, sometimes by train.

Come harvest time Jane realised that she was with child again, and so the peaks and troughs of life continued, and Alec and Jane marvelled at the way life had shifted and evolved for them both. If any more bairns came they would have to top and tail in the beds, as there was little room, but if Jane's granny and granda had managed with eleven bairns in one room, then so could the Farquharson's.

In the same year that the beautiful Central Library building in Aberdeen opened, and the original Jenners department store in Edinburgh was destroyed by fire, Margaret's husband, Willie, died with his wife by his side, leaving a daughter not quite ten in years. Margaret held her husband's cold hand in hers as she quietly spoke to him.

"My love, ye gave me thirteen happy years and the miracle o' a third bairn. I watched ye work hard to become a farmer o' yer own land and provide us wi' a good life. I thank ye for all o' that." She slowly leant forward and kissed him for one last time.

There were some savings put by but Margaret now had to go out and find work to support herself and her bairn. At the age of fifty six she was starting out in life again, and it was not a thought to be cherished with a gaping hole in her heart. But Margaret, being Margaret, mourned in her own quiet way, lifted her head, and carried on.

MOTHERLESS BAIRNS

JAMES FLEMING SOLD his distillery in 1892 to Robert Thorne and Sons but he remained a shareholder and distillery manager. A great deal of money was invested into the business and steady work continued as before for the employees. Alec worked hard and saved what money he was able, as there was no knowing what lay ahead or how many more bairns would come. Jane was thrifty with money and had learned from a young age how to make and mend clothes and how to cook a meal with few ingredients. Everything she knew had come from watching her mother and grandmother, but there had been times when she was younger and had tried to do things her own way, it had not gone down well. There was a certain order things had to be done by and a 'mother knows best' attitude, or a look of irritation given, if done the wrong way.

Jane was stirring the porridge for her bairns' breakfast and was aware of her great granny standing by her. With her fifth bairn almost due and four others girning to be fed, her temper was short and she became exasperated.

"For goodness sake, has anyone ever made porridge to your liking? Sit your auld erse doon and leave me be!"

Great granny's lips pursed and her eyebrows shot up into her hairline as she turned and passed through the wall, not to be seen again for several days. Sarah was laughing at the table, although Jane had her back to her so was unaware of this. The bairns were a bit bewildered as they were already sitting down and did not consider themselves old, but recognising their mother's mood they thought it best not to mention it.

Jane was restless throughout that day, her time was spent washing and cooking alongside looking after her bairns, and just when she felt that she was on top of one chore another appeared. In the afternoon Isabella appeared from upstairs to help Jane sort out some clothes for the upcoming jumble sale which raised money for the orphanage in Aberlour.

"I will take yer clothes for the Jupp sale down to the church wi' mine, Jane, to save ye having tae go yersel'."

Jane sat down heavily. "Thank you, quine, I dinna seem tae hae much time today - the hours are running as fast as a hare."

"The years too. I canna believe the orphanage has been open for seventeen years. I remember when there were just a few bairnies there and Reverend Canon Charles Jupp first started to fundraise across the shires."

"Aye, before we moved here we had heard o' the 'Beggar of the North' and his good work. To think there are nearly a hundred orphans now living there."

"It makes ye hold yer own bairns close at the thought o' them being motherless. Having an orphanage just along the road brings it home to us all how fortunate we are. I ken Peter next door often gives his time freely to fix something or other for them, him being a carpenter."

"Aye, Alec always encourages me tae spend more than we sometimes hae at the sales. I think it makes him think o' his own childhood and losing his father. If his mother had been taken too, his wee siblings would hae ended up in an orphanage."

There wasn't a soul in Aberlour who did not feel sadness at the plight of an orphan, except those who had no heart. As Jane carefully folded the clothes the thought went through her mind,

Being illegitimate was one thing, but to have no parents at all, quite another.

*J*ANE HAD JUST finished sorting the clothes with Isabella when she felt the beginnings of birth pains and knew that there would be no sleep for her that night. As fate would have it, her bairn was born at five o'clock in the morning, the exact same time as her two previous bairns, Jane and Marjory. What that signified no one could say but Jane and Alec were overjoyed, yet again, with another bonny, healthy quine, born that Saturday 9th April, to be baptised Magdalene Kynock Farquharson, and known as Lena.

The young woman, whose spirit lived in their home, kept vigil by the cradle, and Jane gave thanks again for her happy home, remembering with a shiver when Alexander was born in Tomindongle, with its discontented spirits. But discontent came from another quarter as James, now six, stated, "I dinna want another sister!"

Alec smiled and said, "Perhaps one day you'll hae another brother," which cheered the loon but brought a retort from Jane,

"I think I have delivered quite enough bairns into the world!"

She looked over towards her granny and wondered how on earth she had managed to do that eleven times.

THE EYES CAN SEE

OUT OF ALL her bairns, Lena appeared to be the most content. She would only greet when hungry, the rest of the time spent babbling quietly or sleeping. The other bairns made a fuss of her and helped Jane to fetch and carry things, and of course the house people were ever present, watching over them all.

As the months passed, Alexander started school, walking there alongside his brother, leaving Jane with her three quines. Their neighbours upstairs, James and Isabella McKenzie, had eight bairns, two of whom were grown, but their youngest - Sophia and Isabella - were similar ages to Marjory and Jane and often their mothers took them all into the garden to play together. Having lived at number 121 for four years now, the two families had grown to know each other well, and often child care was shared, to enable one mother or the other to go out to buy food or carry out some other chore.

It was a happy time for Jane, her five bairns were healthy, and naturally they bickered and quarrelled at times - thrawn blood flowed in their veins as it did their parents' - but they were kind hearted and affectionate too, and it made Jane smile to see one of them comfort the other with a bosie, following a fall or some mishap.

Often Alec and Jane would wonder, as all folk did, what would become of their bairns, what work they would do, who they would marry and where they would bide. It was a good trait to work hard for your bairns and want them to know a better life than yours, but it scared Jane's heart to think of them being far from her. She felt comforted by the house people and in some ways protected too, and having never been without them she worried about her bairns not having anyone to comfort them when they were alone and in need. One day, when they were much older, she hoped to find the right words to let them know that they were never truly alone, without scaring them or giving away her secret.

One morning, Jane set off along the high street with Lena, now ten months, in the pram, leaving her other quines with Isabella. On entering the baker's shop she left Lena outside whilst she went in to make her purchases. It was a cold winter's day but there was no wind in it and spring wasn't too far off. Lena was well wrapped up and clutching her wee ragdoll, happily babbling away to it as she waited for her mother.

As Jane was paying for her goods she suddenly heard Lena greeting and could see, through the window, that she had dropped her ragdoll and that appeared to be the reason for the tears. Jane waited for her change as the wailing outside grew louder, but then suddenly stopped. Looking out Jane could see that wee Elizabeth was by the pram, smiling and making funny faces and Lena was giggling.

On receiving her change she bade the baker good morning and slowly walked back out the door and stood quietly by the side of the pram. She watched Elizabeth's gestures and expressions and noticed how Lena reacted to them and how she put both arms out towards her as if to be held.

Jane picked up the dropped ragdoll and handed it to Lena who immediately tried to hand it to Elizabeth, and Jane knew for certain that Lena could see Elizabeth.

It was with mixed feelings that Jane returned home that morning. Her granny was in the kitchen and when Lena crawled over to her, Jane asked,

"Can Lena see ye?" Sarah smiled and nodded and gave Jane a reassuring look which put Jane slightly more at ease.

"I always watched the minister's hands carefully during baptisms and never noticed any stray water reaching my bairns' eyes, but perhaps, like the colour of eyes or a thrawn character, it is something that is passed on down through generations."

Jane thought of Alec as she spoke to her granny.

"I ken Alec questions the beliefs o' others at times, including the Kirk's, and he always seems tae find his own answers for things. I stopped questioning why I can see those who hae passed a long time ago, but now that I ken that Lena can see them too, I wonder if there will come a day where such things can be talked about, without fear of being accused of having the Evil Eye."

Sarah sat by Jane, her hand on the quine's arm as Jane continued, "I winna tell Alec. I canna put it into words, it just feels the right thing to do, for the time being anyway."

So life carried on, and before anyone knew it summer had arrived and with it aunty Ann's health deteriorated and Jane found herself, more often than not, in number thirty four, tending to Ann as best she could.

T HE DOCTOR SAID it was cancer, so Ann's time on earth was short. Margaret visited her sister as did Ann's other siblings, and Jane noticed that Sarah was seldom in the Farquharson house, she was to be found sitting with her daughter. As much as Jane feared losing folk, when it came to her own passing she believed that she would be guided and comforted by the spirits around her, perhaps making it easier to leave her loved ones behind. She wished for Ann's sake, that she could see her mother by her side, but Jane had no words that sounded right to be spoken, to let Ann know.

Her aunt passed away in September, in the middle of the afternoon, and on hearing the news, Jane asked if Isabella would mind keeping Jane and Lena, the others being at school, and she took herself off for a walk, over the packhorse bridge and into the countryside, breathing in the comfort of nature and soothing her heart.

Top And Tail

Life continued to twist and turn much like the Lour Burn, fast and furious at times and flowing steadily at others, and come the following summer of 1894, Jane found herself expecting her sixth bairn. James, now nine, was growing fast, and Alexander and Marjory weren't far behind, with Jane and Lena aged four and two, so bedtime was already a tangle of bodies on two mattresses.

There were often squeals and shouts when a foot hit a shin or an arm fell across another's face, such was the life of working class bairns of the time. Sometimes Jane would snuggle in beside them and make up a story or sing a rhyme to her bairns. On one such occasion Marjory was sitting on her knees, with no sign of sleep appearing, wee Jane was cuddled down, eyes still open, and Lena was already in the midst of her dreams. "Sing, Hey Diddle, Mam."

Jane clambered into the bed and Marjory thrust her legs onto her mam's lap in anticipation. Jane took a wee foot in either hand and began to sing, lifting and shaking each food in turn,

"Hey diddle dumpling, my son John,
Went to bed with his trousers on,
One shoe off and one shoe on,
Hey diddle dumpling, my son John."

Marjory giggled and giggled. "He's so daft going to bed wi' a shoe!"

"He is that, quine."

Wee Jane giggled too. "Sing it again, Mam, sing it again."

So Jane sang it again, holding Jane's feet this time and repeating the gestures to the delight of her bairn.

Later that evening before retiring to her own bed, Jane peeked round the door and it made her smile to see all five bairns snuggled together, limbs entangled, some upsides down, yet all fast asleep.

Sharing was only a problem when one of the younger ones wet the bed, then there would be a commotion as if a spark from the fire had landed on their laps.

$\mathcal{J}$AMES AND ALEXANDER applied themselves to school as much as was required. Mr McPherson had a good reputation as a teacher, being firm but fair, although learning came more easily to James, who was an easy going bairn in nature. Alexander, the more sensitive of the two, tried hard to earn his master's praise and struggled with the thought of failure if he was incorrect with an answer.

Marjory followed her brothers everywhere but was very much the boss. Alec often stated that she would make a good foreman, quine or no quine. Jane, just four, already acted like a mother, mollycoddling Lena and forever giving her bosies, and Lena - unbeknownst to anyone but her actual mother - enjoyed the attention of the house people as well as her living family.

So the Farquharson brood was growing and Jane worried about them all every second of every day, her fear of losing one of them never far away, but kept tightly bound to her like a rope around a bull.

$\mathcal{J}$ANE WAS FORTUNATE in that she was rarely ill when with child, unlike her friend Elsie who could keep no food down for months and was forever pale. Her neighbour, Isabella, always looked as if she was carrying three bairns and waddled in a slow, cumbersome manner, which belied her otherwise petite frame and quick footedness. Standing no taller than the Queen herself at four foot eleven, Isabella became as wide as she was tall. She complained that her bairns were never in any hurry to see the world and had tried various means to hasten them along. Jane neither grew too large nor awkward, but having bairns born early perhaps relieved her of the final weeks of discomfort and being unable to see her feet, but her bairns were always so tiny, although thankfully strong.

Both Jane and Alec would marvel at how different their bairns were, both in appearance and character. It was as if someone had made soup with all the things that made Jane and Alec who they were, and every ladle produced a different combination. Some families were the opposite, where they all seemed identical. The Raffans at number twenty five were like that and as their bairns grew folk would say "There goes a Raffan, I'd know that face anywhere."

The death of the Scottish novelist, Robert Louis Stevenson, on 3rd December during a particularly harsh winter, preceded the birth of William Farquharson on 20th December, at seven in the morning, breaking the tradition of bairns being born at five o'clock. Dark haired and blue eyed, like his mother, he had his father's face and was to be known as Willie, whether called after the rugby player Willie Neilson, only his father could say, but it had long been established that Jane named the quines, and Alec the loons.

So James got his wish for another brother, and Willie was born into a home whose inhabitants, both living or otherwise, were thrawn, quick witted and fiercely loving, as only a Farquharson could be.

T HE HARSH WINTER continued into 1895 and come the 11th February, Braemar was to experience the lowest ever recorded temperature in Britain registering a nippy -27.2 degrees centigrade.

Jane was thankful that she had a good working lum and a supply of peat, and Alec was thankful that he was working indoors, as the invention of earmuffs hadn't quite reached Aberlour and a man's cap didn't quite cover the lugs.

The bairns had the look of peddlers who carry all their possessions at once, as Jane had them wearing layer upon layer of clothing, whether it fitted or not, and she was glad, as surely they were too, that school was but a short walk away. Too many bairns and auld folk had died from colds in the chest and, with a newborn to care for, Jane's inner fear of losing folk again rose to the surface.

As nature would have it, that winter was to be the last of ten harsh winters, but poor folk still huddled together in their shared beds and would do so for many years to come.

Cusp Of Change

ABERLOUR DISTILLERY FOLLOWED the tradition of pouring some whisky into the Lour Burn each year to bless the water. Many such traditions took place regarding births, marriages and deaths, and folk of the time continued to be superstitious and fearful of both fairies and the Evil Eye. They had long since stopped burning witches, but in March 1895 one Michael Cleary in Tipperary, Ireland, was imprisoned for manslaughter, following the killing and burning of his wife, Bridget, his defence being that he believed that he had not killed his wife, but had killed a changeling, left in his wife's place by the fairies.

Had this happened fifty years previously perhaps he would have walked free. Fairies were blamed for everything from illness to unruly behaviour, but as a new century was approaching, beliefs were slowly beginning to change, but fear of disrespecting the fairies lived deep in some hearts, perhaps more so than disrespecting the church, and many years later there would still be those who believed in the power of fairies.

The water kelpie was another creature in folklore, which was believed to dwell in the deep pools of rivers and burns and thus be the cause of many a drowning. It would appear in the guise of a black horse near old bridges and encourage travellers to mount it, where it would then plunge into the water resulting in the death of the rider.

James Fleming, who died in June 1895, when Willie was six

months old, left money in his will for a bridge to be built over the Lour Burn connecting Charleston with Knockando, as folk had died when the ferry had overturned in flood conditions. Victoria bridge, known as the Penny bridge, as a fee of one penny was asked of those wishing to cross, undoubtedly saved lives and perhaps deterred the water kelpie also. He also left nine thousand pounds to be used to build a cottage hospital in Aberlour, housing fifteen beds.

Science was advancing, and as new understanding emerged regarding the causes of illness and the treatment to be given, even cures in some cases, some long held beliefs gradually morphed into myths and stories.

Later that year, one Svante Arrhenius, a Swedish scientist, presented a paper on carbon dioxide and its effect on the global climate, to be known many years later as the Greenhouse Effect, so it wasn't just medical advances that were being made.

The Farquharsons were living in a world on the cusp of change.

IT CONTINUED TO be the golden age of whisky and following James Fleming's death, plans were drawn up for an extension to be built onto the distillery. Business was booming and wages were good, allowing folk to have more than they had been used to, including bigger and better houses alongside full bellies. A sea captain, by the name of James Campbell, commissioned a marine architect to design a public house in the shape of a ship, in the heart of Aberlour, where the locals could partake of some whisky.

As 1896 dawned, The McKenzies, who bade above the Farquharsons, decided to move along the street to a bigger house, leaving the upstairs part of the house empty. Seizing the opportunity, Alec contacted the proprietor in Cullen to secure tenancy of the whole house, providing his family with two further main rooms, a large attic and a total of five windows throughout.

At a cost of nine pounds a year it was more than double the current rent but Alec was confident that they could afford it.

Jane was somewhat dazed with the plans, as it all happened so fast. "I feel like the gentry wi' so many rooms, wooden floors and light from windows, not to mention having two hearths. Two!"

Alec was glad to see his wife enthralled but she was worried. "Are ye sure we can afford it, Alec?"

"Aye, quine, ye ken the whisky trade is booming and we have always been careful wi' money. Let's enjoy our good fortune."

Jane watched as her bairns careered around the house as if it were a castle. "Ye are right, Alec, let's enjoy our good fortune indeed."

The quines shared one room and the loons another, and there was still one for Jane and Alec, as well as the attic. Another mattress was procured which meant only two bairns to a bed and not only did they gain more rooms, they also acquired an addition to their house people in the way of an auld man whom Jane found in the attic, sitting in a chair, book in hand.

With a living family of six, two permanent house people and two occasional house people, sometimes three when wee Elizabeth appeared, it was indeed a busy home and Jane had never known such contentment.

T HE RIVER OF life meandered steadily, carrying them safely as it skirted and journeyed through the following year, but there came a time when the seasons changed and the water again altered its path and at the age of seventy one, Alec's mother died. Hers had been a hard life, being widowed and left with ten bairns, but as the years had passed she had watched each one forge a life for themselves and three had even ventured to the city of Glasgow. Alec mourned his mother as any loving son would, but it brought him some comfort to know that she had been proud of all her bairns.

Jane too gave Alec comfort with the news that she was with child again, a happening that often followed a death in her life, and reminded all that the world kept moving forward, pulling folk with it as the engine did the carriage.

EARLY ONE SUNDAY morning Lena was helping her mother to make breakfast, having the kitchen to themselves, when Alec walked in. He leaned against the door, taking a moment to watch his wife and bairn blethering happily as they went about their work, enjoying for a second the feeling of pride that came with having a family of his own. He was about to say good morning to Lena when she spoke.

"See, Granny, I'm doing it right," as she held up the bannock in her wee hand.

Jane then spoke. "She approves indeed, Lena, see her smiling?"

Alec backed silently out of the kitchen as the realisation hit him that Lena too could see those who had passed. He took a minute to compose himself and re entered the room.

"Jane, a word."

Jane heard the suppressed anger in his voice and was confused. She looked up and on seeing Alec's face, turned to Lena and told her to go into the other room for a minute.

"How long have you known that Lena can see who you see?"

Jane's eyes widened and her heart hammered in her chest as she answered, "Since she was one."

"One," he roared. "That's four years! She's my bairn, I had a right to ken."

Jane lowered her head and closed her eyes. "I was protecting her."

Alec roared again, "From her own father, who loves her?"

"No I….. I thought the less folk that know the better. I don't want her persecuted."

"I ken how other folk think, but I am not other folk. I am her father. How could you keep that from me?"

Jane looked up at him. "I'm sorry, Alec, it just felt the right thing to do."

"I don't believe in the Evil Eye or in fairies for that matter, not since I was a loon. I've no wish to upset folk, or the kirk, but I winna be told what to believe. I keep my opinions to myself but times are changing Jane. Yours and Lena's awareness will stay between us, but there will be no more secrets in this house." Alec stormed out, slamming the door behind him.

THE WIND BLOWS

A BELL TOLLED IN his dreams and Alec awoke to the sound of hammering on the door and shouts of "Fire!" His body was out of bed and pulling on his breeks before his mind registered what was happening. He heard folk in the street bellowing that the distillery was aflame and for a second his heart steadied with the realisation that it was not his home that was alight and that his wife and bairns were not in immediate danger. The church bell was ringing informing folk of the danger and Jane too had woken to the racket but her movements were laboured with her unborn bairn only weeks away from entering the world.

"There's a fire at the distillery, quine. I need tae go!" He kissed Jane on the cheek and as Alec flung the door open and disappeared to help, he shouted to Jane, "Get James and Alexander up! All hands will be needed!"

A fire in a distillery was always a risk and the thought of how big an explosion could be sent a shiver down his spine.

Jane shook James and Alexander, "Wake up, loons! Quickly! the distillery is on fire and ye need tae help!"

The loons dazed - but aware of the urgency - quickly dressed and their mother hastened them out the door with a warning. "Be careful and stay high up on the burn away from the fire."

She stood by the door, peering into the darkness as she heard the shouts of instructions, her hand on her heart. Just as she was about to close it ten year old Marjory bolted out the door after her brothers, her thrawn, bossy nature coming to the fore as she yelled, "I'm awa' tae help. I'm strong enough tae carry buckets!"

Jane frantically tried to stop her but Marjory was too quick on her feet and Jane turned back inside to soothe her younger bairns who had woken and were fractious at the commotion, sending up a prayer.

Jane paced the floor, one eye on the clock which had read half past one when Alec left, and the other on the window peering through the darkness, desperately trying to see the long line of folk passing buckets up from the burn to the distillery but it was too dark and folk were too far away. Jane could hear the roar of the fire and the occasional shouts for more water, carried in the wind and as the hands on the clock dragged themselves round, lugging her heart with them, she feared for her husband and her bairns. The tendrils of fear that burrowed deep within her heart tightened their grip as she desperately tried to keep the thought of losing Alec or one of her bairns, at bay.

She knew that Alec would be at the mouth of the fire desperately trying to save both the buildings and his livelihood, and as she lulled Willie back to sleep she sang a lullaby by way of quelling the rising fear in her. Sarah sat by Jane's hearth providing comfort as always, and the ghost of the young woman who also lived with them walked alongside Jane, a reassuring hand on Jane's arm.

As the hours passed, the dark January morning was filled with the anguished shouts of folk to hurry and Jane felt helpless as she listened to them. At half past five her three bairns returned, exhausted, James told his mother, "We were sent home. The fire's nae out yet but it's under control thanks tae the direction o' the wind."

Jane breathed a sigh of relief. "Get yourselves back tae bed and Marjory - dinna ye ever worry me like that again." Although they protested at first, they acquiesced and were asleep within seconds.

It was another three hours before Alec returned to a relieved wife, and later still before the full story emerged of the extent of the damage. Alec, worn out and filthy, told Jane, as he washed,

"Alexander Davidson, the distillery carter, was the first to realise that the distillery was ablaze, living so close to it. He was woken by the roar of the malt barn roof falling in and ran to wake the manager. Mr Morrison and the brewer, Mr Gauld, organised folk and directed us where to throw the water. They did well as it was chaos at first no one quite knowing where to start but we got a system going and the younger ones stayed high up on the burn passing down buckets as quickly as they could. Thank goodness the wind favoured us or there would be no distillery left at all. Daylight will reveal the full extent of the damage but I ken that there will be nae whisky being produced for some time."

Alec had no way of knowing how he would feed his family if that was to be a permanent situation.

LATER THAT SUNDAY, the 16th January 1898, the folk of Aberlour gathered in daylight to assess the damage of the distillery. The malt mill which had housed a large amount of malt, the tun room, mash house, still house and both the brewer's office and excise office had all been destroyed, alongside a large quantity of whisky. It was by luck of the wind direction and the valiant efforts of the locals that the kiln had been saved, preventing the fire from spreading to other buildings.

It had been known that a small explosion had occurred the day before in the mill, and perhaps some unseen sparks had been smouldering overnight resulting in the fire, but the cause was to remain unclear and an estimated six thousand pounds worth of damage was the result.

Thankfully work began within a couple of weeks to rebuild the distillery and it was all hands on deck to get things up and running as soon as possible.

*

Six weeks later as the sun rose on the 28th February, the cold, north east wind blew in, clattering the windows, and howling in the lum. Pushing and forcing its way through, as it battered the streets, its howling echoed Jane's, as her final bairn was thrust into the world.

No sound came from the wee loon's lungs, his eyes closed tight, his body still, and for a second no soul moved or dared to breathe.

Isabella, unsure, passed the bairn to his mother. Jane's heart thudded in her ears and her hands trembled as she lay her tiny newborn on her breast. She could feel a scream rising up from her belly as her breath came in spasms. Her desperate eyes searched the room for answers and the onlookers lowered their heads as little Elizabeth appeared and lay down beside Jane, her wee hand on the bairn.

Jane closed her eyes, thrusting reality away, as her hands stroked her son's back, feeling the softness of his skin and the weight of him against her. Her scream subsided as she immersed herself in the feel and scent of him, her fingers caressing a cheek, an ear, a nose, and her lips softly kissing a tiny palm.

A quiet humming could be heard in the air and Jane realised that it was she who was singing as she rocked her child and held him close, her heart righting itself, beating softly and steadily.

The others looked uncertainly at one another at the sight of Jane cradling her son, as she gently sung to him, and Margaret stepped silently from the room to fetch Alec, tears caught in her throat.

As the hand of the clock moved forward another minute warm air was felt on a breast as five tiny fingers clenched and a wee heart began to beat.

The room sighed with relief as the wind outside paused for breath and Jane smiled through tears at the son who looked so much like her.

Thomas Farquharson, fourth loon, seventh bairn, last born

of Jane, fought for his first breath as the weather waged war, and folk battled with the elements. In years to come, young Thom would leave the world as he entered it.

A New Era

It took only six months to rebuild the distillery, larger than before with the most modern equipment being installed, thanks to insurance money. It was the leading distillery of its day and folk were confident of the future. Alec was back working as a maltman, having been employed as a general labourer during the rebuilding, and life continued on what appeared to be a straight path.

News arrived from Elgin that James and Ann had had another bairn, Florence, and all were well. Jane was delighted for them following the tragic loss of Ernest, eight years previously. Both at home and further afield there was much hype about the coming of the new century and with continuing industrial, medical and political advances, the future looked bright in Britain.

Jane and Alec's life was secure, with enough money for all to have full bellies, shoes on their feet and more than one change of clothes. Life had been tough for farmers the last few years and Alec, for one, was glad that he had steady work in the distillery. Friends and neighbours raised a glass on Hogmanay 1899 to toast a new century and a better future for their bairns, little knowing that some of those same bairns would go to war and never return.

Time moved like the river, sometimes caressing the rocks, quietly and gently, and at others battering and punishing, but always moulding and shaping, and never stopping.

Jane had been lured into a place of safety. Her childhood years were long gone and tongues no longer spat at her. She had seven bairns and a good marriage and her awareness of ghosts added their layer of comfort to her life. They were a part of her, and Alec's acceptance of that had allowed her fear of exposure to be hidden away in her mind.

Lena was eight years old and kept her secret close - but not through fear, like Jane, but through being asked, and understanding that it was something belonging only to her and her mam.

Jane was leaving the butcher's shop one morning with Willie and Thom toddling alongside her when she encountered a face unchanged in eighteen years. The portly figure imprisoned in its corset and the hair that refused to behave, atop a head that gesticulated excitedly, suddenly sent forth with such loudness the words, "Well, goodness me, Jane, fancy meeting you."

Jane's mind was pulled back in time to the wee room at the back of the grocer's shop in Dufftown, having her tea leaves read.

"Good morning, Mrs MacKenzie. Ye are looking well. I was sorry to read in the newspaper o' yer husband's passing."

"Thank ye, quine, it was a lovely piece, all about his life's work and how he provided folk wi' food for o'er fifty years. I was right proud to read it."

"He was fair wi' his prices too, unlike some. I was in yer shop most days buying food for my employers and never had any complaints."

Jessie MacKenzie smiled, "Dae ye bide here, Jane? Are these your loons?"

"Aye. They're my youngest. Been here twelve years now."

"I have just moved here to bide wi' my second loon and his wife. My eldest, Frank, has taken o'er the grocer shop." Her face fell, "So many memories."

"I'm sure," replied Jane.

Jessie perked up, "I still read the tea leaves. Nae need tae keep quiet aboot it now, the kirk seems to think it's harmless enough. I could tell some stories though. A lot o' folk carry secrets."

Jane felt a ripple of fear and her body shivered as the wind picked up. She looked into Jessie's face but could see no malice in it.

Jessie saw the flicker of fear in Jane's eyes and leaned into her. "Dinna worry, quine, I have never told a soul of what I saw in your leaves. Some secrets are best kept."

Jane nodded but could not find the words to reply. Thankfully wee Thom was tugging on her hand to leave so she managed to extricate herself without appearing rude. Jane's heart thudded the entire length of the high street as old fears came rushing forth and her granny's words of warning rang in her ears.

On entering her home she attempted to put water on for some tea but her hands were shaking so violently that the task was impossible. Leaving her loons to play she sat at the table and tried to assemble her thoughts in order.

She had lived her life terrified of being an outcast, or of being feared by others, for having the awareness of those who had passed. Being illegitimate and carrying the Cantlie name had made her an outcast as a child, she had no wish to feel that way as a grown woman. She certainly did not want to be feared.

What had lain dormant for so long was thrust into her present, and as she thought of her bairns she berated a world where secrets had to be kept.

*

QUEEN VICTORIA DIED suddenly from a stroke in 1901, just three weeks into the year, ending her reign of almost sixty four years and in turn ending the Victorian era. Her son Edward V11 succeeded her, and so began the Edwardian era with its boom in technology and relaxation of Victorian morals, if not corsets. A time of peace and prosperity dawned, alongside social and economic change, and Britain led the way in trade, finance and shipping, as the Suffragette movement rose alongside the first aeroplane. In America, two bairns were born who would go on in life to be famous for their work, namely Louis Armstrong and Walt Disney, and in Elgin the last bairn arrived for James and Ann - another loon, named Alfred.

Jane and Alec's bairns were growing with James and Alexander both now working loons. James, sixteen, was a horseman on Balliemullach Farm and Alexander, fourteen, worked with cattle at Knockside. Both talked of moving to the city of Glasgow, lured by what they believed to be more opportunities, but Jane hoped it was just talk and that her bairns would stay closer to home. The other bairns attended school, bar Thom who was now three years old.

Lena continued to see the house people, and others out and about, but like Jane had been as a bairn, she seemed to know how to keep it to herself. Having overcome his anger, Alec accepted things as they were and made it known to Lena that he wished her to talk of the house people to him, just as she did her mother. Jane had not told Alec about meeting Jessie MacKenzie, knowing that he would try to reassure her. There was no point, her fear was deep, its roots held fast in her mind, like the anchor of a ship.

News came to Alec that his sister Jane in Glasgow had died in childbirth, leaving an illegitimate son, Thomas. Their brother Robert and his wife Margaret, also biding in Glasgow, took their wee nephew in to bring up as their own, alongside their own wee ones.

Alec was distraught, but thankful that his wife had survived all seven accouchements as it was a dangerous experience for a woman and her bairn. Jane, though she loved her bairns dearly, hoped that there would be no more, as she had no wish to see them motherless, nor go through the agony of waiting for their first breath, as she had with Thom, but knowing her own mother was forty six on having her last bairn, Jane could only hope.

The Edwardian era may well have been a time of prosperity

but with regards to whisky, the industry went into decline due to a number of reasons. Distilleries had been over producing whisky for years. The huge upfront cost in terms of equipment and employees and the fact that it had to be held in casks for years before selling, contributed to overproduction in the hope of increasing revenue, but having so much whisky on the market caused prices to drop and distilleries to go out of business. The Pattison brothers, who were imprisoned for fraud and embezzlement within the industry, affected whisky's reputation, and had a domino effect across the industry in terms of securing investors, ultimately causing its near collapse.

Aberlour survived but production greatly reduced over the next few years, resulting in less work for employees and less money as time went by. The Farquharsons continued on, managing to maintain a decent standard of living but there would come a time when things had to change.

*

Both JAMES AND Alexander had decided to leave for Glasgow after all. A letter had been sent to their uncle Robert, Alec's brother, and the reply was that the loons would be welcome to stay till they had work sorted. Standing on the platform the brothers shook their father's hand, excitement emanating from their pores. "Tak care and be respectful. And write often, ye ken yer mother will worry otherwise."

"Aye, father."

Jane could feel the knots of her apron strings unfurling as the knots in her stomach tightened.

Emotion would not let her hug her loons, the farewells having been said in the house, and she stood straight backed, a wide smile plastered on her face, defying the emotion in her eyes, as she let her bairns go.

"Dinna worry, Mam, we'll be back for a visit soon enough."

Jane nodded and the loons boarded the train. The doors were shut one by one but just before their carriage door was slammed James hopped off, kissed his Mam on the cheek and jumped back on again just as the door shut behind him and the whistle blew, signalling the start of their journey.

Jane stood, her hand going up to her cheek as her eyes filled with tears and Alec led her home.

ONLY TWO WEEKS passed when a letter arrived for the Farquharsons,

> *Dear Mother and Father,*
>
> *Hoping this letter finds you well.*
>
> *Excuse this joint letter but we have good news and little time to get ourselves organised. I (James) have secured a joiner's apprenticeship with Donald and Son, in the east end of the city, and will move into a room above the workshop on Monday. By the time you receive this I will have moved and started work. I am fair delighted and the city is indeed a place of awe.*
>
> *Alexander, by some Godly intervention or sheer good luck, answered an advertisement in the paper looking for a loon to learn how to drive and look after a motorcar. As I write this he is packing to leave for the abode of a gentleman banker named George Morrison. I fear we will lose him to the gentry and he will soon be speaking like the King himself!*
>
> *Robert and Margaret send their regards and Alexander and I will both write soon.*
>
> *Your sons, James and Alexander.*

Alec placed the letter on the dresser, smiling. "Well, Jane, the loons have done well finding honest work. Imagine oor loon driving a motorcar! Times are changing, are they nae?"

"That they are. I remember the excitement of my first time on a train and I wonder if travelling by motorcar holds the same thrill. I ken James wis kidding but I hope we dinna lose Alexander to the gentry."

Alec chuckled. "That loon loves both his mother and her cooking. Dinna ye worry, quine, he'll always come hame, even if it's only for yer scones."

Loss

MARGARET HAD SECURED work as a housekeeper in various places over the years since the loss of Willie, but she did not marry again or indeed look to do so. Wee Maggie was now grown and had turned into a sweet natured quine and had procured work as a dressmaker. The two had forged a life for themselves following Willie's death, and theirs was a close bond, Maggie choosing to bide with her mother till such times as she married.

1905 found them living in Fife Street, Dufftown, five miles from Aberlour. Margaret, a sprightly sixty six year old, still worked as a housekeeper and enjoyed regular visits to and from Jane and her family. She was in awe of the large house in which her daughter bade and her heart was glad that Jane had found such a happy existence with Alec and their bairns. She hadn't forgotten Jane's troubled childhood and the nastiness of others with their coorse words, or her own past for that matter, but they had both survived and gone on to live better lives.

James was happily settled in Elgin with his family and Margaret hoped that he had come to terms with his father's actions as she had, although it was never talked of.

MAGGIE HAD AN understanding with a postman named John Gray, ten years her senior, and Margaret was delighted that her quine had found herself a solid, hard working man, much like

Maggie's father, who appeared to care for Maggie a great deal. She was apprehensive at the thought of living alone when Maggie married, and had already decided that she would look for a live-in position, near one of her daughters, when the time came.

AT TWENTY PAST three in the afternoon on Tuesday 5th September, Margaret suffered a stroke and died, quite unexpectedly.

Margaret's quiet strength of character had carried within it a fierce belief of doing what was right, nestled together with a romantic view of the world. Her genuine soul, sometimes overshadowed by others, and her couthie nature and quick smile, had drawn folk to her. Her three bairns, all so different, had felt the love she had bestowed on them and a part of her lived on in each of their characters.

So the river of life battered Jane once more.

Jane swayed slightly and crumpled to the floor, the shock reverberating through her, as the heaviness in her chest stopped her breath from coming. No sound came at first, as Alec held his wife tight, rocking her as if she were a bairn.

James led the funeral procession, his two sisters either side of him, as their mother's body was carried to Mortlach Kirk to be laid to rest. The minister's words drifted over heads as the mourners, locked in their grief, said their farewells.

Memories

J ANE WALKED ALONG the road towards her childhood home and knocked on the door of Milton Cottage. All had been arranged and the occupier left Jane on her own, to shroud herself in memories as she sat by the hearth.

Jane lowered herself into the chair, briefly closing her eyes, then tenderly scanned the room. She saw herself on her mother's knee, coorying in, listening to a story as her granny and granda blethered away, and her uncles read their school books, and her wee brother toddled towards his granny who scooped him up in her arms.

She saw herself winding the eight day clock and coming in from outside with eggs, and helping granny to make oatcakes, and she saw bedtime, her mother recounting a nursery rhyme and the tickles that followed.

Jane gently touched the nook where her granda's pipe had nestled, as her mind travelled forward and she heard him playing his fiddle and saw the family dancing in the kitchen, laughter in the air as they biirled round and round. She saw neighbours gathered around the hearth as granda held court with the weekly reading of the newspaper and the "oohs" and "aahs" on hearing the news.

She saw soup being cooked over the fire and felt the ache in her arms from holding the wool to be wound, and she heard banter and teasing. She saw the house people living amongst them, always present and always comforting.

Jane touched the hearth lightly, and her fingers gently brushed the walls, as her eyes caressed the room. She felt love. She felt comfort. She felt bosies and kisses.

Her mind's eye saw, her heart felt, and her ears listened to the years gone by, as a smile lingered on her lips.

As Jane turned to leave, she gathered all the memories together and locked them in her heart, as the old man, and the woman with the bairn who never grew up, smiled with her and walked her to the cottage door. The air heard her whisper and the walls absorbed the words,

"I thank ye."

A quietness now lived in Jane, deep within her, a place where those who raised her, bade.

*

MAGGIE MARRIED JOHN Gray on 12th January 1906 in the Gordon Arms hotel, Keith, in front of family and friends, and Jane and Alec's own daughter Marjory was a best maid. It was a happy day despite the loss of Margaret being felt, and when a bairn, baptised Margaret Jane, was born the following November, the family could smile again and be thankful for the safe arrival of a healthy bairn.

Marjory had answered an advertisement in the newspaper for a nursemaid in Elgin and had acquired the position just a few weeks following the wedding. Yet again Jane struggled with the letting go of a bairn as she said farewell to her eldest daughter.

Jane and Alec heard often from James and Alexander, their letters full of urban life and how different it was from Aberlour. James was now in Greenock but Alexander had settled in Glasgow. As Alec read the letters to the family Jane could see the excitement in both Jane and Lena's eyes, and her heart sank at the thought of them following their brothers. Both quines worked hard as domestic servants but times were changing and the lure of pastures new was strong for many young folk in the area. Marjory was away but at least it wasn't too far and there was family there too.

The loosening of the apron strings was painful to Jane, as each one tugged at her heart, but she knew however much she wanted her bairns by her, they had to live their own lives.

T HE 16TH APRIL 1907 saw the death of John Cantlie, aged seventy two, from heart disease. Her cousin Ann told Jane the news and the two sat with a cup of tea at Jane's kitchen table.

"When we were at school, Jane, I never really understood why the other bairns called you names and laughed. It wasn't till I got older that I realised what being illegitimate meant and how not being acknowledged by John Cantlie made you different from other illegitimate bairns, especially with you carrying his name."

Jane looked up. "Aye, bairns can be cruel but it comes from hearing their folks speaking at their hearth. I didna understand a lot o' the words they called me at first, and Mother always told me to ignore them, but it wasn't easy. I carried the Cantlie name but some saw me as having nae right to it, though it was not my doing. I never really felt comfortable wi' me name till I married, although I was in nae hurry to do that. Your name is something you should be proud to carry. I was proud within myself, but always felt as though I was stuck between two places. I lived life as a Smith but was called a Cantlie."

"Do you think you would have liked to hae lived the life of a Cantlie?"

"Oh, Ann, I canna answer that. I grew up surrounded by them, Francis along the road and half brothers and sisters at school. William up at Keithmore and John working for him. When I was wee I wanted to sit at their hearths, but as I got older all I wanted was to be acknowledged and claim a right to the name that I carried. No Cantlie was ever cruel, I just did not exist tae them. Nay to exist in someone's eyes is an awful feeling."

Jane became aware of Sarah sitting beside her, her hand on hers.

"How does it feel now John is gone?"

"I gave up looking for acceptance many years ago, but I suppose a wee part of me hoped that it would happen one day. Nay chance o' that noo. I suppose there is a feeling o' loss for what could hae been, and I would have liked Mother to have been believed. She held her head high but I know it must have hurt her. Thankfully Granny and Granda were good, loving folk otherwise me and Mother could well have been flung oot and had a much harder life."

Once Ann had left, Jane took herself for a long walk, and slowly became aware of tears on her cheeks which she quickly brushed away as little Elizabeth ran towards her, birling around Jane's skirt and bringing out a smile.

Steel Blankets

As the world kept moving forward Jane and Alec decided to move also. The whisky industry was still in decline and with the older bairns now away they thought it best to move to a smaller home with lower rent. It had been a luxury living at number 121 but they were fortunate that a house had become available just along the road at number 129. It was very similar, just smaller, and the rent was six pounds a year. Having lived at number 121 for nearly twenty years, and five of their seven bairns having been born in that house, it was in some ways a wrench to leave, but being able to bide still in Aberlour, and so close, meant that life would not change much at all. So they packed up their belongings, bade goodbye to the bricks and mortar, and carried their memories along the road.

Jane and Lena climbed the stairs to the room in the eaves where the ghost of the old man lived. "I used tae come up here wi' a book sometimes and just sit alongside him, reading. Usually when I needed some peace fae my brothers."

"I wish I could tak the ghosts wi' us. I'm sorry that you will lose them, Lena."

"Dinna be sorry, Mam. Ghosts are a part of our lives, and they will always come and go. I quite like knowing that there are many others I will meet."

Jane marvelled at her quine's outlook. "Ye see them differently fae me. Tae me they are a part o' me, nae just a part o' life, which is why I find it hard tae leave them behind."

Lena linked her arm through her Mam's. "Come away. He is content."

The two quines left the old man, who smiled warmly as he turned the page of his book. Downstairs Jane bit her lip as she looked upon the ghost of the quine, once the same age, but now Jane had moved on in years. Lena smiled broadly and announced, "Maybe you'll hae a handsome loon move in to swoon over. Ye have looked upon my brothers unlovely faces long enough!"

"Lena!" Jane chastised, but her laugh came easily, and with a nod and a wee smile at her ghostly friend, she turned for the door.

THEIR NEW ABODE was home, not to a human ghost, but a dog. A black and white collie was to be found by the hearth and greeted them warmly, its tail wagging. Jane never knew the names of most of the ghosts that had lived alongside her, and even as a child had never given them her own names, as it didn't seem right somehow, but this dog seemed such a lively and smart creature that she decided to call him Birkie, the doric word for such a fellow.

YOUNG JANE, NOW seventeen, was a domestic servant, locally, but hankered for city life like her brothers and Jane and Alec knew it was only a matter of time before she went further afield. Lena, Willie and Thom were still at school but the years were galloping by and Jane often wished she could pull on the reins and slow down the growing up of her bairns. Having always held tight to those she loved, Jane struggled with the fact that her bairns wanted to move so far away from their home. It was a pull she could not understand but she was proud of them all the same, going out into the world and making good lives for themselves.

It was a fast changing world and Jane and Alec had marvelled at the news of aeroplanes, finding it impossible to believe that such a thing could exist. They would look up at the sky with nothing in it but clouds and birds and could not for the life of them fathom out how on earth it could be true. A shiver went through Jane at the thought of any of their bairns in one.

ALEC'S FIFTY SEVENTH year pummelled into him and he felt the weight of it. Having worked physically since a loon he was strong and fit but was beginning to tire easily and found it difficult to catch his breath at times. He became slow at his work and a moment of dizziness almost caused him to fall into the boiler but luckily another labourer pulled Alec back. Word got back to the manager and Alec was asked what the problem was, and Alec being unable to answer was told to report to a doctor because if things carried on he would be out of a job.

Dr Sellar examined Alec thoroughly and listened to his symptoms. Putting his stethoscope down he sighed and looked him straight in the eye.

"I'm afraid to say that there is a problem with your heart, Mr Farquharson, and I am sorry, but there is nothing to be done about it."

A sudden feeling of coldness passed over Alec as his muscles froze, and his eyes closed momentarily.

"You will continue to feel tired and dizzy and short of breath, and you may have some swelling in your legs and chest pain as time goes on."

Alec lifted his chin. "How long do I hae?"

"A year. Perhaps more."

The words hung in the air, suspended, before plummeting into the pit of Alec's stomach, forcing the breath from his lungs. He stood slowly, his ears unhearing of the doctor's apology, so loud was the beating of his heart. The irony was not lost on Alec and he dragged his legs home to Jane.

The walk cleared Alec's mind enough for him to decide that he would not tell Jane of his diagnosis. He knew how she feared losing him and he wished to spare her the awful news for as long as he was able. On entering their home, as Jane rose to greet him, seeing his distraught face, Alec's resolve crumbled and he was unable to utter a single word. She moved to him and he clung tight to her and grat till his tears were spent.

Jane held her husband, her heart terrified, as she waited for his words and when they came, stilted and flat, her own anguish rose up, catching in her throat as she too wept. Together they sat, entwined in a fog of numbness, neither speaking, each caressing the other.

ALEC APPROACHED THE distillery manager to inform him of the situation in the hope that he would be able to maintain some sort of work. Twenty years he had given them but he was well aware that the industry was fast declining. It was agreed that it was not safe for Alec to be in the boiler room but could be employed as a day labourer, as and when fit, and paid according to what he managed to do in other parts of the distillery.

For a time Alec managed to work most days, albeit quite slowly, and for less money, but as the months staggered on it became more and more difficult for Alec to do so and eventually he had to admit defeat and stay at home.

It was time to tell his bairns.

Alec wrote to his eldest loons with the news. A short letter, no point in waffling he said, as he copied it word for word, an identical letter for James and Alexander.

My dear son,

There is no easy way to write this letter. The doctor has informed me that my heart is diseased and there is nothing to be done about it. I have perhaps a few months left on this earth but I have no pain and I dinna want ye to fret. Yer mother is a strong woman but I ken you will support her when the time comes. Please know how proud I am of ye,

Your affectionate father.

The other bairns were told one Sunday, following kirk. Alec spoke quite matter of factly, as Jane tried to comfort her stunned bairns. Wee Thom, just nine years of age, ran to his father and clung to him, scared and unsure, whilst Willie, now thirteen, mumbled some excuse to leave and left the house, running as fast as he could along the road, past the distillery and into the countryside, tears coursing down his cheeks. Lena went to her mother for comfort as her sister Jane sat in silence. It was Marjory who spoke, asking her father questions, the nurse in her needing answers.

And so the wait began for the Farquharson family.

*

*J*ANE SAT BY her hearth early one morning staring into the newly lit fire, watching the red and orange flames lick the stone, as her mind, weighted down with dread, reflected the heaviness on her shoulders. Crossing her arms she held herself in comfort and rested her head on the wing of the chair.

She could not allow her eyes to close as doing so would pull her into a place she did not wish to visit. Instead Jane looked for pictures in the flames, as she had as a bairn, and imagined she could see birds, hills and far away lands. A flicker of colour at the corner of her eye caused her to turn slightly, and there kneeling beside her was little Elizabeth, her wee hand on Jane's lap and her smile that Jane knew so well.

"Oh, Elizabeth, is where ye bide free o' worry? I am going tae lose Alec and the thought o' it terrifies me."

Elizabeth rose and began to birl and dance, her arms out wide and her feet skipping, as her fair hair fanned out behind her.

Jane watched the bairn who had been three years old for forty eight years. "Sometimes ye look at me with wise eyes and I wonder if yer mind has grown somehow in death. Ye always seem content and for that I am glad, and I am grateful that ye choose tae visit me."

Elizabeth did not stop dancing but she cocked her head in that wise and thoughtful way before disappearing through the wall. Jane felt some lightness seep into her which provided enough energy to enable her legs to move, and for her to start making breakfast. As she gathered together what she needed she whispered into the air,

"Please let Alec be happy and content in the next world."

ALEC WAS GLAD that over the years he had managed to put by a little money and moving to number 129 had been fortuitous as they could never have afforded to stay at 121 now. Lena was now bringing in money, working as a domestic servant and Jane continued to sew and mend for others, as she had always done.

They were managing.

News had come that Maggie was with child again which lightened the mood a little. Jane started to knit some clothes for the new bairn to come, a distraction from the lead weight in her chest. The fear of losing folk she loved, that had always had a stranglehold on her, threatened to consume Jane, its tendrils spreading and intertwining, piercing her heart and hounding her thoughts. Some days a surge of panic would rise up, cutting short her breath and Jane would slump down, desperate to feel a sense of calm. She desperately tried to protect herself from its grasp but she knew deep down that they were going to lose Alec, and there was nothing anyone could do about it.

It was confusing because Alec did not look ill. He was tired and breathless but he looked well enough, and it gave false hope to his family that he might live for years to come. They had been together for twenty four years, conceived seven bairns and lived a happy life, and she was not ready for it to end. Her mind leapt from despair to anger and back again and she pushed away her granny and great granny who tried to comfort her.

Alec himself was quiet at times but he revelled in being at home, being with Jane all day and seeing his younger bairns in the evenings. He could manage short walks and it was like courting again as he and Jane walked slowly hand in hand to the other side of the bridge or just along part of the high street and back. He never lost his quick tongue and their minds sparked, as their hearts beat together, as they had done for twenty four years.

Alec's heart stopped suddenly at half past noon, Sunday 10th May 1908, just nine months on from seeing the doctor, leaving the still beating hearts of his family, shackled by grief.

*

IN THE DAYS and weeks following Alec's funeral Jane could be found slumped by his grave: her hair tangled and dark circles under her eyes. She could not bear the screaming silence in the house or the haunted looks of her bairns, and the empty side of their bed mocked Jane each night, so she took to sleeping by the hearth.

Her friend and neighbour of twenty years, Isabella, took to visiting daily, ensuring that the loons were fed and sent to school, and she cooked dinner for Jane which was rarely eaten as food had no taste. Others also rallied round, her cousin Ann and dearest friends Eliza and Elsie visited, shocked at Jane's appearance, and all tried to cajole her into eating.

Jane herself felt nothing but a numbness. No thoughts formed in her mind, and if she tried to speak no words could come. With nothing but hopelessness in her heart, and loneliness that engulfed her, she was pulled down into a place of darkness. She felt as though fear mocked her, revelling in its win and smothering any fight left in her mind.

Her bairns were wary of her, unsure how to be around her and scared of the tears that flowed silently down their mother's cheeks. It was her uncle John, Ann's father, who broke through

Jane's silent prison. With a voice that seemed to come from a distance he sat with her and talked of losing his bairn, wee Elizabeth, and just a year later his wife, and how he didn't think he could go on living without them, let alone bring up his remaining bairns. As he spoke, Jane was aware of little Elizabeth sitting by her father holding his hand: the wee bairn who never grew up, and her life long friend.

"Yer bairns need ye, Jane, and we are never truly alone, however much it can feel like it. Bring up yer bairns and watch them make Alec proud."

Jane looked at him and hesitated before answering. "I'm scared tae face the world again. What if I canna dae it?"

"Ye put one foot in front o' the other and ye walk slowly at first, till ye get the hang o' it again."

His words slowly seeped into Jane's mind and as Sarah sat by her, Jane leaned in to her granny, gently breathing in comfort and gaining strength. John smiled at Jane.

"Ye can see my mother, Jane?" Jane was startled and nodded as she saw her uncle smile at his daughter, Elizabeth.

"I thought I was the only one who could see them. My granny said none of her bairns had the awareness."

"I've always seen them, Jane, but I never told. Seeing wee Elizabeth has been of great comfort tae me o'er the years."

"Why do you think only some folk come back as ghosts? I dinna think I will see Alec."

"I dinna ken, quine, it's something I have always wondered aboot myself. Maybe they are all with us, we just canna see them. I like tae think so."

"Aye, I like tae think so too."

John took Jane's hand and asked, "Do you hae dreams, Jane, ones that tell ye things?"

His look was so earnest that Jane pulled her hand back. "I dinna ken what you mean, John. Everyone has dreams."

"Many years ago, Jane, when I was about ten, my mother lost a newborn bairn and she was distraught. I came across her doon by the burn, and she was shouting angrily with tears streaming doon her face. Her own mother had passed the year before, but I saw her there and realised that my mother was shouting at her. I was too scared to approach my mother as she was so upset so I crouched down behind the bushes and listened. Some of her words were in Gaelic but she was saying what was the use of seeing dead folk, and having dreams that told of the future, when she could not stop bairns fae dying.

I left as quietly as I could, realising that my mother too could see those who had passed, but her talk of dreams had frightened me and I never told her of what I had heard that day."

Jane took John's hand. "Poor Granny - she had two secrets to keep, fearing the wrath of folk and the minister."

John had left soon after, satisfied that Jane would be all right. He had been surprised, but pleased, that she too shared the awareness of seeing those who had passed and found comfort in them.

After John had gone Jane sat for a long while. She did not dream as her granny had done but she knew in her heart of hearts that one of her bairns did.

She had chosen not to acknowledge it and years before had sternly told her child not to speak of their dreams. Perhaps if she had known of her granny's ability to dream of the future she may have reacted differently, but fear was powerful and she had to protect her bairns.

Jane slept in her own bed that night, deep and dreamless, and awoke with a tiny spark of purpose gently glowing deep inside of her.

SLOWLY JANE RETURNED to the world around her, comforting her family and finding work as a housekeeper so they could eat. As they were learning to adapt to a new life without Alec, Jane received the devastating news at the end of July that her wee sister Maggie, and her unborn child, had died in hospital from Enteric fever, leaving one year old Margaret Jane motherless.

Jane's mind went fleetingly into a state of madness but she clawed it back, determined to be a good mother for her bairns. A sense of anger in her grew, and that alone now allowed her to get out of bed each day. She shrouded her heart and mind with a steel blanket, lifted her head and took one breath at a time.

T HE NEWSPAPERS THAT summer told of the first Olympic games to be held in Britain. Originally intended to be held in Rome, Mount Vesuvius had erupted putting financial strain on Italy, so the venue was changed to London. Having only won four medals at the previous games it was quite a feat for Britain to not only win 146 medals, but to win the Olympic games overall, by a large margin. Bairns across the country, including Aberlour, raced each other along the streets and in the fields, played tug of war with old ropes, and scored goals and tries, all pretending to be gold medallists like their heroes in the newspapers.

Meanwhile, King Edward visited world leaders to discuss the growing power of Germany. Talks were held with Tsar Nicholas II in Russia and he met with the German Emperor to discuss the increasing size of Germany's navy. Later in the year the King met with Emperor Franz Joseph of Austria to persuade him to advise Germany against anti-British policies. There appeared to be political rumblings reverberating around the world which unbeknownst to most, would become catastrophic.

1909 saw Willie leave school at the age of fourteen to work with horses, training as a ploughman on a local farm, leaving Thom, the only bairn now attending school. James was still biding in Greenock, and Alexander in Glasgow, and both loons continued to write home regularly. It appeared that James had met a lass named Mary, and Jane could tell from reading between the lines that she might soon have a daughter in law, a thought that made her smile. Marjory was still working in Elgin, and Jane and Lena, both domestic servants, were close by and visited often, but Jane knew in her heart of hearts that her quines would move away, the pull of city life being strong. When Jane had borne her bairns it had not dawned on her that she would only keep them for a short time.

It was a loss that had no name.

1910-1914

As DRESSES AND skirts straightened in the name of fashion, and the Suffragette movement headed towards what would be known as Black Friday, a new King was crowned in England. Following the death of King Edward, his second son, George, succeeded him. George's elder brother, Albert, had died some years earlier and George had married his brother's fiancee. To lose one's crown, and wife, to one's brother could be seen as rather unfortunate indeed! Jane felt rather sorry for the late brother and the hand that life had dealt him.

In Scotland James Farquharson married one Mary Allison on 9th July 1910 in an irregular marriage in Glasgow. No one was present other than two witnesses. The law at the time in Scotland stated that mutual consent made a marriage, and that no religious minister or ceremony was required, and it was viewed as a civil contract. Hope Street Glasgow housed a solicitors office where many irregular marriages took place until they were made illegal in 1939, and following a declaration by both parties that they were living as man and wife, they then went to the sheriff's office along the road to have the marriage registered legally.

Jane was saddened not to see her first born married but was shocked to learn that he planned to visit Canada with a view to emigrating.

Meanwhile, unbeknownst to the world, Prime Minister H.H. Asquith held a secret meeting with his cabinet to formulate

Britain's strategy in case of war with Germany. As folk went about their daily lives political rumblings were beginning to grow louder.

On 18th November three hundred Suffragettes marched in protest against the failure of the Conciliation Bill to secure voting rights for women. They were met with a brutal response by police who allegedly beat and sexually assaulted many women and threw them into already hostile crowds who were against the Suffragette movement. One hundred and nineteen of the women were arrested but released, without charge, the following day, on the order of Home Secretary, Winston Churchill.

To be known as Black Friday, it marked the beginning of an underground and militant movement where women armed themselves and used destruction against the government in their struggle to gain their vote. On reading the newspaper at home young Jane and Lena were incensed. "What's wrong wi' the world? We hae machines that can fly for goodness sake, yet a woman has no rights."

"I ken, Jane, and to beat women for wanting what men hae is disgraceful," replied Lena.

" I hope neither o' you go to such marches," Jane interrupted.

"Mother!" young Jane retorted. "It's more important than ever now to join such marches. Women must be allowed to vote."

"She's right, Mam, we must fight for progress. The world is growing and modernising every day and women must be a part o' that."

Jane looked at her quines, with a furrowed brow, "I dinna ken what tae think." The steel around her heart dug in at the thought of any harm coming to her bairns, and anger rose in her as her body tensed and she grabbed the newspaper throwing it away, as she shouted, "All I ken is that I dinna want my quines hurt! I forbid ye to go!"

Lena and Jane shared a look, but remained quiet. They were used to their mother's anger since their father had died.

ODERNISATION CONTINUED APACE. The world's largest luxury passenger steam ship, to be named RMS Titanic, was under construction in Belfast, whilst horse drawn buses were being replaced in London by motorised double decker buses. The first ever flying unit of the British military was formed, as aeroplanes became more commonplace and the first electric escalator was installed in London. Jane had quipped at the laziness of folk who didn't want to walk up stairs as Thom dreamt of what it would be like to fly in an aeroplane. His excitement reminded Jane of when she first saw a train at the grand opening of Dufftown station and how she had known that travelling in one would be the most exciting adventure. As much as aeroplanes frightened the life out of her, she hoped that one day her loon's dream would come true and that it would be everything he hoped it would be.

It was also a time of industrial depression in Scotland, which caused unrest in the mines, railways, factories and docks. Many Scots were committed to Scottish independence and the 1911 Scottish Exhibition of Natural History, Art and Industry, held in Glasgow, strengthened their case. Attended by more than nine million people it showcased Scotland's history and culture. Alexander visited the exhibition and his letter home was full of what he had seen:

Dear Mam,

I hope this letter finds you well. I too was surprised at James joining the Constabulary. He is certainly one for surprises and I am never sure what he will do next! My work is steady and I continue to enjoy driving. Perhaps I will be able to take you out in a motorcar one day, I'm sure you would enjoy that very much.

I have much to tell you about the Scottish Exhibition that I attended yesterday. I have never seen the likes and I must admit to feeling like a wee bairn, there was so much excitement in me. I wish you could go Mam, and knowing how you love to read, you would

enjoy the literary gallery with its many famous books by the likes o'
Walter Scott and Robert Burns. It was held in the vast Kelvingrove
Park and some of the buildings were very grand - I was glad to have
worn my Sunday best! You ken how I liked history at school - well
you can imagine my feelings looking upon relics o' Bonnie Prince
Charlie and Robert the Bruce. The Art gallery had every famous
Scot you can think o' - and the size o' them! You could see them
quite clearly from the other side o' the room.

There was a Highland village and an African village which
I couldn't begin to describe, it was so interesting. I was amazed at
the prehistoric gallery with objects that have survived thousands o'
years. Imagine looking upon a bowl that folk used so long ago!

Outside a band stand was built and music played the whole
time I was there, but the most surprising thing outside was a mile
long mountain slide. No, I did not go on it but it was fascinating to
watch others career along, skirling wi' excitement!

As much as it was a sight to see I noticed that there was nothing
to reflect the poor of our country. It was maybe a bit one-sided but
we are indeed a country to be proud o' and I was glad to have had
the chance to go. Scotland certainly has a history and culture o' it's
own.

Well that's enough o' my ramblings. Like you, we are having
a lot o' warm weather and I must admit that it's good when I am
tasked to drive Mr Morrison out into the countryside to his country
residence, as it allows for some fresh air away from the smog o' the
city. Those times remind me o' the hills surrounding Aberlour and
I think I'm maybe a country loon at heart after all.

In answer to your question – no, I am nae courting but as
you said I probably wouldn't admit to it anyway. Better to watch
out for Thom as he is the handsome loon in the family.

On that note I will away and take a stroll before supper.
Affectionately,

    Your son, Alexander.

A GLORIOUS SUMMER THAT year led to drought in many parts of Britain and the highest ever recorded temperature of 36.7 degrees was recorded in Northamptonshire. As Jane baked in the heat of that summer she both marvelled at, and feared, the changes around her, as life seemed to be progressing rapidly, both in terms of the world's advances and her own advancing years. The future pulled the world and her bairns along with it and God only knew where they would all end up.

Three years had passed since Alec and Maggie had died and Jane still shrouded herself in a steel blanket. Too scared to let it go in case her heart and mind crumbled, she wrapped it tight around her each day as she walked step by step through life.

Her bairns saw the new hardness that lived in their mam, sometimes portrayed by a harsh word or glower, but there were glimpses of her softness now and then, with a gentle touch of the hand, or light kiss. Her true nature fought to be released but Jane's thrawn mind resisted: unable, unwilling and unforgiving towards a cruel world. She still felt the loss of Alec as a physical pain.Tiny needles pricked her heart when her thoughts turned to him and there was never any warmth on his side of their bed no matter how long she lay there.

Occasionally Jane would find herself laughing at some comment and the sound was strange to her ears but she would see the delight on her bairns faces and something in her would soften momentarily. She felt the encouragement from the house people to feel the life around her and she remembered from her past that a wall around her heart stopped the good as well as the bad from entering.

It was Thom who melted the steel with a simple gesture of helping an old man who had fallen on the street. The man was just in front of them and although the rain, which had been heavy, had now stopped, there were large puddles covering the path and he slipped causing him to land heavily. Thom immediately left his mother's side.

"Here, Sir, take my arm and I will help ye up."

Thom extended an arm whilst he wrapped his other arm around the man's waist and hoisted him upright, not letting go till the man was steady on his feet. "Are ye hurt, Sir?"

"Na, na, loon. Just my pride. Thank ye for yer assistance."

"Nae trouble." He gathered the apples that had fallen from their bag and handed them to the man. "Are ye fine to walk hame?"

"Aye, lad, nae damage done. Thank ye again."

Thom nodded. "Good afternoon to ye."

The man continued on his way and Thom turned back to his mother. Jane pulled him to her and landed a kiss soundly on his cheek.

"Ye have made me proud, Thom, and for the first time in a very long time I feel grateful for what I have in life."

Thom, now thirteen, was embarrassed at his mother's outpouring of affection, but she laughed, and he grinned unwittingly at his Mam's affection and sudden lightness in mood, though he checked to see that no one had witnessed the kiss from his mother.

His immediate kindness in helping the man filled Jane with pride and love for her young loon, and for the first time in a long time, Jane felt alive and grateful for what, and who, she had in life. A part of her had died with Alec but the rest of her was alive and needed to live accordingly.

The steel blanket slowly receded and the gloomy atmosphere lifted from the Farquharson home over that summer as Jane's quick wit and gentle soul was again present, but there would forever be some steel wire running through her heart.

HAVING SEEN THE return of their mother's true nature, a relieved Jane and Lena decided that the time was now right for them to leave Banffshire and experience city life. Edinburgh was to have the honour of receiving the quines and both had managed to procure work as domestic servants in the city.

216

The house bustled with the packing of clothes and a few treasured possessions, as Jane scurried behind her quines issuing instructions. "Stay together on the train, ye don't ken who might be travelling wi' mischief on his mind."

"Oh, Mam, of course we'll be together, and we can tak care o' ourselves. Have ye forgotten we hae four brothers?"

"That's different and ye ken fine it is, Lena," retorted Jane.

Young Jane, intervened. "We will be careful, Mam, and we ken how to behave. We winna disgrace ye."

Jane smiled at them both but she couldn't help but worry about them going off to live in the city.

With tight bosies and promises of frequent letters, Jane waved her quines off at the station, a soft smile on her lips as she saw the excitement in their eyes, and an awareness of the loosening, yet again, of apron strings. Her sense of pride in them mingled with her sense of loss but as the world beckoned her bairns, Jane turned for home, wee Elizabeth skipping alongside her.

1912 SAW AN AMERICAN, Albert Berry, parachute out of a plane to the disbelief of the world, and the sinking of the great Titanic with the loss of over fifteen hundred lives. Jane was thankful that James had returned safely from his trip to Canada via ship, but his letters were full of how much better life was there and she knew in her heart that it was only a matter of time till he left for good. His first bairn was on its way and Jane was delighted at the thought of being a granny but knew that she might not get to see him or her grow up. Jane being Jane, whenever life was difficult she stopped thinking altogether and the steel wire tightened its grip.

Thom, now fourteen, had completed his Higher examinations at school, receiving his Leavers Certificate in English, Maths, Latin and Greek, enabling him to go on to further education and seek a profession, the first in the family to do so.

Jane held the certificate in her hands and shook her head in awe of her clever loon. "Yer father would be proud o' ye, Thom."

Thom's head lowered for a second but he smiled and told his mother, "I plan tae go tae the training college in Elgin and become a teacher. I think I would enjoy that."

Jane's eyes widened. "Well ye have kept that quiet, loon."

"I was waiting tae see if I did well enough in the examinations afore saying anything."

"Well, Thom, I think ye would make a fine teacher."

A bright loon with the world at his feet, and he talked of nothing but aeroplanes, Jane wondered where his own wings would take him and her apron strings tugged against her and try as she might to tighten the knots, her bairns were adept at unravelling them.

Often she longed for the presence of Alec to calm and reassure her. The house people comforted Jane, as they had always done, with their knowing looks, but as each bairn moved away she felt bereft and a little lost. Coming from a long line of farming folk, on both sides, it surprised Jane that so many of her bairns did not have a love of the land, preferring the busyness of a city. Jane and Lena wrote frequently and Jane was relieved that both seemed happy and settled in Edinburgh. She had never envied other folk for material things but there was a part of her that wished she had bairns who lived and worked close by, being able to see them often and watch them bringing up their own bairns.

The newspapers were full of adverts for folk to emigrate to the other side of the world. Domestic servants and farm workers were in great demand in Canada and Australia, offering seventy two pounds a year including free passage. The lure of greener grass was strong and it pulled James and his dreams of a better future.

James had become a fully fledged policeman in Greenock, and his first bairn was born on 18th January 1913, named Alexander Angus. Jane was sure that Alec was looking down, proud of his first grandbairn, named after him, and James informed her that Angus was after his Chief of Police, John Angus, who had procured a year's absence for James to travel to Canada.

Jane took her first train journey south and spent a few days with James and his new family. She had marvelled at her wee grandbairn but was disconcerted, as times had changed alongside folks' beliefs, and like Alec had in his lifetime, many now no longer believed in the power of fairies, and bairns and their mothers were no longer being sained. When Jane had enquired on who had watched over Mary and her new bairn till they had been sained it had been met with awkward laughter.

Jane had held her tongue but perhaps she had more reason than most to believe in the old folklore having the awareness of seeing those who had passed. She knew ghosts lived amongst them and just because she had never seen a fairy or a kelpie it did not mean that they did not exist, and she had been brought up to fear them and their wicked ways.

Jane visited Alexander in Glasgow before boarding the train home and was fair delighted to meet his lass, Margaret, whom he planned to marry that coming December. It had been a fine visit with much laughter and well wishing, and although Jane and Lena had not managed to get any time off and travel to Glasgow, their letters spoke of them both thriving on city life.

Jane was content that her bairns were happy and settled and although she was sad to leave them she was glad to return to the hills of home and to her own folk.

On her return, Jane wrote to her friend Elsie in Aberdeen telling her all about her wee grandbairn and Alexander's lass.

Dear Elsie,

I sit here wi' a cup o' tea having just returned from Greenock yesterday. It was fine indeed to meet my first grandbairn, and you will ken the feeling well, having three o' your own now. Ye forget how small they are when first born but oh how times have changed. I was met with laughter on enquiring about being sained and I must admit to feeling a bit hurt and a little dismayed that the young no longer see any danger following accouchement. Maybe I'm just getting auld!

It was a grand visit all the same but it passed quickly. Fortunately I was able to meet with Alexander in Glasgow and he introduced me to his lass, Margaret. They plan to marry in December and there is no doubt both are smitten, so I am reassured that Alexander has made a fine choice.

Yer last letter made me chuckle, Elsie. Ye are an awful quine, the way ye tease yer husband o' thirty years. Remember when Jessie read yer tea leaves in the back room o' the Grocer's and said ye would marry twice in quick succession? I sometimes wonder if he would hae preferred it if you had done just that, the way ye speak.

You mentioned the amount o' political talk in Aberdeen wi' Germany's growing fleet but I dinna think we need tae worry. There's enough worry on our own doorsteps without worrying about other countries.

I will away now, and I hope this letter finds ye all well. Let me ken how ye get on wi' yer Suffragette meeting. My quines are forever rambling on at me tae be more involved.

Your friend, Jane.

As Jane signed off she smiled to herself as she thought of her old friend in Aberdeen. She had not married twice in quick succession but had held on to her man these past thirty years. Her flighty ways had never left her and she had threatened to leave her man several times over the years claiming she would fend for herself and take a lover, and he was never quite sure if she meant it!

They had both been lucky with their husbands and as much as Elsie jested, Jane knew that Elsie would choose no other life.

T HE NEWSPAPERS TALKED of Germany's growing naval fleet and political rumblings continued with the Balkan War, but life in Aberlour continued along in its own quiet way. Jane's wee holiday had been good for her. She had needed to see with her own eyes that her older bairns were indeed happy and she felt more at peace than she had in a long time.

Willie had proved himself a hard worker and good ploughman and Marjory was still in Elgin which wasn't too far away, with Thom busy with his studies there too. Neither Willie nor Thom talked of yearning for city life, so Jane wondered if perhaps she would get to keep her two youngest bairns closer to home. Willie had a love of horses and Thom loved the hills, like his mother.

Maybe some farming blood had seeped into them after all.

The annual Jupp jumble sale came round and Jane busied herself helping the women in the church to organise donations. Canon Jupp had passed away in 1911 but the sales had continued and a new boys' wing had been built, named in his honour. The orphanage had grown over the years and now hundreds of bairns called it home. When their schooling came to an end they, like everyone else, went out into the world to find work, and the home where Jane worked as housekeeper had just taken on a quine, Mary, from the orphanage, as a domestic servant.

She was hardworking and far more capable than Jane had been at that age, remembering her early days when she was all fingers and thumbs, and mistakes followed her like a fox chasing a rabbit. Jane recounted the story of dropping a whole roast beef on the floor which gave Mary much amusement and the two got along just fine.

Willie, now a fully trained ploughman, had been to the Feeing market and secured work for the next six months. The usual bartering of wages over whisky had taken place with some procuring better positions than others. On his return, despite a successful day, his mood was foul and Jane could not prise an explanation from him. "What on earth's wrong wi' ye Willie? Ye said ye bartered a fair wage."

"Nothing's wrong, Mam, I hae work and the wage is fine," he mumbled.

"Well, Willie, yer face does not seem tae agree wi' ye, and I can tell that ye have had mare than one whisky and ye ken I dinna like that." Jane rose to lock the door as Willie quietly spoke again,

"I'm sorry. I'm away tae my bed."

Willie stood and went over to his mother. He hugged her goodnight quite unexpectedly, and kissed her cheek, before taking himself off to bed leaving Jane with a look of bewilderment.

Whatever happened that day, years later, on his marriage certificate, Willie would write his mother's maiden name as Smith, and not Cantlie, the only one of Jane's bairns to do so.

T HE YEAR ENDED with Alexander's marriage to Margaret Cooper on 6th December in Glasgow. Jane sat proudly as she watched her loon marry and imagined Alec by her side sharing the joyous occasion. By the time their first born, Agnes, arrived, Britain was on the brink of war, and life, like the River Spey, carried them all forward with no way of turning back.

WAR

PRIME MINISTER ASQUITH took active steps to protect Britain's ports following the assassination of Austria's Archduke Franz Ferdinand in June, and the subsequent declarations of war that followed, all for a number of reasons.

Whispers of impending war grew louder causing fear in the hearts of some, and excitement in others. The young, who thought themselves invincible, imagined heroic battles over love for their country, and Governments who relied on such feelings, plucked at heart strings and gathered in the fodder.

The 4th August 1914 saw Britain declare war on Germany, the evening after Germany's declaration of war against France, and what was to be known as The Great War began. By the time it ended the world would be struggling to comprehend the slaughter of an incomprehensible forty million folk.

On hearing the news that her country was at war, Jane made herself a cup of tea and for the first time in a long time, read the tea leaves. She saw downward arrows and crosses portending wrong direction and death, and with a hand that shook, slowly placed the cup back onto its saucer and vowed not to read them again.

In the days that followed, many men enlisted in the army or spoke of doing so, and there was much talk of the war being over by Christmas. James was again in Canada but his wife and bairn were still in Greenock and Jane was unsure what that would mean for them. Following church that Sunday folk gathered outside to talk with their friends and neighbours, some adamant it would be a quick victory for Britain, others portending a time of hardship, but no one could have predicted the true outcome of that war.

POSTERS STARTED TO appear encouraging men to enlist and on Friday the 28th August a large meeting was held in the Fleming Hall, Aberlour, to make arrangements for dealing with a national emergency. Similar meetings were held up and down the country as the realisation of war hit. Plans were laid down for everything from protecting yourselves from bombs, to the knitting of socks for soldiers.

Jane, Willie and Thom attended the meeting, sitting alongside friends and neighbours and there was a mixed sense of unease and excitement in the atmosphere.

The chair of the meeting welcomed all. "We find ourselves at war, and although we believe it will be short lived we must prepare for all eventualities. Our first priority is to do all we can to help our soldiers at the front. Regular supplies will be needed in way of clothing, food and other essentials, and as a community we can help the Government by preserving food, knitting the likes o' socks and blankets, and sending whatever is asked for."

Heads nodded in agreement. "We must also consider the safety of ourselves, in the unlikely event of any bombs being dropped."

There were several audible gasps from some quarters and the folk started to talk amongst themselves.

"Quiet please - we have a lot tae get through this evening. It is not my intention tae scare ye, but we must consider all possibilities and prepare for them. We need volunteers to help set up procedures to be followed and there will be a chance for folk of all ages to help in some way. If ye are willing tae do so, please leave yer name wi' Mr Nicol on yer way out."

He ended the meeting with words portending certainty and hope.

"Our brave soldiers will bring victory, swift and sure, and peace will reign again - of that I am certain."

As the meeting came to an end, there was the same mixture of unease and excitement, but for some the lure of going to war had taken its grip, and its fingers were curling round minds, reeling in lads with the promise of glory.

*

SEVERAL DAYS FOLLOWING the meeting Jane was dishing up supper for Willie when, with no warning, his words came quiet but firm. "I have decided to enlist in the Scottish Horse Regiment. I have already told work and I plan to take the train to Elgin on Monday. I have to enlist there at the Drill Hall."

Jane stopped short, clutching at the edge of the chair. "No, Willie, ye canna mean it. Ye work on a farm and are exempt fae going."

"I ken, Mam, but I want tae go and fight for my country, and my mind is set."

Jane saw the streak of stubbornness that ran through his blood, as it did her own, and closed her eyes. The steel wire tightened its grip once more on her heart but her mind fought against it and she refused to give into the fear as she declared airily, "Right ye are, loon. Well the war will be o'er by Christmas, so ye winna be gone long."

The lightness of her words belied the heaviness in her heart, but it was such a foreign situation that she had no way of knowing how to react or how best to speak to Willie.

Willie looked at her, uncertain at the tone of her words, but not wishing to prolong the conversation merely answered, "Aye, Mam," and proceeded to eat his supper.

IT WAS WITH a heavy heart that Jane watched him leave to catch the train to Elgin, whereby shortly afterwards he was sent to Dunkeld for initial training.

Come September the newspapers were calling for men to enlist, the Seaforth Highlanders claiming that they were five hundred men short. A carriage full of wounded soldiers had arrived at Craigellachie train station en route to Aberlour hospital, and they were greeted with hearty cheers from the locals and offers of help. The country's pride held its head high, believing politicians' words concerning atrocities, victory and peace. As momentum and energy surged folk were carried along on its coat tails, oblivious to the slaughter and horror that lay ahead.

Thom was busy with his studies in Elgin but more often than not took the train home to see his mother at the weekend, especially since Willie had left and she was living alone. One of Jane's neighbours, a sour faced gossip by the name of Doris, declared that men who did not enlist were cowards, and seeing Thomas standing with Jane one Sunday following kirk, said,

"A fine strapping lad like yourself should be off fighting for yer country."

Enraged, Jane retorted. "He's a loon o' sixteen, and nae old enough for war. Away with your daupit talk!"

But a seed had been planted and just a few days later Thom had taken himself off to the Drill Hall in Elgin and lying about his age, saying he was eighteen, had enlisted with the Seaforth Highlanders.

The following weekend he visited again but unsure of how his mother would react, Thom left telling her till just before he had to leave for his train back to Elgin. Jane sank into her chair at the news, stunned into silence. Slowly her mind refocused and she looked sharply at Thom.

"Ye will go back tae the Drill Hall and tell them that ye are only sixteen. They might be angry but they will not want ye, being so young, and ye will carry on wi' yer education."

Thom stood tall. "I need tae go, Mam. I am fit and healthy and they are in need o' young, strong men tae fight. I want tae be a part o' it and fight for what is right."

Jane's voice rose alongside her anger. "Ye will not go! I winna allow it!"

"It's done, Mam. I have signed the papers and I leave in a week. I promise tae write as often as I can and it will just be for a few months. No one expects it to be a long war."

Jane felt a rush of helplessness and as her loon bade her farewell with a kiss on the cheek and words of "Dinna worry," she sat slumped for she knew not how long. She heard the whistle of the train as it left the nearby station and as it rumbled on its way, she became aware of a feeling rising up from her belly and only just managed to reach her sink before vomiting.

Wiping her hand across her mouth, Jane's distress turned to anger and she left her home, her strides lengthening as her anger rose, and she hammered on Doris's door. As the wife herself opened it Jane's hand struck her hard across the cheek and in a low, angry voice spat the words, "If anything happens to my Thom, it will be your fault."

W ith Willie and Thom both now away for training, soon her loons would be off to war, and as Jane read *The Northern Scot* newspaper that December its words rang true:

"The war cloud is now hovering nearer. Now that a number of Aberlour Territorials are on the scene of action there are many anxious hearts awaiting the latest news from the front."

As Jane thought of her loons, tears fell silently, but the steel wire wound itself tighter around her heart, her way of finding strength, as she knew that she had to be strong for her bairns whatever lay ahead. She turned to her granny.

"I will not hide behind a wall and hope it all goes away, but I will stand strong and proud with my bairns and face whatever is to come. I canna fight on the front line but I can help fight in other ways, and worrying will not bring my loons home sooner."

Her granny nodded as Jane wiped her eyes and vowed that no tears would fall again till her loons were home safe, and then there would be tears of joy.

As Christmas came and went it became apparent that the war was to last, although no one seemed to know by how much longer. No leave had been granted and it was a quiet Christmas for many, and Jane had no way of knowing when she would see her loons again.

News came that Jane's uncle John had died on 29th January, peacefully, aged eighty five, his heart tired from disease. Jane imagined that his mother, Sarah, and perhaps wee Elizabeth would have been by his side, to both comfort and guide him to his long lost wife who had been gone for nearly fifty years. John had worked hard following the death of his wife Elizabeth, becoming a farmer of his own croft, and with the help of a housekeeper and family, had managed to bring up his bairns alone, never remarrying in all that time, his heart belonging to one quine only.

He had shared with Jane his awareness of seeing those who had passed and it comforted her to know that he would have been aware of them there in his passing. Death was feared by most folk, fear of the unknown lying in wait, and a journey to be taken alone, but for those with the awareness of ghosts she imagined it less fearful, and she herself trusted that they would guide her when her own time came.

The many deaths that Jane had experienced throughout her life, particularly in her younger years, had brought with them immense grief and added to the fear within her of losing folk that she had loved, but for the first time, her uncle's death, although sad, brought a small smile to Jane's face as she thought of his long life with his bairns who had grown into fine, good folk, and of how he had been such a good and loving man, who having waited so long and worked so hard, was now reunited with his darling wife.

Jane was also glad for wee Elizabeth, who now had both her mother and father with her again. She too had waited a long time.

A LETTER FROM ALEXANDER arrived shortly afterwards,

Dear Mam,

 I hope this letter finds ye well and that ye are managing fine on yer own. I am writing to tell ye that I have enlisted wi' the Army as a driver, and am about to leave for basic training.

Jane's hand slowly lowered and the rest of the letter went unread. Her eyes closed and her heart constricted in her chest as the realisation hit that she now had three sons in the war.

W INTER BROUGHT WITH it more casualties home and news of trenches which folk could not fully appreciate. Letters spoke of the need for parcels with warm socks and comforts of home to lift spirits, and the postal service was inundated with mail, resulting in a feat almost miraculous in the delivering of parcels and letters to and from soldiers at the front.

 Letters from Jane's loons became very infrequent and although she wrote to each one religiously every week, she did not know if her letters had been received. It did not deter her though, and the ink flowed religiously, scratching words on paper, carrying sentiments of hope and affection.

My dear son,

 I have no way of knowing if all my letters reach ye, but know that ye are always in my thoughts and I will continue to write till ye are home safe and well. The newspapers reported that ye were having a bit o' trouble wi' the weather and the trenches were full o' water. I hope ye were not affected and are managing to keep dry. I have sent more socks and another blanket just in case, alongside a new book for ye.

I have also enclosed my last letter from yer uncle James, as ye ken how he has a way with words, and his letters are always entertaining. I thought ye would appreciate a bit o' humour. I especially liked the bit about the very odd parcel the post office received.

Spring is here and the wee lambs are skipping in the fields and the flowers are beginning to bloom, bringing a splash o' colour to folks' gardens. I have acquired some salmon from auld Mr Muir, the river still being high, and fish in abundance. If I could send ye a fish pie I would, but I promise to make one when ye next come home.

There was a bit o' excitement here last Saturday, as the laird o' Netherton has bought himsel' a motorcar and he drove it along the high street, right past our house! I must admit to going out to see it better. It was a deep green colour and his wife was sitting in the front, all wrapped up as it was cold that day and the roof was pulled down. Isabella thought they were just showing off as it was cold and no need for the roof to be down, but it gave us a better view so I was quite glad.

I had a usual week at work with nothing much to report there. The Simpson lad, Gregory, has joined up, so his mother is asking if ye will look out for him, as he has joined the same regiment.

I will sign off now and pen a letter to yer brothers. Let me ken if ye need anything at all.

Take care, loon,

    Yer loving mother.

S︎HE LOOKED UPON the photograph taken of Willie and Thom, standing proud in their uniforms, before they left for the front, and prayed that they were safe. She had no such photograph of Alexander but she conjured up his image in her mind and sent up a prayer for him too. James was working for the railway in Canada and for the time being not in the war, and she hoped things would stay that way.

Heavy losses were reported following the lost battle of Gallipoli and it had been a full year since she had last seen any of her loons. Willie was the first to come home on leave, home for just three days that August, as travelling took up most of his leave time. When he arrived he was thinner and there was a seriousness about his eyes that Jane had never seen before.

"It's good tae eat yer homemade stew, Mam. I miss yer cooking."

"Eat up, lad. Ye need fattening up. Do they nae feed ye well?"

"They do their best, I suppose. I worry more about the horses than mysel'. They dinna understand what all the noise is…"

His voice trailed off and Jane was unsure what to say.

Willie rallied. "It won't be for much longer though. I want tae hear all about life here, Mam, and maybe we can take a walk along the river in the mornin'."

So talk turned to Aberlour and Jane, although she could have no concept of war, she understood that her loon needed the familiarity and peace of home.

Three days passed in the blink of an eye and suddenly Willie was off again.

" I will write as often as I am able. Take care o' yersel, Mam."

Jane kissed his cheek and forced her words to be light. "I will write every week and send ye parcels o' food. I hope ye see yer brothers."

Willie turned and boarded the train, leaving Jane not knowing when she would see him again.

Thom returned from France two months after Willie, his regiment having fought at the Battle of Loos. Jane had to squeeze her eyes tight as she hugged her bairn, as the change in him shocked her. He had left a bairn of sixteen but stood before her with the look of a man haunted.

"Oh, ma loon," were all the words Jane could muster, and she swore in her mind at the men who had caused the Great War, and berated a God that allowed bairns to suffer.

Thom was quiet, but unlike Willie, he spoke a little of the war.

"I stay at the back, as they ken I am young, so ye dinna need tae worry. I like to read, when I can, and one o' the officers has a wee dog and we take it in turns to take him for walks. He's a wily wee fellow and it's strange to be playing wi' a dog in the midst o' war, but I like to spend time wi' it. Makes life feel normal, I suppose."

"I'm glad, Thom. Maybe we'll get a dog when ye come back home after the war is over."

"Aye, Mam. I think I would like that."

As his days home came to an end Thomas left much in the same way as Willie, with promises to keep safe and write often. He told his mother that her letters of home were a great thing indeed and how much he looked forward to them.

Jane allowed herself to cry on each one's departure but made sure that the last thing they saw was her smile, before the tears came as the train pulled out. These were the only times throughout the war that she allowed her heart to soften and the tears to fall.

*J*ANE SAT WITH Isabella, her friend and neighbour since moving to Aberlour twenty six years previously. Over a cup of tea the two women talked initially of having watched each other's bairns grow, and the happy times sharing their home at number 121. Both had loons away fighting, as had many of their neighbours and friends, and a way had to be found to keep those at home occupied in work that would both help the war effort, and keep minds sane. Too much time allowed worry to overtake the thoughts so Jane surmised that the best thing to do was to keep busy.

There were fundraising events throughout Banffshire and of course the whole country. Baking was sold and chores done all to raise funds to purchase goods for the soldiers. Letters home asked for everyday items like books and footballs and even instruments and records. Jane was forever sending parcels of baking, clothing and books to her sons. Herself and Isabella were also involved with the sending of parcels to the lads from the orphanage.

W ITH SO MANY men away fighting Jane saw how women were now having to replace them in the fields, the trains and the post office and how capable they were, and those working on farms even wore breeks! Letters from her quines, Jane and Lena in Edinburgh, spoke of women working in factories and offices there. The world had turned upside down and Jane wondered how it could possibly ever be the same again.

In January 1916 James enlisted in the Canadian Overseas Expeditionary Force and found himself in France alongside his brothers. February saw what was to be the longest, bloodiest battle of the war, lasting nine months, where Germany attacked Verdun. Heavy losses were reported on both the French and German front but it was hailed a French victory. March brought military conscription by the British Government, forcing all able men between the ages of eighteen and forty to enlist in the war, as the need for more soldiers rose and this resulted in a manpower crisis. A booklet was published by the Government called *"Women's War Work"* detailing a list of jobs previously done by men in order to persuade employers to hire women.

April 1916 saw the first bombs landing in Scotland and Jane near fainted on hearing that it was in Edinburgh where her quines bade. Thankfully both were unharmed and had had the sense to send a telegram to their mother as soon as they were able, to reassure her that they were fine. Marjory visited her mother shortly after the bombing.

"I am going to stay and work in Edinburgh, Mam. They are desperate for nurses and I want to go and do my bit. Dinna argue wi' me, my mind is made up and I am leaving in a few days."

"Oh, ma quine, as if I dinna hae enough folk tae worry about!"

Up until then Jane, and many others, had viewed the war as something taking place far away but now it all seemed very close to home, and Jane now worried for all her bairns and not just her loons.

𝕴N MAY THE Government took the decision to move clocks forward one hour to increase the working day, mainly for agricultural reasons, and it was a strange thing indeed for folk to get up and move the hands of their clocks forward, denying an hour of time which seemed wrong and wicked almost, to do so. Jane thought of all the bairns born in the lost hour and how the time of birth recorded would always be untrue. It was a thought that would stay with her till she died, as no Government changed the rule back again following the war.

If truth be told, many would have gladly moved the hands forward to the end of the war that day, sacrificing time in order to have their loved ones home again.

𝕵ANE CONTINUED TO work as a housekeeper in Aberlour for the Simpson family, but her role changed, as so many middle class women were now out working and young bairns needed looking after. Young Mary from the orphanage had moved into farm work so Jane had more work to keep her busy, and between that and the constant letter writing, knitting of socks, sending of parcels to her loons, growing food in her garden and constantly preserving, Jane's days were long and tiring, but that was how she wished them to be till the war ended.

Meanwhile the newspapers reported the first Battle of the Somme, the first day resulting in the largest losses suffered by the British in one day of battle. It was to last from 1st July till 18th November with over a million casualties on both sides. Unbeknownst to Jane all four of her loons were there, entrenched in heavy bombardment, covered in lice and living in rat infested trenches full of the stench of death.

There was a rule that no men under twenty years of age

were sent to the front lines but although further back, would have witnessed the many dead and wounded carried back from the front. As their comrades and friends fell all around them, the thundering noise, terrifying screams and scenes of horror, imprinted on their brains, as men were annihilated, mutilated or disfigured.

LETTERS AND SCRAN

T HE NEWSPAPERS WERE full of news on the Battle of the Somme, and Jane had not heard from any of her loons for months. The descriptions of the battles and lists of the many dead filled folk with fear and dread, and the postie was pounced upon each day as kin grew desperate for news.

Finally, a letter arrived, crumpled and muddy but a letter all the same and Jane ripped it open before her door was closed. Jane read the words quickly:

Dear Mam,

I hope ye are well. There has been no reprieve from fighting, therefore little time to write. All we seem to do is fight and sleep, fight and sleep. I have seen Alexander, who heard news o' Thom, and Willie managed to get word through a friend, so we are surviving. I received three letters from ye at the same time, dated a while back, such as the way at the moment. Forgive me for such a short letter but I must find some food and grab some sleep while I can.

I will write again soon,

Yer loving son,

James.

It was short but the words told her that her loons were alive and she allowed herself to breathe again.

Many of the loons who bade in the orphanage in Aberlour enlisted in the war and they too wrote letters to the only home they knew, with their news. Often their letters were printed in the monthly Orphanage Magazine and some locals took it upon themselves to start corresponding with them, as the wardens could only reply to so many, there being a total of two hundred and eighty nine boys over the course of the war who joined up. Many loons throughout the country had no one to write to and women took to writing to these soldiers in the hope of providing some comfort and support to them whilst they were at war. The Government recognised the need for letters in keeping up morale and it was actively encouraged. For some, over the course of the war, these letters brought strangers together and deep friendships, and sometimes more, developed as a result.

Jane's old friend Eliza in Dufftown, had taken to writing to the son of a neighbour who had passed away, knowing that he now had no mother to write to him. She herself had two loons away fighting and felt some motherly feelings toward the lad, having watched him grow up next door. When news came that he had been killed, Eliza mourned him as she would a son, and like Jane and so many others, she shrouded her heart and mind in metal to protect them till her bairns returned.

Newspapers printed stories, most masking the true horror of battles fought overseas, but the ever growing lists of the dead told their own story, as did the number of telegrams and letters holding tragic news of men missing in action, captured or dead. Whenever Jane saw a young lad, or more often than not a woman, cycling along the high street with a satchel of letters, she held her breath in case a letter from the war office was amongst the mail for either herself or a neighbour.

Letters from her brother James in Elgin were full of both pride and worry for his own loons away fighting but his steady, calm nature which came through in his words, always perked Jane up as he talked jovially of common life, bringing a smile to Jane's lips with his descriptions of everyday happenings that he made comical. Often Jane would relay his tales to her bairns, in her own letters, always mindful of keeping her words light hearted so as to contradict the war, and to give them a letter worth reading for its happier news.

Letters also passed between Jane and her two daughters in law, Mary and Margaret, and they both kept Jane up to date with their growing bairns. Mary and James's son Alexander, was now three. Mary was living with her sister and her family for the duration of the war. Alexander and Margaret's daughter, Agnes, was now two, and Alexander had been home on leave to visit Margaret at the end of 1915 and she had delivered a second bairn, Alexander, on 28th August. It was a reminder that life continued on, war or no war, and folk could only pray that all the wee bairns whose fathers were away fighting, would have them returned safe and well.

W ITH WOMEN HAVING to take on the jobs previously done by men before the war this meant that some young quines who volunteered to help the war effort were sent far from home, living away from their parents for the first time and earning a wage for themselves. Isabella's daughter was one such quine and she confided in Jane.

"Sophia has never been past Dufftown and now she is away working in a factory in Aberdeen. What if someone takes advantage o' her?"

"Isabella, ye have brought her up tae ken right from wrong. Dinna be listening to the auld biddies who talk o' loose morals. Ye hae to trust yer bairns to make good choices, and a war will not change that. Aberdeen is nae too far away and ye ken Elsie is there if needed."

For many quines this newfound freedom led to their social advancement, as they proved themselves capable and intelligent in the world of work.

Jane continued,

"I have never actively been involved in the Suffragette Movement but I have certainly heard their arguments and read their pamphlets. I remember, as a young quine working in Dufftown, my employer Christina Morrice, being a staunch advocate for women's rights, but I had not thought it to be something that included myself, believing such things to relate to those above me in station. At that time I could not see how the world could possibly change to become a place where women could vote, be financially independent and do a man's job. Now aged fifty nine, with war raging and quines doing every job imaginable that have previously only ever been done by men, my outlook has changed. I hear not only my own quines' opinions but I see with my own eyes how women in Aberlour have adapted to take on male roles, and how many appear to enjoy their work and even thrive on it."

"Aye, ye hae a point, Jane. One of our neighbours is a conductor on the train, another works as a butcher and one even works as a teller in the bank, something I thought we would never see in our lifetime."

It appeared that it wasn't just armies that were advancing and the two women looked upon these leaps of change with astonishment, but they made them smile with pride and they wondered what their mother's would have made of it all.

$\mathcal{J}$ANE HAD ALWAYS been grateful for the ghosts in her life, for their comforting presence, and they provided company for her, with her bairns all away, so she had less need to feel lonely than some. She also had the company of the dog, Birkie, who occasionally accompanied her on a walk into the hills, with wee Elizabeth running alongside him. Many women felt the loneliness of an empty home especially in the silence of the evening when that time would have been spent regaling stories of their working day.

Although Jane was not overly lonely she did miss the sounds of blethering and movement in the house, so it became commonplace for neighbours to visit one another in the evenings, taking their knitting or sewing with them and spending time blethering over a cup of tea, keeping one another company. Sometimes the older women, like Jane, would sit together in a younger quine's house to watch over her young bairns whilst she sat at a friend's hearth. It was a routine that continued throughout the war, strengthening bonds and friendships, and as socks were knitted and mending done, the folk of Aberlour, and indeed across the country, fought their own fight, to keep themselves strong in mind, for their kin.

It was easy at times to forget how to laugh, with the weight of worry heavy on folks shoulders, and sometimes folk would feel guilty at having allowed themselves to laugh at some humorous occurrence, thinking themselves selfish when their husbands and sons were out in some God forsaken field fighting for their lives.

One evening, in Isabella's house, four women, including Jane, had gathered together with their knitting and one of them had commented on feeling as such, and an auld wife, named Grace, put down her knitting and said,

"Laughter is good for the soul, and the soldiers themselves will be looking for humour wherever they can find it to help lighten their load. I pray that they find something, or someone, or some memory to make them smile often."

The quines nodded in agreement and Grace continued,

"When I was a young quine, many moons ago, I had an older brother, Matthew, and one evening he had fallen foul of too much illicit whisky and had fallen asleep by the hearth, too drunk to drag himself into bed. I had risen first the following morning finding him half on the kitchen chair and half sprawled on the floor, snoring loudly. The sun had not yet fully risen so the kitchen was fairly dark and being somewhat a mean brother, always teasing me, I decided to play a trick on him, knowing that he had an awful fear of fairies. I tied his laces together and standing behind him I roared in his ear,

"Fairies! The fairies are here, brother, come to take you away!"

Matthew sprung up, belying the whisky in his blood, and with a skirl, attempted to leap from the chair and out the door, but of course the laces made it somewhat impossible and Matthew found that he could neither run nor leap, and as his bewildered state grew so did the volume of his shrieks as I continued to bellow,

"Fairies! Fairies!"

The commotion brought mother and father running and as my laughter grew, Matthew slowly recognised the predicament he was in. Matthew received a clip around the lug from mother for waking the house, and me a tongue lashing, followed by a wink, from my father."

The women laughed, its sound breathing life into the walls of the house, and lightening the hearts for a while.

*

No LETTERS HAD arrived for Jane for some months and then a bundle came all at once. She tore them open, desperate to hear her loons' voices through their words. At first she read quickly, going from one to the next, the words running past her eyes as fast as the river,

Dear Mam,

I hope this letter finds ye well. Yer parcel arrived today and I am eating yer wonderful cake as I sit here writing. It's nae easy keeping it away from the rats, some are as big as cats, but I am determined to enjoy every morsel tae mysel'...

...We had a game o' football today, Privates against Sergeants, and the Privates won. The prize was extra tobacco and the use o' a whisky barrel for a bath!

...When I get home I'm going to go fishing for three days straight, just sit and soak in the peace and quiet and catch a week's worth o' dinner. How I miss our hills and the singing o' the birds.

....met a city loon last week, never been anywhere in his life, and had nae idea of one end o' a horse to the other. He was told to mount the beast and take it to another area and I had tears streaming doon my face watching him trying tae get on.

...I miss my wife and bairns and I have yet to lay eyes on our new son.
...Lost two friends yesterday. One had just married, last time he was home on leave.

...thoroughly enjoyed the book. Maybe ye could send me another by him.

...met up wi' my brother. He was a sight for sore eyes. Had a beer in the 'estaminet' and talked o' home.

...When I am a teacher I will bide in a wee place wi' a country school near ye.
...a lad lost his legs. He won't be a police constable again.
...letter from a quine!

...no idea what month it is, never mind day.
...the lice have a good feed on us.

...sending ye a wee carving o a flower made by another soldier. He is a stonemason.
... heard about a tank race. That would hae been some sight.

As her heart settled, Jane's eyes slowed, and she drank in every letter one by one, reading and rereading till she knew them by heart.

So little was said and yet so much. Some words spoke of what they would do when they returned, some simple things like watching the sunrise over the hills and fishing on the river, and some grand things like taking her out in a motorcar and living like the gentry.

As Jane read her sons' dreams they mingled with her own, and she prayed that their dreams were stronger than their nightmares.

COME DECEMBER, POLITICAL discontent came to a head when War Secretary, Daivd Lloyd George, and senior members of the Conservative Party lost faith in Prime Minister Asquith's ability to win the war and threatened to resign from their posts unless Asquith agreed to give responsibility for the running of the war to a small war cabinet. Asquith himself was not to be a member of this cabinet. Refusing such a deal, Asquith resigned and two days later Lloyd George formed a new coalition ministry, and as Prime Minister set up a war cabinet of five people, replacing the previous twenty three members, which resulted in crucial decisions being made far more efficiently.

As men in London fought across tables, losing their tempers over how to win a war, men all over the world fought across trenches, losing their lives, limbs and minds, over a war in which they had no choice.

News of the end of the Battle of the Somme filtered through into the newspapers. What had set out to be an offensive, to inflict as much damage as possible on Germany, had become a war of attrition, lasting a hundred and forty one days with severe casualties on both sides and not much gaining of territory.

For every mile gained 125,000 men were either killed or injured.

Page after page told of the ravages of war and death notices listed the names of men never coming home.

*J*ANE TRAVELLED TO Edinburgh just after Christmas to visit her quines. Young Jane was to be married and she had managed to secure a few days off work. It was the coldest winter since 1895 and the journey was slow going and extremely cold by train, as it travelled through snowy conditions. Marjory had to nurse during the day but she joined them in the evenings and Jane cooked a meal for them, doing what she could with the little food available but relishing being a mam to them all.

Jane and her quines laughed and marvelled over the front page adverts in the previous week's newspaper,

"Well - have ye ever seen such disgrace? Imagine advertising low bust corsets in the paper. And on the front page!"

The quines giggled at their mother's appalled face. "Mam, ye dinna have to ask for them discreetly in the store anymore. Folk purchase them quite openly."

"Well I think it very unladylike."

"It's getting harder to buy most things we need so I suppose we should be grateful there are corsets at all," replied Marjory.

Jane sniffed, but her comment on seeing the next advertisement caused her quines to erupt.

"And how anyone these days needed pills for constipation is beyond belief as surely the mere fact that war is raging and you could be bombed in your sleep is enough to keep anyone regular."

Huddled together with her quines around a small fire, it was the happiest Jane had been for a long time and she devoured every morsel of every word, laugh and bosie, enveloping her heart with the love of her quines, and strengthening each other's hope that life would soon be peaceful and safe again.

*J*ANE WAS DISAPPOINTED not to see James or Alexander, as neither had leave at that time. She had seen neither for such a long time and although letters were exchanged as often as was possible her heart ached to see them with her own eyes.

On 29th December, Jane, aged twenty six, married one Peter Lowe, aged forty, a shale miner. Another ordinary event in extraordinary times, and Jane was glad that her quine had found someone to love and navigate through life with. It was a small wedding held in Kirknewton, near Edinburgh, and Lena was bridesmaid to her sister.

Jane sat proudly, imagining Alec by her side, as their quine said her vows and she hoped they would have a long life together.

It was a flying visit, no one having much time off, and as Jane returned by train the following day she was happy to see her quine settled in marriage. There was promise of a family gathering to celebrate properly when the war was over, and all prayed that the whole family would be in attendance.

1917 brought the closure of distilleries, as barley was in short supply and needed for food, so Aberlour distillery closed its doors and lay in wait till the end of the war. The wheat harvest of 1916 had been poor and tattie crops had failed in Scotland and some parts of England. Food prices were at an all time high and with Britain reliant on imported grain, meat and sugar, Germany sought to starve its enemy by its campaign to sink all allied ships, including merchant ships, in order to prevent the safe passage of food. Folk in poorer areas suffered the most: between the high prices and lack of food, many became malnourished.

Jane worried for her quines as she knew that in cities folk had to queue for hours to buy food and with many having no gardens, could not grow any food for themselves. Often fights broke out with folk grappling over food and looting became common. The Government encouraged the setting up of allotments and suggested self-rationing and preserving of food, printing leaflets encouraging folk to eat less in order to maintain stocks and allow men at the front full rations.

The Women's Land Army was established to train women in farm work as so many male farm workers had enlisted, adding to the shortage of food being produced, and farmers were instructed to turn pasture land into crops to increase grain production.

Meanwhile Russia was in the throes of a revolution resulting in the abdication of Tsar Nicholas II and the rise of Vladimir Lenin, the head of the Bolshevik Party. The USA declared war on Germany in April sending 14,000 troops into France, and Greece entered the war on the side of the allies in June. July saw the start of the Battle of Passchendaele and the Battle of Ypres, which were to be two further long, bloody battles with horrendous casualties.

𝕵ANE'S NEIGHBOUR AT number 6, James Robertson, a Signaler with the Royal Field Artillery, had been killed in the war, and the closeness of the horror of war was brought home once again, his name added to the already long list of men lost in battle.

But the tide was turning.

BROTHERS

Late one evening at the beginning of August there was a knock on Jane's door and on answering it she found standing before her Willie and Thom. It took a second for their presence to register with Jane as she had not seen either of them for a year and a half and as she pinched herself to ensure that she was not dreaming her two loons picked her up and held her tight.

The shock having passed, Jane wanted to know everything from how they were to how they got there, questions pouring from her as the tea did from the pot.

Willie started. "We bumped into each other at the train station in London and travelled the rest o' the way together. Our leave coincided by chance. There was nae time tae let ye ken we were coming, so here we are."

Jane looked from one to the other, her mind hardly believing what her eyes could see.

"How long are ye home for?"

Thom answered. "We hae ten days but it's three days' travel each way so we hae four days here."

Mrs Simpson allowed Jane some time off and she spent the time fussing over her bairns, as to her they would always be her bairns, no matter how old they were. They talked and talked and talked, but not of war, and Jane tried her best to ignore the harrowed, haunted looks of her loons which had aged them and robbed them of youth.

They talked of childhood happenings and fun, and of future things. "I want tae continue working wi' horses after, and I want the peace o' the countryside. Ye winna find me in a city."

Jane smiled, "Aye, ye are a country loon, Willie. And what about you Thom, are ye still set on being a teacher?"

"Aye." No more words were forthcoming and sensing maybe she had said something wrong, Jane changed the subject and talked of safer things. Each loon had suspended the future in a sack to be picked up after the war.

On their last day, Willie and Thom took themselves off for a walk into the hills, breathing in the fresh air and soaking in the peace and quiet of their countryside.

"It's good to be surrounded by quietness."

Willie glanced at his brother. "Aye. Sometimes all I want is silence."

A kestrel hovered, surveying its prey, soundlessly.

Thom noticed the bird. "No birds sing over there - hae ye noticed?"

"Aye. They ken more than we do."

"What's the point o' it all?" a voice asked the wind.

The two brothers climbed, side by side, each lost in his own thoughts, both remembering easier, carefree times as young bairns. The trees whispered stories of having been climbed. The river trickled memories of fishing. The wind carried thoughts of laughter and fun.

On reaching the highest point, overlooking the fields, trees and river of what was their home, they took in the view in silence. As they stood looking out Thom spoke in a quiet voice.

"I dinna want tae go back, Willie."

Willie nodded in understanding. He saw the ravages of war etched on Thom's face, mirroring his own.

Both had seen the horror of war and felt its weight on them.

Both had heard the terrifying screams of fellow soldiers and friends, as they were mutilated.

Both had felt unimaginable fear and the closeness of death.

Both were fodder and neither really understood why.

"Aye, Thom, but ye hae to. Otherwise the Military Police will be at Mam's door."

Thom nodded, knowing before he spoke that staying was never an option. The two brothers walked back down the hill towards home, where their mam was waiting.

*

Saying goodbye was incredibly hard, as always. Jane held tight to her loons and her tears, as they said their farewells at the station. As they boarded the train, Willie first, followed by his brother, Thom squeezed his Mam's hand one final time and Jane smiled into his eyes. Her heart breaking as the whistle shrieked and the thundering, clacking of the engine and wheels began,

Jane held her smile till her bairns were out of sight and turned for home, tears silently coursing down her cheeks.

The Beginning Of The End

September saw German air raids in Kent, England, with bombs resulting in over two hundred casualties. Battle continued in Ypres till November when Canadian troops captured Paschendaele, ending the offensive with five hundred thousand casualties from both sides. Many of the wounded had drowned in mud filled trenches due to the amount of rain that Autumn. In Russia, the Bolsheviks overthrew the Government and installed a Communist one under Lenin, who immediately announced the end of Russia's involvement in the Great War.

As battles, both political and military, continued to rage across the world, the ordinary things in life continued also, with bairns being born, meals being cooked and children attending school. Sometimes, walking along a country road, folk could be forgiven for forgetting that they were in the midst of war.

Surrounded by the quiet of the hills, only the sounds of nature making itself known, Jane liked to walk slowly, allowing her mind to soak in the sights and sounds of the river and the birds, watch the rabbits darting to and fro, and the sheep ambling with lambs in their bellies. She took this rare time to forget her great fear and worry for her bairns and to restore her strength, silently sending the strength she gained to them, that they needed to come through the war.

ENTHUSIASM FOR THE war was now gone, from both civilians and soldiers, due to the heavy losses suffered and the severe lack of food. Lloyd George made a speech in January 1918 outlining Britain's aims in order to persuade folk in Britain that it was worthwhile continuing to fight. Food availability was at a critical level as a result of continuous German submarine warfare on merchant ships, so the Government now had no choice but to impose compulsory food rationing. At one point only four days' supply of sugar and a few weeks' worth of flour remained in Britain.

Ration cards were issued to everyone and folk had to register with their local butcher and grocer in order to procure the staples of sugar, meat, butter, milk and flour. Fixed maximum prices were set on these foods as well as on bread and tea. Jane consulted The Win the War Cookery Book containing recipes to help women cook with rations, and how to substitute one food with another, in particular flour, in order to preserve what food was available. Where once flowers had bloomed, now hens pecked, and tatties and carrots grew. Every garden was being used to feed folk.

The role of women throughout the war had not gone unseen and on the 6th February women over the age of thirty, who met property restrictions, were given the vote, alongside all men over the age of twenty one. A smile formed as Jane read the news. She had observed the Suffragette movement over the years and the war had proven how capable and intelligent women were. All three of her quines held strong views on the subject and she knew that their next letters would be full of what had been achieved, but - knowing them - it would not be enough and the fight would continue. And so it should.

As war continued to rage, Spanish Flu arrived and would silently kill more people across the world than the Great War, but it was not written about. There were no articles in the newspapers, no Government warnings or procedures. The pandemic silently raged its own war, claiming lives, with the public largely unaware of its scale.

As July arrived the second Battles of the Marne began which would prove to be a turning point in the war and Germany's last offensive. On Sunday 28th July, Jane attended kirk in the morning, as always, and despite the warmth of the sun that day she felt a chill in her bones that her cardigan did not suppress. As the day wore on, feeling out of sorts, she decided to take herself off for a walk in the late afternoon and set off following the well worn path over the bridge and up into the hills, Birkie alongside her.

She wandered through woodland and skirted fields full of wheat, and was glad to see her granny walking with her. Jane smiled at her but did not feel the need to talk, allowing her feet to carry her where they wished, her shoes enveloped in the long grass edging the fields and her thighs ploughing her body upwards towards the sun. She was aware of her muscles as she climbed, and her breath shortened with the exertion reminding Jane that she was no longer a young quine.

Her loon too was climbing - up through trees, rifle in hand, side by side with his comrades advancing on the village of Buzancy in France. Battle had commenced at 12.30pm and his battalion, alongside the French and the Gordon Highlanders, had taken Buzancy by 1.30pm but by 2.10pm the Germans were moving from the North East with reinforcements.

His muscles ached with the climb followed by the charging of his battalion, and his mind was on full alert as they advanced, sometimes running, sometimes crouching, always skirting offensive fire. His ears were bombarded with the bellowing of orders and the screeching of shells, and his nostrils filled with the scent of smoke and the stench of blood.

Jane stopped to catch her breath and turned to look down on Aberlour below her. Her eyes took in the River Spey, the houses and distillery behind and further back in the distance, Ben Rinnes, shrouding the other hills. A buzzard swooped high above her and the breeze toyed with Jane's hair, grey now and held back with pins, and she brushed the blown tendrils away from her eyes, noticing the sweet scent of the wild gorse bushes. The peaceful scene before her and the quiet of the countryside belied her heart, as it raced unexpectedly, a feeling of panic enveloping Jane as the breeze stopped suddenly, leaving an empty abyss, and the long, plaintive note from the buzzard echoed through the hills before it too stopped.

Jane sank down onto the grass, grasping for her granny's boneless hand, her breath taken from her and her body shaking.

At 4.35pm an SOS signal came from the South East corner of Buzancy as the Highlanders were driven back. He was bombarded with the immense screams and screeching of shells and shrapnel as they repeatedly hunted the air, killing and mutilating mercilessly as they tore their way through flesh and bone. The screams of men clung to his ears as they meshed with the screams of shells.

Outflanked and outnumbered, the Scots retreated, awkwardly stumbling and flailing, rows of machine gunners behind them, clacking rapidly. The thundering noise was deafening as war raged, the Scots turning, when they could, to fire back, plunging bayonets into advancing stomachs.

The young soldier sank down into the rough ground, his knees giving way beneath him, his breath thrust from his lungs, as his flesh was ripped and blown away. Then all was still and silent.

*

T HE LETTER FROM the Army arrived three weeks later - only officers' next of kin received telegrams. Jane took it unopened to the graveyard and sat by Alec, gathering strength to open what she knew would be crucifying news. Which bairn it would entail she did not know but a bond had been severed she knew, and the strongest welded metal could not hold her bairn to her now.

She was unaware of how long she sat there but eventually her trembling fingers gently tore the envelope to reveal its contents. Her eyes transfixed themselves to the top of the letter, unwilling to read the words below knowing that she would not be able to unread them. She repeatedly read the heading, *Army Form B. 104-82,* before tearing her eyes away and allowing them to lower.

Madam,

It is my painful duty to inform you that a report has this day been received from the War Office notifying the death of

(No.) *202789*   (Rank) *Private*

(Name) *Thomas Farquharson*

(Regiment) *Seaforth Highlanders, 8th Battalion*

which occurred   *in France and Flanders*

on the   *28th July 1918*

The report is to the effect that he   *was killed in action.*

A scream reverberated through the cemetery as she read Thom's name, and the searing pain in her heart scorched and tore every fibre of her being.

PEACE, DEPARTURES AND DELIVERIES

JUST EIGHT DAYS following Thom's death, what was to be known as the Hundred Days Offensive began, involving a series of attacks by the Allies resulting in the defeat of Germany and the end of The Great War. On the eleventh hour, of the eleventh day, of the eleventh month, 1918, Germany signed an Armistice agreement with the Allies in a railroad car in France.

Thom had fought for nearly four years, from the age of sixteen to the age of twenty, sacrificing the end of his childhood, as well as his life. Jane struggled with having no body to bury, leaving her with a tiny spark of hope that her bairn was merely lost and would return, but her heart told her the truth, as she felt the loss in her, and she believed that she had felt his passing, that day on the hill.

The tiny piece of hope had been extinguished with the arrival of another letter from the Army, informing Jane of where Thom's body was buried, some place called Buzancy, far from his home where he belonged. Sitting by her hearth, the letter in her hand, Jane let out a long, slow breath, and as her granny appeared in the opposite chair she looked into the eyes of her ghost. "My poor loon, he is so far away."

SOME WEEKS LATER a letter came, crumpled and muddy, the address barely visible, that Jane was surprised it had been delivered at all. She tore it open to be met with words that broke her heart. It was dated October.

Dear Mam,

Do ye remember when I was a wee loon and I went fishing wi' my father. It was different from other times as it was just the two o' us. Can't remember why but it was the first time I had him all to myself. I think I was maybe five at the time.

The rabbits ran around and it was a fine, warm day and I remember we sat on the bank in the sun. Ye had given us a meat sandwich each and we ate it watching the line for any movement and whispering in conversation so as not to scare the fish away. Dad kept telling me funny stories and I was trying so hard not to laugh loudly, covering my mouth with my hand.

He caught the first fish, a trout, and showed me how to reel it in and I couldna believe my luck when my line started twitching and shaking and I hauled in my first ever catch all by mysel'. A trout, same as dad, and it was a big one too. He hoisted me up on his shoulders and ran round in a circle whooping in delight wi' me laughing. It was the best day o' my childhood.

I wish I could be at home and fish wi' father again.

All my affection,

Alexander

All the reports of death and rats and atrocities and mutilation that Jane had read, paled in comparison to the emotion that she felt on reading that letter, written by a man who just wanted to return to a simple time.

As NEWS OF the end of the war filtered through, Jane was busy hanging out the Simpsons' washing, the day being clear and dry. On receiving the telegram, old Mr Duncan from the post office had rushed into the street shouting,

"The war's over! The war's over! Germany has surrendered!"

Cheers and shouts erupted up and down the street and lanes, as folk celebrated the long awaited news.

Jane let the pegs fall and quietly walked back into the house, gently closing the door behind her. She sat on a kitchen chair and closed her eyes, the sounds of cheering filtering through the open window. No smile or tears came, but she was conscious of a weight lifting from her shoulders as the news filtered into her mind, but she wouldn't fully believe it until her three loons were home safe.

It took a long time for soldiers to return home as demobilisation had to be organised with the most needed, skilled men, returning first. About forty groups were formed with miners and agricultural workers being in group one, so Willie was lucky to be sent home first. He had sent word to his mother as to when he would arrive, and Jane felt as though time was crawling through treacle as she waited.

The train pulled into Aberlour station, a large crowd waiting to greet the returning soldiers, and at first Jane could not see her loon among the throng of folk. Her heart pounding with anticipation, Jane's eyes scoured the platform and suddenly he was before her, his arms wide.

Folk of the time, who kept their feelings and affections in check, discarded such notions and succumbed to openness that day. Where soldiers had left with shakes of a hand, they returned to warm embraces.

Jane clung to him, relief flooding through her at seeing her loon home for good. It was an emotional reunion, both glad the war was over but both mourning the loss of Thom. Jane saw the raw grief in his eyes and Willie saw a woman who had aged way beyond her sixty one years.

James had to return to Canada with his regiment preventing him from seeing his family till his wife and son emigrated in January 1919. Jane ached to hold her loon, following the end of the war, but she would never see her first born again.

A LEXANDER HAD TO wait, which was detrimental to his health, as the war had taken its toll on his mind, and continuing to be surrounded by soldiers in uniform only allowed his mind to deteriorate further. His wife, Margaret, gave birth to a daughter, Margaret Jane, on 19th December, so when Alexander did return he was father to three bairns.

On hearing of his homecoming Jane and Willie took the train to visit him, and although physically well they could see that he was not himself. As Jane held her son she berated a war that had taken another son from her, as the man before her was not Alexander. She prayed that time would heal and that he would recover from whatever horrors he had endured.

J ANE'S QUINES HAD come through the war, much as she had, and were to continue bide in Lothian. The year 1920 was a period of adjustment, with most soldiers now back and trying to find a place for themselves at home, post war. Many women too had to readjust to no longer doing the jobs of men and of living again with a husband - if indeed he had returned - some of whom had changed beyond recognition, either physically maimed or mentally scarred.

As the Irish War of Independence raged, the Spanish flu was reaching its devastating end, both claiming yet more lives, as if the war had not taken enough. At the same time there was a feeling of optimism in folk, and the beginning of what would be known as the Roaring Twenties, with great social and economic change.

Like a set of scales, life had to be carefully balanced, every thought, feeling and sensation, weighed against every word, deed and occurrence.

It seemed to Jane that life caused either anger, bitterness and hostility, or appreciation, passion and courage. She surmised that folk made choices in life and lived by those choices. Old Doris -who had spurred Thom to enlist - avoided Jane in the street, scurrying away whenever she saw her. Jane let it be. There were a hundred reasons as to why Thom no longer lived, but one reason for her to get up each day and live life. Hope.

𝔍ANE TOOK A stroll one summer evening and found herself by Alec's grave. She sat on the grass and lifted her face to the sun, its warmth soothed her and the surrounding hills enveloped her as they always had done, providing comfort and strength. The scent of the distillery filtered through the air and a small smile teased the corners of Jane's mouth as she closed her eyes and saw the man that had been her husband.

She saw the broad shoulders and the red hair and the eyes full of mirth. She heard his strong voice that carried across a room and the thrawn-ness that flowed in his blood. She smelled the scent of him as he held her, and felt his arms around her.

"Oh how I miss ye, Alec. We had a good life and I thank ye for it."

Jane rose, her memories meandering in her mind, causing her smile to widen. As she turned to leave a thought made its way into her consciousness.

"The war took Thom and a part o' Alec too, but it gave me something in return. I grew up wi' fear: fear o' losing folk, fear o' not being accepted and fear o' my secret being exposed. War made me face my fears and that is something I never thought I would be able to do. I'm nae saying the fear has gone; I just feel differently aboot it now."

Jane felt the comfort of Alec as she slowly walked home again.

*

$\mathcal{H}$APPY NEWS CAME that year with Lena, then twenty eight, declaring that she was to marry one Andrew Martin, aged thirty five, in September. The wedding was to be in Kirknewton, a few miles from Edinburgh and on the day itself, Alexander, who had periods of better days, had been able to borrow his employer's car and had transported Lena and their mother to the wedding in style. Jane found the journey enthralling.

"Oh, Alexander, the seats are so soft and I love the scent o' leather. It reminds me o' my very first pair o' new shoes."

Jane perched herself on the edge of the seat, her eyes looking all around her as the motor car travelled sedately along the road in the busy city and out into the countryside. Lena chuckled as her mam continued,

"It's very different fae a train. The wheels are so nifty."

"Aye, it's different altogether, Mam."

Jane wound down the window a little, feeling the breeze on her face. "Can ye go faster, Alexander? I want tae feel the wind more."

Lena laughed again. "Are ye in a hurry to marry me off, Mam?"

"Nae, quine, I'm just revelling in the experience. I might nae get another chance tae feel like the lady o' the manor."

It was a thrilling experience and Jane did indeed feel like a lady of the manor as she stepped from the car, sorry to have the ride end but excited to be attending her quine's wedding.

It was a bonny, sunny day and smiles came easily, as folk celebrated with the happy couple. Lena was radiant and very much aware of her great grannies and wee Elizabeth, smiling alongside her. A knowing look passed between Lena and her mother and they couldn't help but giggle when wee Elizabeth walked reverently down the aisle, curtseying at the guests and doing a twirl at the end.

$\mathcal{J}$UST A FEW weeks later news arrived from Canada,

Dear Mam,

Thank ye for your last letter. It sounds as though Lena's wedding was a grand day and I am glad ye had the chance to travel in a motorcar! I write wi' happy news. We hae a quine, Beatrice, born on 19th October and all are well. Wee Alec dotes on her as much as their mother and doesn't seem put out wi' nae having a brother (unlike me, if I recall!). Mary thinks Beatrice has a look o' me, but maybe she will grow oot o' it and adopt the bonniness o' her mother.

Life here in Palmerston continues to suit us and we intend to bide. I enjoy my work with the railway and it pays well enough. I think we are finally getting used to the heat o' the hot summer here and I must admit to liking it. We both miss things about Scotland but there are better opportunities here for a family. The downside, ofcourse, is not being able to see you, but you are thought of often and are always in my prayers.

I promise to write a longer letter soon. I just wanted to let ye ken about Beatrice.

Your affectionate son,

James.

JANE WAS THRILLED for them, her heart glad that they had a good life, but sighed with the knowledge that her son would likely never return and she would never know her grandbairns. Willie had made it known that he was angry with James for emigrating but Jane was aware that each had to follow their own path and do what felt right.

HAVING SETTLED BACK into farm life following the war, Willie had decided to spread his wings a little and took work on Greenbank farm in Buckie, as a milk retailer, about twenty five miles away. Jane reassured him that she would be fine on her own, having got used to her own company over the four years of war. Some of the older women had kept up the habit of gathering together some evenings, that had helped them through the war, and Jane, who continued to work as a housekeeper during the day, enjoyed the blethers over a cup of tea whilst they knitted. Jane had fallen in love with books as a child and at times would read to her circle of friends from one in her possession, each following the story and commenting on either its interest, humour or awfulness. *The Importance of Being Earnest* by Oscar Wilde, with its wit and lovers' entanglements, brought much hilarity to the evenings, each one enjoying it thoroughly.

Come 1921, life had settled into a rhythm for Jane and she flowed alongside the river of life, continually changing and adapting and always moving forwards. Letters flowed, as they always had, providing a tether.

Jane was delighted to receive a letter from Lena telling her all about married life in Kirknewton.

Dear Mam,

Sorry I have taken so long to write. It's been a hectic time sorting out the house but I think we have finally managed to make it a home, and thankfully the roof no longer leaks.

I wish I could tell ye in person, Mam, but I have exciting news. I am to have a bairn in the summer (July) and although I am sick most days I am very happy, and Andrew is as excited as myself. As much as I enjoyed life in Edinburgh it is good to be living in the countryside again. I thought I would miss the hustle and bustle o' the city but I do not. Spring has sprung here and I am surrounded by hills and trees and birds, and it reminds me o' home. It will be a grand place to bring up a bairn.

It is good having Jane so close and with her wee Jane just born I am able to help her. Our bairnies will grow up together.

Andrew has settled into his new work as a boiler fireman and we have good neighbours, so all in all Kirknewton suits us very well indeed. Andrew's mother calls in everyday - which is a bit too much for my liking - but she means well, and I shouldn't complain, but I ken ye will understand!

My home is also home to the ghost of a young bairn. He looks to be around five or six years old and he has the most infectious grin. I imagine he was a cheeky loon in life, who ran his mam ragged! I am glad to hae him here, and if my bairn has the awareness he will be company for him or her too.

I hope ye are keeping well and that we can see one another soon. Drop me a line and let me ken how life is.

Your loving daughter,

Lena.

Jane felt a rush of happiness for her quine and could not wait to spread her news, so it having been a while since she had written to Elsie, she promptly took pen and paper from the bureau and proceeded to write to her friend.

Dearest Elsie,

I am so glad to hear that ye have recovered from yer bout o' illness, and I know that yer new grandbairn will bring ye much joy. My Jane has had her first bairn, a quine named Jane Smith. I have not had the chance to meet her yet but there is talk o' them coming here soon. As ye already ken, Alexander's wife, Margaret, is wi' child again, but I have just had a letter fae Lena to say she expects her first bairn around July. I am fair delighted for her too, so there is plenty o' knitting for a granny to do!

It seems minutes since they were all bairns themselves, but time marches on. I promised myself after losing Thom that I would live life how both him and Alec would want me too, so I revel in my bairns exploits and I have surprised myself at the joy I can feel in this life, despite their loss. I must be getting auld, Elsie, as I sound content!

I can hear the gasp of horror in you reading such a word! You will be sitting down to reply immediately insisting that I take a husband and find some excitement in my life. Considering how often ye berate yer husband and bellow about the rights o' women I am surprised ye recommend marriage.

Ye think I am lonely, but I am not.

Anyway you give me enough excitement and more laughter than anyone else I ken. I would not be surprised if one day ye end up in Government, with the Prime Minister as yer lover and the King as yer confidant! Ye enthral me with yer capricious nature.

Eliza visited last week and nothing ever seems to dampen her spirit either. We had a fine afternoon and too much cake was eaten. She was saying she would write to ye the following day so no point in me telling ye the same news.

Willie is courting a lass named Annie, and I am tae meet her next Sunday, so I will write then and tell ye all about her. Till then,

Your friend, Jane.

WILLIE HAD BEEN to a dance in Buckie and met a quine named Annie Paterson. The two enjoyed dancing and often frequented the local dances, even winning a competition, dancing the Highland Schottische together. When Willie took Annie to meet his mother that Sunday afternoon, Jane could see he was smitten, so no doubt there would be a wedding, and her heart was glad for them both. He had confided in his mother later that Annie was a Catholic and that her parents weren't too keen on her courting someone who wasn't. Jane looked at Willie and announced,

"Well, Willie, my mother once telt me that dry shoes winna catch fish, so if you are intent on marrying the quine you will just hae to get your shoes wet."

COME JULY, THE whole of Britain was in the midst of the hottest year on record and Jane was sitting writing a letter at the kitchen table, the day being Sunday 10th, the heat from the day still high by the evening, when there was a wee knock on the door followed by the appearance of her quines, Marjory and Jane. An excited Jane jumped from her chair to greet her bairns, her tongue full of questions as to how did they get home, how long were they staying and were they hungry? In the midst of fussing and blethering Jane suddenly stopped, taking in the harrowed looks on their faces. Slowly Jane sat herself down again, her quines following suit. Marjory took her mother's hand and quietly spoke the terrible words,

"Lena is gone, Mam. She died in childbirth last night. The wee bairn was never born."

The shock ripped through Jane, the steel wire strangling her heart, forcing her breath from her and claiming another piece of her soul, as her mind thrust itself back into the hell of grief that she knew only too well.

T IME WAS A strange thing. Sometimes it dragged like an ancient plough pulled by an old horse, and at other times it swept along as if it were a river in spate. As the months passed Jane had little concept of time, her mind focusing on the practicalities of work and life, whilst her heart grappled to salvage itself. She allowed her house people to comfort and nurture her with their presence, realising that she would not survive otherwise. They - and only they - truly understood the meaning of death, and the whys and wherefores of who were taken, so she trusted in the gentle smiles of her granny and the lively energy of wee Elizabeth to pull her through hell.

A LEXANDER WAS A father again, to a wee loon named Thomas, which lit a spark in Jane's dark heart that Thom's name would live on in his nephew.

Willie's wedding was fast approaching: he had taken his mother's advice and by converting to Catholicism had 'wet' his feet and gained the blessing of Annie's family. So the world kept turning and Jane slowly lifted her head and breathed.

The hottest year ended abruptly with the arrival of severe cold, and the 24th November was a particularly nippy Thursday in Buckie where Willie and Annie married in the Roman Catholic church. It was a different service to what Jane was used to but just as joyous all the same, and Willie stood next to his bride, his infectious grin stretching from one lug to the other. Jane's heart beat with pride and she smiled, wee Elizabeth sitting on her knee, her feet dangling.

The World Of Fashion

T HE YEAR 1922 brought two more grandbairns for Jane. Alexander became a father for the fifth time, a loon by the name of William being born, and James's wife, Mary, bore a loon by the name of Cyrus, that July. Her growing family continued to ignite sparks in Jane, spurring her on through life and giving her joy. The pace of life hastened, even in the small town of Aberlour, and motorcars were seen more often, driven by the local gentry or by guests staying in the local hotel.

The year also brought the death of Jessie MacKenzie, the auld grocer's wife who had read Jane's tea leaves all those years ago. Jane heard the news in passing, whilst out shopping in the town, and was surprised to notice a knot unravel in her stomach at the news. She took a walk along the river and when wee Elizabeth joined her Jane spoke, almost to herself.

"I remember feeling scared when Jessie told me that she knew my secret, but so many years have passed that I thought I was fine about it. Our paths rarely crossed but a part o' me is glad she has passed and I feel guilty for feeling that way. It's a wicked thought, Elizabeth. As far as I ken she kept my secret and was never a threat tae me, yet I am glad still. My secret is mine, and mine alone, now and I prefer it that way."

Little Elizabeth gave Jane her usual wee smile, and shook her head as her hand beckoned Jane to look upon the hills she loved.

$\mathcal{M}$ANY WOMEN HAD returned to working in the home but there was still evidence of the war years with some quines continuing to work jobs where husbands had not returned and bairns needed feeding.

Fashion too continued to change, the shortage of metal during the war hastening the demise of corsets for some, much to Jane's horror. As uncomfortable as they could be she saw it as extremely unladylike to be without one.

"What do you think, Jane? It is the new fashion and so comfortable."

Jane had to bite her tongue as she looked at her employer wearing a low waisted, short dress with the obvious omission of a corset.

"The material is very nice," she replied, but her tone said otherwise and Mrs Simpson looked at her sharply.

"We have to move with the times, Jane. Yer own quines will be wearing the same." She twirled in front of the mirror.

"Yes well, I must get on and see to dinner," and Jane left the room as quickly as she was able.

On visiting Eliza she told her of her employer's dress. "I consider mysel' someone who moves wi' the times and I agree with the emancipation of women, but surely that does not hae to mean going against what is decent."

"I agree, Jane. Why my own daughter has taken tae wearing breeks, and I was black affronted walking through Dufftown wi' her. It's one thing tae wear them on a farm but quite another whilst out shopping!"

"Marjory is just as bad. She showed me a magazine with pictures o' some famous French designer, wearing breeks and with hair cut to the nape o' her neck, in what is called a bob, and she expressed her liking o' the fashion."

"Well, Jane, look at this letter fae Elsie, full o' the new freedom for women and saying how she herself has cut her hair into a bob and frequently wears breeks, even to kirk!

It wasn't just clothes that were changing. Farms now grew soft fruits and bred poultry and large tractors could be seen in the fields, doing the job of horses. Jane often wondered what Alec would have made of the changes, perhaps embracing the easier ways of doing things alongside lamenting the loss of old ways.

He had always been a progressive thinker so she chose to view these changes as being for the better, although for her the lack of corsets would take some persuasion. Some new things were easier to swallow than others, especially with the arrival of new foods like a spicy pickle sauce which she had been instructed to buy from the grocer's shop for Mrs Simpson who implored Jane to try some on a cheese sandwich. It amused Jane's taste buds, its tangy zing tingling her tongue and she resolved to treat herself to a jar, now and again, when money allowed.

Something called a fridge had been invented, a contraption to keep food cool and fresh, and seemingly the hotel had purchased one for sixty five pounds, a criminal amount of money that Jane was sure would have been better used in the orphanage, or to employ men who still struggled to find work following the war. The newspaper had reported that new houses being built in London had indoor toilets and that eventually every home in Britain would have one. Isabella had been quite shocked and had retorted to Jane that the idea was simply disgusting and surely no decent person would want such a thing inside. Jane secretly liked the idea as she was not keen on going outside on a freezing, dark, wintry evening, but fearing a tongue lashing from Isabella had merely nodded in agreement.

The year wore on and political rumblings were again apparent in London resulting in Prime Minister Lloyd George being replaced by Andrew Bonar Law. The fight for independence in Ireland was finally won in December, but it would quickly be followed by a civil war, and Jane wondered if the world would ever learn how to resolve its issues without bloodshed.

TIME

IME BEGAN TO flow gently again for Jane, her heart forever scarred with her losses, but her mind keen enough to be inquisitive about what each new day would bring. Through her bairns' letters she saw rural and urban life in Scotland and Canada, each treasured word describing work and social events, grand buildings and gardens, friends, neighbours and bairns. Jane knew the wonder of new things, through her own experiences, and so could share in the joy of her family's exploits and encounters.

The apron strings were no longer tethered but an invisible thread existed between her, and her loons and quines, one that was stronger than any metal.

The Farquharson family continued to grow, with Willie and Annie having their first born in August 1923, a quine named Elizabeth Mary, and the following summer, James and Mary had another loon, named Donald. Jane was forever knitting and sending parcels, but the highlight for her was receiving photographs over the years of her growing family. She cherished them all and had Willie make her a frame for each one, so she could display them on her dresser and see them every day.

It saddened her not to have any of Alec or her mother and grandparents, as no such thing existed for the poor, back when she was young, but she could see them when she closed her eyes, which she often did, conjuring them in her mind and revelling in her memories.

She remembered her granda telling her once that the older you get the faster time moved and Jane could see how true that was. She would look upon the River Spey and it was like watching her life rushing by, its speed and force at times overwhelming, unable to stop it or slow it down; but then she looked upon the hills, so still and comforting, and she would imagine that that was where her feelings and memories lived, buried deep within them, forever ensconced.

Life's river carried Jane forward and the following year three more grandbairns were born, all loons. Alexander's sixth and final bairn was named James Cooper; Willie's first son to be born was named Alexander; and Jane's second bairn was named Peter.

If there was one thing you could say about the Farquharsons, it was that they were certainly fertile.

At the age of thirty seven, Marjory was Jane's only bairn not yet married and Jane wondered if perhaps she would not marry and have a family of her own. She had always been fiercely independent and headstrong, and the progression of women suited Marjory. When she had last come home to visit her mother, Marjory had burst into the house all smiles, bobbed hair and an air of confidence in her. Jane remembered how Alec, when Marjory was wee, had said she would make a good foreman with her bossy ways and confidence, and he was right. Jane imagined that she made quite the formidable nurse, but with a big heart beating inside her: love and tenderness in her blood.

Alexander was the one that worried Jane. Following the war he had never truly returned to his old self, and no one seemed to quite know how to get him back. She was concerned for Margaret too, as it could not be easy living with a troubled man, and she was sure that at times she felt helpless.

Alexander and his family visited his mother early in 1926 and whilst laying flowers at his father's grave he announced to Jane,

"The Canadian Government are giving out land grants and

we hae decided to emigrate. It's a new start, Mam, and one I think we all need. I have been offered land near Prince Albert, Saskatchewan, a place that is in the countryside and I plan to farm there."

Jane looked at her loon, now thirty eight years old, and saw the need in his eyes for a life of peace. Jane took a breath and as she held him she whispered, "Go with my blessing, Alexander, and find contentment again."

Jane knew that she would not see him again, not in this life anyway, but if that's what it took for him to be able to return to his old self then it was a sacrifice worth making.

Alexander and his family left on a ship named the Anthenian, from Glasgow, on 30th April to start a new life on a pig farm.

ℐT WAS HARD for Jane knowing that her contact with Alexander could only be through letters, like James, but she resolved to make her letters interesting and reassuring. Canada was a big place and her loons were very far apart, which worried Jane that Alexander had no family nearby if needed. She knew that the rest of her bairns wrote regularly so she had to trust that that would be support enough.

Come December, news came that James and Mary had had another quine, Emma Elizabeth, completing their family of five. Jane was now sixty nine years of age with fifteen grandbairns and another on the way for Willie and Annie.

1927 began with severe gusts of wind battering the whole of Britain, and Jane found herself being blown to work, pushed and buffeted as she went. A giggle rose up in her as she remembered the feeling as a child, playing outside Milton Cottage in the wind and imagining that she looked like old Mr MacPherson after a few whiskies. She watched as bairns lifted their coats and used them as kites, their skirls and laughter carried in the wind, and a part of Jane wanted to lift her coat and copy them.

Wee Elizabeth, unaffected by the wind, seemed to sense Jane's excitement and skipped and hopped in front of her. Running and stopping, waiting for Jane to catch up, and running off again.

The child in Jane ran with her, as she imagined herself playing with Elizabeth as they had done as bairns. She saw coats being lifted in the wind and hens being chased, as mothers laughed or scolded, as washing was hung out to dry and wee fingers plucked worms from the mud.

The wind seemed to blow time along, quicker than ever, and the seasons flew by with it.

A LOON, NAMED WILLIAM, was born to Willie and Annie that January, as the wind howled and walloped the windows. They now lived in Guthrie Cottage, Aberlour, and Jane took great pleasure in watching her wee grandbairns grow in front of her eyes. It fascinated her that she had so many grandbairns, who in turn would have their own families, and so the generations would continue through the years, passing on the colour of eyes, thrawn minds and loving hearts.

She found it funny that her mind often returned to her youth, reminding her of long forgotten times and making her smile. Wee Elizabeth, who never grew up, seemed to emanate vitality into Jane, and she sometimes wondered what the quine thought of her childhood friend and cousin, who was now grey haired and old with a heart that beat erratically.

Jane also wondered if she herself would return in ghost form and if so, who would see her and be comforted.

As the winds passed, and spring awakened the sleeping buds, Jane, as always, took herself off for walks into her beloved countryside, always accompanied by someone who had passed, be they on two or four legs. Her mind soaked in the sights and sounds of her home, soothing, comforting and caressing, as her legs carried her slowly through fields and woodland. No longer fit enough to climb the surrounding hills, she skirted them, allowing their presence to enfold her in a bosie. She was thankful for both the hills and the close-knit community that had healed her childhood heart when she had moved there almost forty years before.

Jane reflected on her friendships with Eliza, Isabella and Elsie, their bond as strong as family, and how fortunate she was to have them. She had written to Eliza in Dufftown to invite her to stay, when she was able, as it had been a while since she had seen her, so that was something for her to look forward to.

*

T HE MONTH OF May arrived delicately, as did Eliza, who had eagerly accepted Jane's invitation and had come to bide for a couple of days. Jane baked enough cakes for a dozen folk and met Eliza off the afternoon train on 12th May, with a skip in her step. The two widows walked the short distance to Jane's home, arm in arm, one short and round with rosy cheeks, the other slim and straight backed with warmth in her smile.

Eliza was ushered in and the water put on to boil for tea, the tea things already laid out alongside the cakes. Weight was taken off weary legs and bottoms were perched on fireside chairs, as tongues blethered and eyes smiled. News of bairns and grandbairns was shared as they caught up on tidings and the happenings in both Dufftown and Aberlour, before talk moved to reminiscing.

"I have lived here almost forty years, Eliza. It's hard tae believe, time moves so fast. Aberlour healed my childhood heart. The folk and the hills absorbed my hurt and accepted me, and for that I am thankful."

Eliza shook her head. "Na, Jane, it's nae Aberlour ye need tae thank. It's yersel' that accepted ye, and allowed ye tae hae a good and happy life wi' Alec."

Jane's brow furrowed and she looked to her friend as if to question her, but Eliza just smiled a wide smile and nodded, "Aye, *you,* quine. Ye made yer life a happy one all by yersel'."

The air stilled for a moment as Jane thought back. She saw in her mind's eye the wee bairn that was, and she said, "I was like a lamb in another lamb's skin; Smith in heart and Cantlie by name."

"Aye, I can see that. What are ye now, Jane?"

Jane thought for a minute and started to laugh. "I'm an auld ewe, too tough tae eat, but wi' my own fleece."

The quines howled and anyone passing the window would have thought they were mad, the racket they were making, with tears of laughter streaming down their cheeks.

They each had tales of early domestic life and disasters, and of childhood games and songs. Wee Elizabeth appeared and sat herself on Jane's knee, and Jane was reminded of a long forgotten rhyme that her mother would recite whilst touching Jane's face:

"Knock on the door,
Peep in,
Lift the latch,
And walk in."

"She would knock on my forehead, peep in my eye, squish my nose and walk her fingers to my mouth. I loved that rhyme and would ask her to do it again and again, and I did it with my own bairns."

Eliza smiled. "Yes, I mind that one, Jane. I loved it as well."

"It's funny how rhymes and games get passed on through the years, Eliza, alongside beliefs and traditions." She looked down on Elizabeth. "Secrets too sometimes."

As Jane thought of her bairns and grandbairns, some yet to be born, she thought about her bairn who was born with the ability to dream of future things and if that secret would ever be revealed. She wondered which grandbairn would pass on the seeing of things to come, and her own awareness of ghosts, down through the generations.

Where these endowments came from, and where they would go, she would never know, but perhaps her descendents would be braver than she and that one day there would be no need for secrets to be kept.

A spark of pain entered Jane as she thought of the bairn she had scolded so harshly when they had spoken of their dreams. "I was wrong. I will write a letter in the mornin'."

"What's that, Jane?" Eliza looked at her friend, confused.

Jane had not realised that she had spoken aloud. "Nothing, quine. I'll away and make some more tea."

She smiled at her lifelong friend. "I'm right glad ye are here, Eliza."

As she rose, a thoughtful smile playing on her face, a piercing pain struck her chest and the room fell suddenly silent, not even the chiming of the clock, marking the sixth hour, could be heard.

Jane's legs gave way beneath her and her body collapsed to the floor. As her spirit rose, the steel wire in her heart melted away and she heard an old familiar voice, as Alec reached out his hand and gently spoke the words:

" 'Tis time, ma quine…yer bairns are waitin'."

The End.

192_ DEATHS in the _Parish_ of _Aberdeen_ in the _County_ of _Banff_

Page 7.—

No.	Name and Surname. Rank or Profession, and whether Single, Married, or Widowed.	When and Where Died.	Sex	Age	Name, Surname, & Rank or Profession of Father. Name and Maiden Surname of Mother.	Cause of Death, Duration of Disease, and Medical Attendant by whom certified.	Signature & Qualification of Informant, and Residence, if out of the House in which the Death occurred.	When and where Registered, and Signature of Registrar.
19	Jane Farquharson Widow of _____ Proctor _____ Distiller Worker	192_ May 5th 6.40 p.m. Aberlour	F	69	Margaret Smith Thomas Farquharson Alexandra Farquharson m.s. Falquhar (deceased)	Senile degeneration Cardiac sync. Arteria sclerosis Acute dilatation M.B. Chb.	William Farquharson Son Alexander Mackie Aberlour	192_ May 13 th At Aberlour _____ Alex Garton Registrar.
20	Christina Grant Wife of Robert _____ Administrated Assets Licensed Grocer's (Wife)	192_ May 14th 2.40 pm Aberlour	F	56	William Grant Distillery Manager (deceased) Margaret Grant m.s. Grant	Pulmonary Oedema Pulmonary Thrombosis Cardiac failure Certified by J. Macrorthur M.B. Chb.	Jan McGregor Aberlour	192_ May 16th At Aberlour _____ Alex Garton Registrar.
21	Peter Henderson Farmer (Aged)	192_ May 22nd White Cottage Aberlour Aberlour	M	68	Lewis Henderson Farmer (deceased) Jane Henderson Mrs McKenzie (deceased)	Judged Senile Decay Heart Disease George Grant Certified by J. Macrorthur M.B. Chb.	Ann Duff Coucowart Brother William Aberlour	192_ May 22nd At Aberlour _____ Alex Garton Registrar.

ACKNOWLEDGEMENTS

WHILST TRACING MY family tree there was always something about Jane Cantlie that intrigued me. I felt a connection to her that propelled me to write about her life and in turn give her a voice. Without having discovered her story I would never have written a book and I am thankful to Jane for the opportunity and I am proud to call her my great grandmother.

Thank you to the professionals who helped shape this book: developmental editor, Gary Smailes, book cover creator, Ken Dawson and typesetter Kate Coe.

Thank you to Alison Massie for your many hours of proofreading as well as support and encouragement throughout the process of writing this book. I am not sure if I will ever get the hang of when to use a colon and semi colon but thank you for trying to teach me!

Thank you to Jean 'Cordelia' Byass for beta reading and for your encouragement.

A heartfelt thank you to my husband, Erlend, who believed I could write a book. You cheer me on and inspire me every day. Love you, always.

And thank you to our amazing girls, Rowan, Ellis and Halle; this book is for you. May you always follow your dreams.

GLOSSARY

Accouchement	childbirth
Quine	female/girl
Spurtle	wooden utensil for stirring porridge
Hearth	fireplace/home
Dreich	wet, gloomy, weather
Burn	stream
Thrawn	stubborn
Coorse	bad
Loon / Lass	male/female
Chiel	young man
Tatties	potatoes
Folk	people
Bide, biding	stay/live
Bade	stayed/lived
Bosie	cuddle
Bonny	pretty
Erse	arse/bottom
Auld	old
Blether	speak/chat
Muckle	big
Kist	large wooden box/trunk
Cloot	small piece of cloth
Greeting	crying
Sain	purify
Lugs	ears
Girning	whinging
Daupit	stupid
Beardie	affectionate rubbing of a beard on a child's cheek

Couthie	loving, caring person
Hae	have
Tae	to
Na, Nay, nae	No
Dinna	don't
Winna	won't
Orraster	loose woman
Lum	chimney
Birl	twirl
Coorie in	cuddle in
Gypit	foolish

Printed in Great Britain
by Amazon